WHAT THE CRITICS ARE SAYING ABOUT

The Chymical Cook

In keeping with *The Celestine Prophecy* but superior in narrative and style, written with the imagination and sense of direct experience, the tension and spiritual depth, of a Carlos Castaneda — *The Chymical Cook* is a decoction of ancient alchemy and the unique folk tradition of our own heritage. Bremyer flavors his prose with his poetic gifts creating a musical continuum that leads the reader into realms between the known and the unknown world. I couldn't put it down.

Helen Lindquist Bonny, Ph.D.
Founder of the Bonny Method of Guided Imagery and Music,
author of *Music and Your Mind*

Fantastic and mysterious, *The Chymical Cook* takes the reader into a world of magic dog bones, crystal skulls, fire and the thrill and confusion of space and time-warps. This altered reality is encountered by five young people who walk into the Georgia woods on a journey wrapped in danger, adventure, and an exploration of consciousness. Bremyer's well-told tale challenges readers to see with new eyes, and know with new hearts, that life is much more than it normally appears to be.

Kathryn Watterson
author of *Not by the Sword*

The Chymical Cook makes the hair on the back of your neck stand up, then sends you home to do something meaningful with your life. Bremyer catches the anxiety and hope of the 1960s, the conflict between idealistic naiveté and the teacher who sets herself the task of turning the student's base metal into gold. This is the kind of exquisitely tuned medicine we need in the 1990s.

Bowen White, M.D.
Columnist, television commentator,
author of *The Cry of the Heart*

A Fast-paced, headlong journey into the intricacies of consciousness – relevant to all who recognize that concensus reality is but a thin veil over a much deeper mystery.

Stanley Messenger
Author, lecturer, and teacher of the New Anthroposophy

Five young people, each in their own way profoundly attracted to an elderly woman named Elsie — a strange communicator of instructions concerning their own identity and destiny — are brought together for a short time in the backwoods of Georgia. They learn that they must undertake to perform certain actions that, according to Elsie, will affect not only their own lives, but the outcome of an ancestral conflict, and the very development of human consciousness on earth. Each person is on their own to understand the strange events of which they are a part; there is no coersion or indoctrination here, no tempting hopes of ultimate teachings, or even further instruction on a "path." There is a sense of awe, of uncertainty, and, most of all, a profound spirit of inquiry that, inspite of doubts and differences, allows them to cooperate in an endeavor each one feels the urgency of. The text is wrought so finely that, as the story unfolds, the reader too is brought into the mystery, and his or her understanding, wisdom and intuitive power — to follow, make sense of, or dismiss what is going on — is developed and brought into play.

Charles Stein
Poet, author of *The Hat Rack Tree*

The
Chymical
Cook

A True Account
of Mystical Initiation
in the Georgia Woods

Jay Bremyer

STATION HILL OPENINGS

BARRYTOWN, LTD

Published under the Station Hill Openings imprint by Barrytown, Ltd., Barrytown, New York 12507.

Distributed by Consortium Book Sales & Distribution, Inc. 1045 Westgate Drive, Saint Paul, Minnesota 55114-1065.

Text and cover design and cover photo by Susan Quasha.

Library of Congress Cataloging-in-Publication Data

Bremyer, Jay.
    The chymical cook : a true account of mystical initiation in the Georgia Woods / Jay Bremyer.
        p.   cm.
    ISBN 1-886449-31-7
    1. Bremyer, Jay.   I. Title.
    PS3552.R374C49   1996
    813'.54—dc21   96-37214
                                                              CIP

"Let us say that this tablet is a gift of Memory, the mother of the Muses." Plato, Dialogues, Theaetetus, 191

I DEDICATE THIS BOOK

to Sara, my muse, mate and partner in our effort to share the story of our time with Elsie, the teacher who broke down our preconceptions and introduced us to our deeper selves; to Karin who facilitated this journey; to Larry, Kathy, and John, who accompanied us; and to Seth and Aaron, our sons, whom we took to meet Elsie while they were still young; and to Elsie, who still whispers in my heart:

"The temple of my teachers is located here
Behind the mountains, within the shade
Where the waterfall glistens
And the high priestess prays.
Prophecies and patterns in the stones,
Water splashing, the wisdom of crones
Is carried by the Ladies of the Lake
For goodness sake," she crooned.
"But if you can't bear the sound
Of this crying earth,
If you can't face the sun,
The moon, the stars of your birth,
Of our wound, of our vision,
Of our pain so dear,
Then know, at least,
That I whisper here."

Lake Raven, Georgia — 1969

Table of Divisions

Preface

Sara and I had read P.D. Ouspensky's *In Search of the Miraculous* and Herman Hesse's *Journey to the East*, but in the summer of 1969 we had no anticipation that, through a series of synchronistic events in the mountains of northern Georgia, we would actually encounter an authentic Teacher. We were twenty-two years old.

Elsie cooked, gardened, and tended crystals according to what she claimed was a mystery tradition combining Goethe's spiritual science with the esotericism of Sri Aurobindo Ghose. She instructed us in reading patterns encoded in everything from fairytales to engineering manuals. She played multidimensional chess and seemed to manipulate time and space.

She said she represented the spiritual hierarchy and was setting stages on which she could introduce us to the mysteries of evolutionary consciousness; but that it would take twenty-five years for us to understand what had happened to us.

In spite of claiming to be a practicing alchemist, she insisted that the occult is the biggest con-game in the world, full of charlatans and rogues. We must not accept anything just because "a voice" spoke through a person we love and trust. Her purpose was to inspire us to take responsiblity for making something valuable of our lives.

The significance of our account is not what specific teachings we were given, but rather the manner in which we were guided through a time which was both beautiful and frightening — like today, on the edge of crisis.

Pushed by Elsie, we faced an apocalypse rising out of techniques and frames of reference which, in some instances, have become the iconographia of the New Age movement. The danger is that we tend to make these usages into idols, new prisons rather than platforms for growth and liberation.

I was tempted to include commentary about how I see things now, after twenty-seven years of additional experience, but decided to avoid interpretations which only became possible much later.

The narrative is therefore limited to how I saw things at that time. I have changed certain names and taken some liberties with time sequences in order to condense the story, but what follows is a true account of our initiation at the hands of an authentic and wonderful alchemical cook.

Jay Bremyer, 1996

Introduction

In the aftermath of the assassination of John F. Kennedy, Sara and I had come out of high school determined to change the world or drop out. College students were taking over campuses and being gunned down. We protested, using guerilla theater, improvising in the streets and football stadiums. We identified with the hippies and flower-children migrating across the country, dressed like dispossessed Indians, their Volkswagon buses painted in psychedelic rainbows. We stuck flowers in rifles — and prayed we wouldn't be shot.

Thich Nhat Hanh, a Vietnamese monk, author of *Lotus in a Sea of Fire*, came to our campus and shared the pain and wisdom of his people during a forum sponsored by the Kansas State University Student Government.

Bobby Kennedy announced his candidacy for President — promising to open the wound, stop the war, and begin the healing. Kansas was his last stop before California and his appointment with death.

Some of our best friends had fled to Canada or gone to prison. Television showed the police clubbing those of our generation who still believed enough in the system to go to Chicago and protest the Democratic Convention. The Chicago Eight were set for trial. Bobby Seal, chained and gagged, was carried into the courtroom.

The Black Muslims had killed Malcolm X. The Black Panthers were struggling to re-establish pride among their people. The Weathermen were blowing up buildings, taking hostages, committing murder. Tim Leary was counselling a radical alliance. Richard Nixon was President.

Over 100 Americans per week were being killed in Vietnam. Our troops were massacring women and children. Black children were being burned in school buses. Martin Luther King had been murdered. "I have a nightmare."

I had been managing a bookstore and taking graduate classes in English, history, and linguistics. Sara worked for the English Department and was taking education classes. She wanted to help children get a better start. But our main interest was our work with Larry and Kathy on *Outlet*, a small literary magazine we founded together to express our rage and sorrow and hope.

In June, we attended the annual Convention of Small Magazine Editors and Publishers in Ann Arbor. When we got back, my mother called and said that if we would drive to Georgia, she would pay our expenses to a Yoga workshop.

We were searching. We had to keep moving. We, like hundreds of thousands of others, were ready to explode.

Into the South

Making great time, we glide down black ribbon highways, through the green flow of the Ozarks, the tear drop lakes, the road stretching before us. We're entering Tennessee, will touch Alabama, the deep South, before reaching Georgia — redneck country, at risk as outsiders, protesters, communist sympathizers — needing to maintain whatever invisibility we can, unable to do so because of wire-rimmed glasses, my hair too long for a man. Sara, soft body and straight hair to the center of her back, is too vulnerable and trusting to be native to these truckstops.

Road narrowing, black men loitering on unpainted wooden porch steps, one stop light in the center of town. It's getting dark. We need to eat, maybe find a room. We've never been in country like this before.

We're not too far from where civil rights marchers are routinely clubbed, kicked, mutilated, arrested, sometimes murdered. The local white supremacists are not Midwest conservative Republicans wanting to lecture us back into line; and we're not native Liberals of good breeding and Northern education interested in social causes, nor student activists willing to have our skulls split open to change the world.

Several whites loiter near a pick-up, with rifles across the back window, next to the filling station pumps.

"Keep going," Sara counsels.

"What if we run out of gas?" I ask, disgusted with my own awkwardness, uncertain about my ability to avoid conflict, something impersonal and awful, which may harm us.

"There's a town up ahead, much bigger." Sara studies the map. "It's not far."

"No motel here, anyway." I speed up, hoping that we don't get stranded on the highway, thinking of rednecks blasting Dennis Hopper and Peter Fonda in EASY RIDER. A near full moon looms over the road ahead of us.

Neither of us wants to talk. This is a tourist motel with attached restaurant — no locals except the proprietor and his solid wife, their kids playing in the pool out front, then shooting off fireworks. Tomorrow is the 4th of July.

Pine trees march up the rise behind our room. There's a small gas station two hundred yards beyond the gravel parking lot. We can fill up in the morning. We'll be at Clearmont by tomorrow evening — safe. We make love, tentative, tender, reassuring, and curl up to sleep.

Moving across the Tennessee River into the rose haze of Chattanooga, then through dense lowlands toward the Blue Ridge mountains, I begin to feel better. But the tight turns still unnerve me. Even curving up into the Chattahoochee Forest, past splendid vistas through rich green valleys rolling up the sides of lush mountains, isolation crowds us.

The Appalachian Trail starts somewhere near here. We travel past mountain lakes on highway 76 toward Hiawasee, Black Rock, and Bald Mountain. Tallulah Falls and Raven Gap— where DELIVERANCE, by James Dickey, took place — are somewhere to the south of us.

Rolling into Clayton, Sara glances around. "I don't see any blacks. Where are they?"

"Mostly in the farming regions, or the cities," I comment, uncertain, then pull into a filling station. "But I'll bet there are plenty of rednecks."

Getting out first, Sara asks the attendant for the key to the lady's room. His eyes float across her breasts, firm beneath a light blue T-shirt, down to her legs, vulnerable and exposed beneath her jean-shorts, to her sandals.

"Around the side, miss. It's open," he drawls, glancing toward me when I approach.

"Which way to Lake Raven?" I'm aware of my Midwestern twang.

"Out 23 to Wiley then take 24." He pushes his ball cap up with a greasy hand. "Where you from?"

"Kansas." I figure he's not much older than we are.

"There's a post office and store at Clearmont where you turn onto the river road to Lake Raven. Fill her up?" He wipes his hands on a red rag and stuffs it in his back pocket.

"Sure." I stretch my arms and breathe the mountain air, the scent of grease and gasoline minor by comparison.

"Coffee's in the office. Help yourself." He opens the hood to check the oil. "The toilet's through there, too."

A Bob Dylan song wafts from the radio in the garage. "Why aren't there any blacks here?" I ask.

"Oh," he glances at me, "the niggers keep to themselves. There's a few, mostly part Indian, up this way. I get along with them, but you better be careful who you ask."

"Why?" I'm a little concerned that the punks who just drove in will overhear us.

"Cause if you're a nigger-lover, you might get killed," he answers, his voice lower, apparently sincere. "And I'd keep an eye on your girlfriend, too."

"My wife," I correct him.

"No matter. She's a give away."

"How do you mean that?"

"People don't like hippies."

"We're not hippies," I overstate, reacting to images of brutes raping Sara.

"She's got beads on." He raises his voice: "All the way to the top?"

"Yeah." I note that the register is passing $5.00, then, voice lowered, ask: "Do the beads mean she's a hippie?"

"People are different here." He pulls the nozzle out. "You don't know what you're getting into."

"No," I admit, appreciating his frankness.

"Any particular reason you're going to Lake Raven?"

"We're signed up for a workshop at the Christian Retreat Center." Sara approaches and gets into the car. Deciding to skip the restroom, I give him a ten dollar bill.

"There's been some trouble up there." He hands me the change. "Not everybody approves of that place."

Turning off at Clearmont, we curve in front of an old storefront. An old man, next to a partly-dead tree, stares at us as we follow a narrower road into the mountains, shadows creeping across the asphalt. Scrub trees clinging by determined roots hang over the turns. A car passes us in the opposite direction. An old lady waves and smiles.

On the right we notice a small "Oasis" sign on white painted wood, near the ground, next to a drive leading up to a small bungalow and garden area. A couple hundred yards further, a stone fence separates an estate from the public. The sign reads: "Hart Retreat." A compound of buildings and an orchard stretch behind the sign.

Around the next corner the road drops and the blue sky expands over the green wave of trees. Some fifty yards away, the lake washes in unhurried undulations. Slowing, we hear the calls of birds. A young boy stands on the strip of pebble beach, his fishing rod pointed out over the water.

On the right, behind a low retaining wall, old hardwoods line the road. A two storied home needs paint but still looks grand. Just past the home, a newer building perches on a stone outcropping, the area excavated to accommodate it.

"CRC Headquarters," Sara reads the sign. A sandy haired man, in jeans, pushes the door open and descends the wooden stairs from the deck.

"I'm Ned O'Riley." He shakes my hand. "Will picked your mom up at Clayton. Easy to tell you're related."

"Jay and Sara!" Mom announces from the door to the kitchen. Naturally curly, fine black hair framing her smile, she moves toward us for a hug.

"This is Will." She turns to introduce us.

"Printer." His voice is soft but friendly.

"Dan Paladin ... neighbor." Lankier than Ned but not as gaunt as Will, dark eyes, sharp and dancing, Dan stretches his arm out to shake hands, revealing a tattoo. "Come over and see me." He holds my eyes a second then moves like a cat past the other guests and out onto the porch.

"Who's he?" Sara asks.

"A damn good writer," Will comments, appreciatively.

A quarter mile further around the lake, surrounded by huge trees and nestled on the opposite side of the road, the Lake Raven Hotel looks like a ship hovering on a wave.

While I unload, Sara and Mom make their way up the wood steps to the porch. A full yellow-white moon hangs over the front gable, facing the lake. A fireball explodes silently in the sky, followed by a whistle then clap of a huge retort.

A swing, suspended by long ropes from a high branch on a sentinel tree in the center of the parking lot, creaks, twisting slightly, barely illuminated by the one light on a wooden pole. The cry of an owl rises in the distance.

Across the way, over the tops of dark trees, a stream of pale light shimmers above the gray sheen of the lake. A string of fire crackers goes off, then several booms in quick succession. Parachute explosions in orange, purple and blue, float through the sky. A rocket careens wildly, leaving a smoke trail. I sense that Indian spirits are retreating, unwilling to celebrate, and wonder about Confederate holdouts still insisting that this is a separate country. The red glare reminds me of cannons and blood, bodies floating in water.

Another barrage then silence, smoke floating, the pungent sting of gunpowder, even at this distance. Crickets, cicadas, and frogs fill the void. In the distance, a car weaves toward us. High above, the beams of yard-lights dot the mountain.

The lounge, dimly lit in yellow light, is filled with heavy tables, four chairs to each. Shelves are stacked with books and magazines. A door opens onto a porch overhanging the slope to the road, the lake beyond. The interior wall contains a large hearth and fireplace.

Two men, sitting in the far corner, with a bottle and glasses, don't stop their conversation to look at us. The ceiling is supported by heavy posts. Cigar smoke is muted in the long habitation of the room. A big, white-bearded man disappears into the room behind the counter.

"We're down the hall on the other side." Mom dangles two sets of keys.

"Is the bar closed?" I ask.

"Yes. But I have a bottle and the proprietor ... "

"Looks like a sea-captain, doesn't he?" Sara whispers.

" ... said we could get into the kitchen for ice."

Following them around the outside corridor, I'm pleased to be the beneficiary of one of Mom's impromptu adventures.

Opening the door to a single bed covered with a home-made quilt, a lamp with a floral shade between a writing desk and the window open to tree scents and night sounds, her Spanish rosary, an overnight bag bulging with pills and vitamins, books and note pads on the desk — we enter Mom's room.

"So," she pours Scotch, "tell me about Larry and Kathy. Why didn't Kathy go to Ann Arbor with you?"

"Kathy's the university artist now," Sara answers. "She had a project deadline."

"What's Larry working on?" Mom looks at me.

"Multi-media," I scoot around to get more comfortable, "mostly documentaries about the protest movement."

"Your draft board confrontation is killing your dad."

"His minister supports me," I comment, knowing there is no good place to go with this discussion.

"Tradition and honor are very important to him."

"This isn't an honorable war," Sara reminds her.

"To him it's a question of loyalty to your country."

"A government which shoots kids for expressing their right to free speech?" I say in disbelief.

"He doesn't see that side of it." Mom lowers her head.

I swallow hard and get up to use the bathroom. Whatever our differences, I respect Mom's effort to bridge between us.

When I return, they are both sitting cross-legged on the bed. Brown hair hanging down her back, pushed behind her ears, blue eyes expressive, Sara is settled in. Content to listen to her relating to Mom about how we first met Larry in front of the Kansas State Union, I relax back into the chair.

"A group of pro-war types were shouting at Jay and over to the side, another group at Larry, and, really, Jay and Larry were holding their own." Sara laughs. "Ever since they've been good friends."

"He's quite a bit older than you, isn't he?"

"Nine years," I answer. "After college he travelled around Europe then worked for a while, was married briefly, then came back and got a masters degree in art."

"Why did he stay in Manhattan?"

"Larry says that friends are the most important thing you can have," Sara explains.

"Friends come and go." Mom starts to refill our glasses. "Family is the only thing which never changes."

"Friends are important to us." Sara is emphatic.

"They are, of course," Mom concurs. Ready for some quiet time to read and reflect, glad they'll enjoy their time together I stand to excuse myself. Noticing I'm about to leave, Mom says: "Sweet dreams."

"We'll wake you up if anything exciting happens." Sara grins mischievously.

"After we ran out of cigarettes," Sara chuckles, "we actually smoked a stoggie we found in the lobby." She has just gotten out of the shower and is telling me about their adventures last night. "I don't even feel hungover."

Aware of my eyes, she smiles. Water beads glistening across soft skin, bird songs and bright light bouncing off full leaves outside our window, she pushes me playfully, wet hair cool against my chest, back onto our bed.

The Retreat

Ray Michael Jarvis, in a tan suit and silk tie, looking the gentleman, moves to the easy chair at the front of the room. Glancing around, I count some fifteen people and settle on a strangely attractive woman wearing a pink blouse with a straight-skirt, her hair blond with a silver tint.

"If I can have your attention," Ned O'Riley announces from the back of the room, "I'll introduce Ray Michael and then you can get started."

For the next hour, Jarvis talks about the lineage of his masters, their pictures spread reverentially on the side table, adding a quick overview of the major yogic schools before announcing a break.

While the others mill back toward the pass-through, I follow Sara to the deck facing Paladin's home. I had hoped he would be in the group. Mom stays behind. When she joins us, she says:"The blond lady's name is Karin. She's from New York. I asked her to meet us for supper."

A falcon pendant on her jacket, every piece of blond hair in place, Karin stands while Mom introduces us.

"You're the daughter-in-law, technically."

"Yes." Sara pats Mom on the shoulder. "But we joke that next time I may be the mother, so she better be nice to me."

"True." Karin smiles, then extends her hand to me. "And you are the beneficiary of much love."

Suddenly flooded with warmth, I fumble for words.

"So," Mom looks from me to Karin, "did you get your business done in Clayton?"

"Let's talk after we order." I am struck by a distinct perfume, rose or desert jasmine, associated with Karin. She seems self-determined and unaffected by her surroundings. Placing our orders then chatting, she treats us like old friends, then opens her briefcase.

Noticing a bound manuscript, I ask if she is a writer. Taking a deep breath while the waitress returns with our plates, she leans forward, her words clipped: "I need to share something and will get right to the point. Okay?"

"Sure." We respond in unison.

"I'm a very practical and realistic person — actually, as I told you," she nods at Mom, "an administrative assistant in the law firm which handled my husband's estate. Therefore, six years ago, when I heard a voice say I had to stop hiding from reality, I thought I had really lost it."

"You heard a voice?" Mom questions.

Karin nods. "I had had a series of dreams in which a spiritual being was trying to teach me something, but I refused to listen, so now he talks while I'm awake." She turns back to me. "He told me I had to study geography, politics, and metaphysics in order to be prepared to write."

"What are you supposed to write about?" I ask.

"About the end of this world."

"Any idea when that might be?" I try to sound casual.

"It's beginning now." She chooses her words carefully. "The wars, population problems, degradation of the environment — are both causes and symptoms. A new level of consciousness is trying to get hold here, while there's still time to turn it around or, to state it more accurately, to drive the camel through the eye of the needle. Whether the old world dies with a bang or a whimper depends on how successfully we attune to the new world which is being born."

Karin picks at her salad. "I'm interested in Jarvis's work as a means of clearing the consciousness of monkey chatter. But that's not the real reason we're here."

"What is the reason?" Mom sets her cup down.

The rest of us have finished eating. Taking a bite, Karin chews thoughtfully before going on: "My Master told me I would meet the people I am to work with."

All at once the room seems chilly. Outside it's grown dark. Everyone, except the waitress, has gone.

"Shall we pursue this further," Karin reaches for her briefcase, "or are you uncomfortable?"

"We're comfortable with you," Mom responds genuinely. "But

the whole thing about voices and the end of the world is a little scary." She starts to get up before continuing: "Probably because of things in my own background."

"We have a lot in common." Karin rises. "And there is much to be frightened of."

"Let's have lunch tomorrow," Mom suggests.

Karin nods appreciatively, then crosses the planks to the parking curb and drives toward Clayton.

Walking in the dark, Sara tugs me to the side as a car, it's headlights like the eyes of a night cat, approaches, slows, then speeds past us. Starting out again, Mom remarks: "How can she know the source of voices?"

"I don't know," I hesitate, "but if you can communicate with them while meditating ... "

"Like Jarvis says about the yogis," Sara interjects.

"Maybe that's what we're here to find out about," I suggest, not certain what I'm trying to say.

"In any event," Mom points up to the hotel, "Sara and I need some sleep." She starts up the steps. "Karin sets off some alarms." She pauses. "You know? But I do feel that she's very special."

In our room, Sara lies on the bed writing in her note book. I sit at the desk, wondering about Karin and what tomorrow will bring.

During the next couple days we are unable to make connections with Karin other than as part of the group work under Jarvis's gentle, but compelling, guidance. Each of us thoroughly enjoys the exercises and explanations of Yogananda's teaching. When we have free time, Sara and I walk the mountain trails. Cosmic rhythms unfold around us.

The tensions of the outside world: redneck, cop, army, war, which had driven so much of our action and reaction for several years, have begun to recede. It is as if Will's claim — that this area has been sacred to the Cherokees and all the way back to the Atlanteans — were true.

On the next to the last day of the workshop, with lunch finished and the entire group in the lodge, Karin suggests we take a short walk before the afternoon session. Moving toward the path, she apologizes for having been unavailable.

"I've been wondering about the Hart Retreat." Sara pauses as we enter a clearing. "Is it connected to CRC?"

"I don't know," Karin answers. "But when I first drove by there and saw the St. Germain flag ... "

"Isn't he associated with Theosophy?" Mom asks.

Karin nods, then walks to the edge of the clearing and back to us, before continuing: "St. Germain is a title used by a school of the spiritual hierarchy which has responsibility for this planet. Historically he was a famous alchemist, occult philosopher, and quite a Casanova. According to his critics, he was a brilliant charlatan. There's no doubt he was a spy and involved in various conspiracies.

"In any event, St. Germain is greatly revered by most occultists, but the dominant viewpoint today is that he was a fraud. Conservative churchmen maintain he represents the devil's work because, as you know," she holds her hands up, "if it ain't in the Bible, it's a delusion or worse.

"But," she glances in the direction of the Hart Retreat, "many of the most advanced adepts of the Western Mystery Tradition are in communication with a Master who identifies himself as the St. Germain who was born over 250 years ago and is associated with the Archangel Michael, the Spiritual Being who is in charge of the transition to the New World."

"New World?" Mom asks, looking up.

"The New Jerusalem, the Golden City, the 'change over' — depending on your school of prophecy. No matter what you call it, there are various centers around the world where the seed work is going forward. The Hart Retreat is one of those."

"Seed work?" I ask.

"Preparing the next generation for what must be done."

Back in our places, Jarvis begins the final afternoon session: "Consciousness is not limited to embodiment. The techniques have to do with clearing the window between us and other worlds.

"There is nothing easy about these teachings. Not when you dig deeper. But I believe that something inside each of you is in touch with a higher consciousness, an inner guide which knows what is good for you and what is not."

Jarvis rolls a piece of polished wood around the rim of a brass pot sending a weird then soothing series of overtones through the room.

"Close your eyes and relax. The techniques of my masters have been practiced for thousands of years, in dedication to the awakening of the higher self. Nothing which we will practice together will violate your own inner guidance."

Silence fills the room, a warm hush, a stillness which folds in and out in slow, peaceful waves. Breath suspended, Sara beside me, the room hovering, the presence of Beings, and Helpers, and Souls, and Attention, and Love ...

Some time later, the entire group having flowed through inexplicable silences full of harmony and light, Jarvis claps, gently bringing us back.

After the session, Karin says she has to meet some people in Clayton and excuses herself. Sara, Mom, and I walk along the shore, breathing deeply and barely talking, then go to the Marina for a quiet supper before returning to the lodge.

When Mom goes to her room to call home, Sara and I wander back outside. Hoisting herself into the swing, Sara suggests we take a drive with the top down. She leans back, legs extended to gain height. "The stars will be out soon."

Rounding the lake, I turn off at a sign to Tiger, a small hamlet we hadn't seen before. Sara sing-songs:

"'Tiger, Tiger, burning bright ... ' what was the rest?"

"'In the forests of the night,
What immortal hand or eye
Dare frame thy fearful symmetry?'"I quote.

Hit by a sudden gust, a chill running up my spine, I turn back toward the lake.

"There's a kid at the crossroads." Sara puts her hand on my leg while I slow to a stop. He's maybe fifteen years old.

"Thanks." He swings himself over the side into the back seat. "Could rain. Might be better with the top up."

"Doesn't look like rain to me," I reply.

"Could be important." He grins. "People are funny."

Under his baseball cap, he's freckled.

"Where are you from?" Sara inspects him, interested.

"All over, really. Been working on my chakras, opening up, you know. Been a little rough, actually." He's serious.

"At CRC?" Sara asks. "We didn't see you."

"Nah, this is the real stuff." He chuckles. "It knocked me out for a while, though. Too much, too quick."

"Do you need any help?" I ask, puzzled.

"I was kind of lost," he answers. "I don't know. Too much floods in."

"You've been lost?" Sara is concerned.

"I'm supposed to tell you to stay."

"Us? Why?" Sara asks.

"Don't know."

Suddenly having the urge to put the top up, I snap it into place just before a pick-up truck passes, rough looking men watching us from inside, a couple others in the bed, going slowly, a rifle in the back window.

"You know them?" I ask.

"Enough to get out of their way," he answers matter-of- factly. "I'm Mike." He extends his hand. "So," he looks at Sara, "you're staying?"

"At least tonight," she confirms then glances at me.

"We better get out of here." He points ahead.

I pull onto the road, wondering if he is spaced out on drugs. Lights on, I curve toward the lake. Sara is facing him across the seat, asking: "How long have you been here?"

"Tell you the truth, with this chakra thing, I've lost track." He turns toward the side. "Could you stop?" I pull over. "It's just that there is so much going on." He smiles, uninhibited. "It's not drugs. I know what you're thinking."

"Well, Mike," Sara pauses, "it's not everyday someone says they've had their chakras opened. Are you okay?"

"Who's okay with the war going on? Who's okay when the world is suffering? There are only certain things I can talk about." He crosses the road behind us and walks in the opposite direction. Head lights approach. I turn to see if he catches a ride. There's no one there.

On our way back to the lodge, Sara says: "If someone else heard that conversation, they'd think he was cracked."

"Or on drugs, but he seemed straight to me."

Returning to our room, Sara peers out the window. Trees move like dark figures through the crisp air against the mountain beyond her. I get flickers of images from the yoga meditations — some Being or Spiritual Intelligence lifting us up. Turning back to me, she says: "I have the feeling we should take an I Ching reading."

After studying Carl Jung's introduction to the ancient oracle, we had decided the I Ching should never be used casually; but handing the three Chinese coins to Sara, I sense she was right. "How would you phrase the question?"

"I want to find out what the effect would be if we stay, and," she brushes her hand back through her hair, "what's going on here."

Writing the question while Sara clears her mind and tosses the coins six times, I think about the thousands of possible answers.

Opening *The Book of Changes* she checks the index for the reading, then flips through the text to the proper page and reads: "'DIFFICULTY AT THE BEGINNING works supreme success. It furthers one to appoint helpers. . . . Everything is in motion: therefore if one perseveres there is a prospect of great success, in spite of existing danger.'"

She pauses, thinking, then moves her finger across the text. "'In order to overcome the chaos' we need helpers ... and we need 'inspiration and guidance.'"

Karin's references to the Hart Retreat and the spiritual hierarchy float through my mind. Sara turns to the next reading:

"'HOLDING TOGETHER brings good fortune.
Inquire of the oracle once again
Whether you possess sublimity, constancy, and
perseverance; then there is no blame.
Those who are uncertain gradually join.
Whoever comes too late, meets with misfortune.'"

Scanning the commentary, she reads:"'... anyone attempting the task without a real calling ... makes confusion worse than if no union had taken place ... He who comes too late to share in these basic experiences must suffer for it, if, as a straggler, he finds the door locked.'"

"That's heavy." I make a note. "Some place it says: Don't ask, if you don't want the answer."

"I know." Sara pauses. "And now we have to ask whether we're up to it. This time you throw the coins."

Sitting on the floor, I toss the coins.

"'Treading (Conduct).'" Sara glances up from the text. "You ready for this?"

"Sure." I go back to the table to write.

"'Treading upon the tail of the tiger. It does not bite the man. Success.'

"That's weird." Sara looks up. "Tiger, you know — the town? Then Mike. Maybe he's a helper?" She reads ahead: "'Treading' is composed of 'heaven above, the lake below.' So," she pauses, "at least we're in the right place."

"What?" I ask, puzzled.

"The lake mirrors heaven." She points outside. "By treading we achieve supreme success. The tiger doesn't bite."

"If we have the right helpers." I refer to the notebook. "And spiritual guidance."

"And if we have sublimity, constancy, and perseverance."

"The last two are just a matter of applying ourselves," I think out loud, "but the sublime is something monstrous, which breaks through and changes everything — what Blake called the marriage of Heaven and Hell. 'Tiger, Tiger burning bright.'" Sara shakes her head as I quote:

> "'When the stars threw down their spears
> And watered heaven with their tears,
> Did He smile His work to see?
> Did He who made the lamb make thee?'"

"What are we getting into here?" Sara reaches for the wine bottle Mom left and fills our glasses.

"Don't know, Babe." I hold my glass up to hers. "But we're about to find out."

After a leisurely breakfast, during which we tell Mom we're staying at least another night, we arrive at CRC excited for the final session with Ray Michael Jarvis.

Glancing around the room, Sara whispers: "Where's Karin? Surely she wouldn't leave without saying goodbye."

His voice a settled sureness, Jarvis addresses us: "When the mind is still, the sound of the universe is a wave. Ahead of you and within you, you sense, then see, a golden radiance shining from a dark core. Coming closer, you see a white light in the very center of the figure. This is the condensation of the Trinity.

"White is Pure Consciousness. Blue is Universal Intelligence. Gold is Cosmic Vibration. Perceiving these lights, surrender to the gold — merge with it. Once you're settled, move on and yield to the blue — feeling yourself to be one with Universal Intelligence, knowing that what sustains you sustains all creatures, all life, all sounds and forms.

"Finally, having felt the vast sweep and intimate nearness of the blue light, surrender to the white. You are being pulled by the Magnetic Attraction, the True Source, to the realization of Pure Being — the highest samadhi, the Realization of Oneness. This exercise is called the Tunnel of Eternity. Stay there. Be at peace."

The blue light flickers and is superseded by white. A roaring then silent glow fills the cosmos. Lost in it, I am still conscious of the platform of my breath; the steps by which Jarvis has taken us through imagination to vision, from sound to silence, by gold to blue then white; that the universe resonates with total and pure Being.

Jarvis fades from my consciousness.

Will taps Mom on the shoulder. "It's time to go."

Sara stirs on the other side of me. My eyes flicker, moving toward focus, the quick farewells with the other students, expressions of appreciation to Jarvis and Ned.

Reoriented and euphoric, we help Will transfer Mom's luggage to the van, so he can drive her to the airport.

"I didn't get to say goodbye to Karin." Mom looks around one more time. "Give her my love."

"We will." Tears in her eyes, full of thankfulness, Sara hugs her. Words can't express how much she has done for us, over and over again.

Holding hands we walk back up the path behind the lodge. Being alone together we celebrate our presence in these mountains. A view over the lake. Sun shining through high clouds — gold, blue, and white.

"What's next?" Sara rises to stretch.

"You took the I Ching." I laugh, feeling good.

"Let's take a drive then get something to eat." She pulls me up by the hand then down the path to our car.

Circling in a large loop, we stop at Clearmont for gas.

Leaving Sara while the attendant washes the window and checks the oil, I approach the porch of the combined grocery and service station. Dirt streaked children are arguing over the coke they are to share. Inside, a man in overalls stares at me as a woman, in a plain, home-made dress, backs away. Suddenly conscious that my wire-rimmed glasses and sandals mark me as an outsider, I pay quickly.

Driving back toward the lake, I note homes tucked neatly into the woods. Tall trees throw shadows across gardens and roof-tops. No cars, no rednecks in pick-up trucks now.

"I feel something but don't know what it is," Sara muses.

"Do you remember any dreams?" I probe, knowing that the sleep world is a place she goes rather than simply a necessary counter-balance to the day.

"I haven't thought about the dreams." She pauses. "Let's stop at the Marina."

"'Sublimity, constancy, and perseverance,'" I quote. "What else?"

"Heaven over the Lake ... Good fortune from waiting. That's how I remember it. It's been good today."

"Sure has," I agree. I remember the sensation in the Clearmont service station but say nothing.

An old fisherman waves when we come in and take a table next to a couple of women talking about the CRC workshop on occult fiction which begins tonight. As they get up to pay their bill, I hear one of them say Paladin is working on a novel based on a race of Olympians trying to save the world, and wonder why I hadn't made the effort to follow up with him.

Finishing my meal, I ask Sara what's next?

"Whatever presents itself ..." She stops, slightly startled. Mike — baseball cap in hand, in jeans and a Led Zeppelin tie-dye T-shirt — is moving toward us.

"Thought I'd find you here." He grins.

Sara gives him the thumbs up sign. "What's going on?"

Leaning toward us, hands on the table, he whispers: "There's someone you're supposed to meet."

"Who?" I recall the I Ching reading and Sara's comment that he might be one of the "helpers."

"Not sure." He hunches his shoulders. "Just stay in the area. It'll happen."

The waitress approaches with our ticket. Mike stands completely still. She doesn't seem to see him. After she's returned to the counter, he says:

"There's a building up the mountain, just this side of the Hart Retreat. Take that road."

"And do what?" Sara coaxes.

"You might stop there." He glances around. "Something might happen."

"Did someone tell you we were to be there?" I pursue it, not wanting to play games.

"That's the best I can do." He points to his heart, walks toward the register, then veers out the door.

He is nowhere in sight when we get outside. "What do you think?" Sara asks.

"We've gone this far." Recalling Mike's comment last night, I note that the roof is still up, then drive toward the purple flag on a high pole above the Hart Retreat.

A mile later Sara points to an abrupt turn off and a building on the rise, barely visible in the trees. Stopping in the parking lot, we study a six sided building with a high pitched roof, encircled by a porch, fairly new, but with no identifying signs. Something is wrong. The windows are broken out. The door hangs open. Against the pine scent of the clearing I sense the vague acid of gun powder.

Pushing in, tentatively, we enter the main room. Stout posts from the wood floors support lofts around the perimeter. The kitchen, on one side, opens to the center. On the opposite wall, shelves for a library are bare except for a few randomly scattered magazines. A sleeping bag and some blankets are spread beneath the windows facing the lake, which is barely visible in the distance.

"Looks like they were attacked." Sara turns to me, concern on her face. "We should get out of here."

Tires screeching — a red pick-up slides into the lot. A man, in his mid-thirties, wearing glasses, brown hair bunched around his collar, hurries up the steps waving his arms:

"We can't stay. They may be back ... "

"Who?" Sara reacts, alarmed.

"Rednecks. Blew the place up last night. Shot the windows out, everything. Could have killed someone."

"Why?" I ask, astonished.

"This was a rehab place for drug-kids out of Athens and Atlanta." He goes to the corner and picks up the blankets and sleeping bag. "Guess they didn't get everything."

"Who?" Sara moves toward him.

"We had to get them out. Terrible. Most are really screwed up: cocaine, acid, heroin. We're trying to put them back together again."

"Who is?" I ask.

"Order of Melchizedek, mostly. Other groups. You know, White Brotherhood, all that. Trying to help these kids and we get this. Somebody was supposed to stop it!"

Sara helps him with the blankets.

He surveys the room, moving with determination. "We better get going. It's still dangerous."

Sara says: "Why did you come back?"

"I was down by the lake. A voice just said ..."

"Who told you about us?" I cut him off.

Looking confused, he says: "No one — but there's someone you're supposed to meet."

"Who?" Sara starts for the door.

"Just follow my truck." He stops and takes one last look around the room. "Wait a minute." He drops the bag and blankets. "Maybe we should walk."

"What about our car?" I'm edgy about the attack.

"Oh," he laughs. "I'm Jack."

"Jay."

"And Sara," she adds.

"Let's visit a bit." He walks to the sliding glass door to the porch in the back. "Sometimes I get out of order. I'm from another planet." He looks at Sara.

"A space man?" I ask, not amused.

"Not even a name for it here." He sits on the steps.

"'Jack' sounds American enough," Sara comments, disbelief in her voice.

"That's my given name." He leans against a post at the top of the stairs leading down into a rock garden.

"What do you mean about another planet?" I ask.

"It's a memory." He surveys the landscape. "The attack's over, for now." He studies me. "Lots of the 'star children' have memories because they're not so attached here. The drugs make it worse for them."

"Who do you work with?" Sara probes.

"I'm sure you're supposed to meet this lady."

"Do you work with her?" Sara presses him.

"Everyone does, though most don't know it. I don't always." He seems humble, reflective.

"What's she do?" I try to get him back on track.

"She cooks." Adjusting his glasses, Jack moves back into the house, pointing for us to move around the outside to our car. "Lock your doors," he cautions.

When we arrive at the other side, he's tossing the bag and blankets into the bed of his truck.

Moving like a leprechaun, Jack leads us into the woods, ducking beneath branches, skirting the bramble which seemed impenetrable from the house.

Just past the tree line, a path opens before us. One hundred yards further, stopping at a clearing, he sits on a stone bench. Taking a deep breath, he seems pleased.

"This is beautiful." Sara turns in a circle.

"This is the back way to Mahdah Hart's."

"Who's she?" I ask.

"She runs the Hart Retreat Center." He looks around. "She and her husband, a scientist. But he's on the other side now, still working with her but not incarnate. Mahdah Hart is the present director under St. Germain."

"Is that where we're going?" I wait for an answer.

"No." He gets up and signals us to follow. "Just behind the back walls, then over to the Oasis."

"A third center?" Sara asks.

"Oh, there are lots of centers, you know — a circle with a circumference, the center of which is everywhere — an alchemical garden."

Following Jack behind a tall stone fence, I ask: "Are they all connected?"

"There are levels and levels of connection, most of which are not recognized." He turns back toward me. "You know about Ezekiel's spaceship, don't you? Wheels within wheels."

"A spaceship to us," I comment, "a fiery chariot in the sky to his contemporaries."

"Well," Jack points off to the left, "there's even a landing site. Some of the scientists have been working with extraterrestrials for years. It's all pretty routine now."

"Routine?" Sara exclaims.

"For them." He takes a few steps in that direction.

Sara stands her ground. "Do you work with them?"

"I know it goes on, but that's not my thing." He returns to us. "I don't even know who they are."

"What about your planet?" Sara asks.

"Sometimes I get images of it."

"How?" She insists.

"Interdimensionally." He studies her. "In meditation, by certain exercises."

He turns to continue along the path behind the stone wall, then pauses, looking back at Sara. "If it's your thing, someone will explain it."

Behind the Hart Retreat, noticing terraced grounds through a wrought-iron gate, I stop to glance in. Several bungalows dot the manicured landscape. Gardening tools line a building made of the same stone as the fence. Rock, vegetable and flower gardens are laid out between the buildings and a small white wooden structure near the edge of the grounds. An older couple work in one of the garden areas. The air is fresh. A white-bearded man sits in a lawn chair beneath a large maple tree reading a book. In the center of the complex, between an administrative building and a lodge, which might once have been a huge stone barn, a purple flag waves peacefully in the afternoon light.

"A lot goes on there," Jack comments, surveying the grounds with me.

"How do you get in?" Sara looks at him.

"Just rent a room." He raises his shoulders whimsically, then turns to lead us along the path behind the fence.

"What are you going to do if the rehab center is shut down?" Sara calls after him.

"They've changed my assignment. We'll have to start up again, in another place."

"Who gives you the assignments?" I ask.

"The lady I'm taking you to. Today I was supposed to find you. Then I'm going to Atlanta to organize more kids."

The path veers into the woods.

"How does she know us?" I ask.

"I haven't seen her for months." He pauses. "Wish I could, but she's busy. We all are."

"So who told you?" Sara pursues her original theme.

"You'll learn how she does it." He holds his arms up while weaving between trees, the trail narrowing, more rugged here. "There's the path to the landing site." He points. "Over the rise."

Backing away from us, Sara says: "Can I take a look?"

"Up to you," Jack answers noncommittally.

Within moments, Sara is back, looking dismayed.

"What?" I ask.

"There is a clearing, with a rope around it. Everything is bare in the center." She moves down the path ahead of us.

The Teacher

Ten minutes later, we weave out of the woods and descend toward a cabin which I had noticed when we first drove toward CRC. Jack signals us to stay where we are while he knocks respectfully on the screen door, calling softly: "Elsie, I've got some friends here to meet you."

A lady, somewhere between fifty and seventy, totally vital, with short strawberry-blond hair, brilliant crystal-blue eyes, solid, barefooted, wearing a gray smock, steps onto the porch stoop. "Thought you might come today." A friendly grin spreads across her face. Turning to Jack, she pats him on the back. "Good work."

"Elsie, this is Jay and Sara." He nods to us, then walks around the edge of the house toward the woods.

"He has these fantastic ideas." Elsie laughs gently, then hugs Sara like a child or grandchild she hasn't seen for years. "Thinks I'm a white witch."

"He's pretty mysterious," I comment. Entering the kitchen — full of clean light, bright smells, spicy — suddenly I sense that everything up to this point has been a meandering on the way to Elsie's home.

"So you're a writer." She opens her ice box and takes water out. "The glasses are over there, Sara." She points. I pull chairs out for us. "I used to write for *Poetry*, under other names, though. You can't do too much as one person. Anyway, I've got plenty of connections, still ... Random House, Yale, the major presses, so we can get something done."

Placing the pitcher on the table, Elsie backs to the window and takes a half-smoked cigarette from a glass ash tray, lights a match, watching the flame, draws in on the cigarette, then puts it out, saying: "Just to keep one toe on the ground. I'm the match girl, you know. One light in a deep forest. One light, then another. So," she looks at me, "you want a printing press — to cut costs for your magazine?" Amazed she's immediately into what I had wanted to discuss with Ned but had forgotten, I simply nod.

She pours water for each of us then backs to the window again. "I used to run a press, in the early days. You're out of money — from your subscriptions ... Right." She relights her cigarette, exhales. "That could work, but it has to be off-set, and that depends on condition. I think there's a man" she pauses, "north of where you live. Franklin, or in Franklin? Have you talked to him?"

"We've heard about him." Sara glances at me.

"In Franklin," I answer, wondering how she could know that. "He prints magazines and fliers, and might have an old off-set to sell. We just don't know how we could buy it."

She spins around on her toes. "We can't give you anything; but we can sell it to you for pennies. Yes. Okay," she answers herself. "You want to look at some things. What you take, that's serious — understand?"

"Take?" I ask.

"Accept." She looks up at me. "You're growing already."

"Don't think so." I laugh, off guard but fascinated.

"Just keep track of the patterns." She points to the door, then potted plants, flowers, pots and pans stacked on top of the cupboards, utensils above the refrigerator, back to the kitchen sink, faucet, trays of beads, a crucifix hanging on the wall, a framed picture, notes pinned to cork board, a stack of cook books. "Everything changes. Be careful what you accept. I can't know what's right for you, but I'm like your fairy godmother. I love having you here."

Patting Sara affectionately, she goes back to the window and fingers her cigarette. "Want one of mine?"

"We have our own." Sara digs in her purse and hands our package to her. Pointing to the logo, then turning it upside down, Elsie says:

"Watch 'Salem' become 'Wales.' Know there's a tunnel between the Celtic underworld and the kingdom of Melchizedek — old Jeru-Salem. We can go on and on about tobacco." She winks at me. "I'm a man in a woman's body, so, like Jay, I need a little tobacco. It's hormonal, but ..." She glances up beyond the ceiling then takes Sara's arm. "He is growing. Hard to keep up, isn't it, dear? Hold on." She ducks. "Some of these boys do grow so fast. Sometimes I smoke the ones with no tobacco."

"No tobacco?" Sara asks. Watching, I'm wholly engaged but also slightly unnerved. There's a strange energy running through Elsie, particularly as she shifts voices.

"I'm an alchemist by trade. Root of chemistry." She points for us to sit down. "Digging around, you know, I combined archeology with a law degree — interesting, right? No one doubts me. That's a laugh, isn't it?" She chuckles.

"Putting them out, the way I do — " she stubs her cigarette, "I shoot for the right amount. Less expensive to watch our pennies than our dollars. Dollars could break a man. But I have lots." She pulls a cupboard open. Cartons of different types of cigarettes are piled on each other.

"We drive onto the reservation for tobacco. Plenty of Salems here, though." She points. "These are all special — a nice mix. Each body needs what it needs." Patting herself, she sighs. "I need this one and it needs tobacco. Have you been to the falls?"

Putting her finger to her temple, she looks up through the ceiling. "Haven't, yet," she answers. "When you get back, maybe. I've just been — afternoon monitoring — checking it out ... you know, Sara ..."

"What, Elsie?" Sara straightens.

"Just got back, actually ... Saw Jack — bless his soul — traipsing around behind Mahdah's. Glad you were with him. It's been a while, hasn't it?"

She waits for an answer. Sara smiles.

"You're a natural." She gazes at Sara. "That's all you need to know. You can't learn it."

I ask: "You were travelling astrally?"

"Terms confine us." Her eyes pierce me. "I'd sweat like a Turk if I took this," she pats her self, "everywhere — particularly in summer. In Pondicherry we use alchemy to transform the bodies. The Mother's cells are the key to the descent of the supramental. Read Sri Aurobindo."

She leads us into the other room. Light diffused here, it smells like an old candy shop but then I catch the whiff of some chemical operation, sense that I'm in a laboratory, but mixed with peppermint, licorice, butterscotch.

"Meanwhile," she glances at me, "we're working on kids blown-up in Vietnam. Jack is one of them."

"Blown up?" Sara asks. I wonder what Jack found when he got back to the rehab center, whether rednecks are after him.

"They're all over the walls. It's terrible, dear." Elsie, full of sadness, looks at Sara. "Just trying to keep the gene-pools together. This is the worst. We're down in the caves literally scraping their bodies off the walls."

"He's too old for Vietnam, isn't he?" Sara questions.

"This is where I work with crystals. See this." Elsie hands a glass container to Sara. "Look deep."

"There's a diamond light in it." Sara seems fascinated.

"It's a start. Jack was an officer. I'm re-growing him; but he has his own ideas. A little care. The right water, right window, right sun and moon — fixed to different planets and stars. You have the knack for it, you know."

"What ... " Sara hesitates.

"You do, Sara," Elsie says emphatically. "Don't doubt it. Jay knows you know, but that won't help if you don't." She looks back to me. "Patience makes perfect." Elsie's smile pulls my heart. "Then it disappears."

"What does?" I ask.

"Perfection." She stamps. "Move toward the edge. A toe here and there. That's my practice — the perpetual practice of the presence of God. The old cook from France. I'm a cook, too. CRC — catch the letters? — " she winks, "has a pamphlet on him — his letters. Pick it up."

Setting the crystal down and turning her attention back to Elsie, Sara says: "How do you interpret the letters?"

"Cosmic Refinement Center." Elsie smiles. "Christian Rosen-Creuz. Cycle of Raven Consciousness. Make of it what you will."

"Are you connected with CRC?" I ask.

"Elsie here, Elsie there, Elsie everywhere — a little match girl. Sara's the same. Lighting fires."

"Does Mahdah Hart own CRC?" Sara asks.

"No." Elsie pauses. "One of the old ladies holds to 'Christian Retreat Center.' That's good, though I prefer 'Cosmic Raven Consciousness' or 'Christos Repair Center' — with earth sciences and alchemy. So they think I'm a dark witch." She rolls her eyes up. "Could be."

Struck by a chill, I sense that the cocoa and cinnamon sticks, the candy store of her kitchen, are gone, leaving the room cold with emptiness. Pulling my head down, Elsie whispers: "Every male wants to get her into bed, but she doesn't know it. Watch her. And Sara," she releases me and raises her voice: "be careful."

"What?" Sara asks, startled.

"The men will leave you if you let them."

"Because I come too late?" Sara pauses. "We had an I Ching reading that said that — about stragglers."

"No, dear. Because they love you."

"That doesn't make sense."

"They're afraid."

"Of what?" Sara looks bewildered, troubled.

"Of love." She leads Sara to the straight back chair by the window. Slanting through sheer curtains, tangled with plants along the shelf, glancing off crystal beds in cut glass containers, the sun hovers in pools of refracted light. Drawing the curtains back, Elsie says: "You can channel, Sara. Listen. Open your heart."

Elsie's hand on the back of her neck, Sara swivels to look out the window. Her focus diffused, she breathes deeply. Standing beside her, knowing she's been frightened by out-of-body experiences, I wonder how she will react.

Bending to her ear, Elsie says: "Voices, Sara, first your own, then others. Beneath the others, around the edges, the fingers of your intuition catch something — tug gently. Open your heart, your throat, your mind. Let words form at the base of your tongue. Give them space. Move to the side. Allow those who hover about you to speak."

Gazing out the window, Sara breathes. Mouth open, she forms the place for words. Blue eyes, she searches Elsie. "How do I know? How do I know it's right?"

"Watch yourself and the world within worlds, here." She touches Sara's forehead then holds her face up. "Taste it. Words form like honey and flowers, morning dew-drops on leaves, sun glistening from a time before we were cut off from the other worlds."

Sara forms the words slowly: "I can see. But I don't know which words are right."

"Nor do I." Elsie nods. "But the beings protect you — your guardian angel holds you firmly in her wisdom and love. There's no hurry.

Learning to speak is learning to wait." Clucking her tongue, turning to me, she whispers: "Not her long suit." Then to Sara, in a normal voice: "Learn to wait, but be alert, ready, willing."

Glancing back out the window, Sara says: "I don't want to lose control."

"Your control?" Elsie swivels Sara back to face herself. "Choo-choo ... I think I can ... well ... the control you fight for is the prison the old men lay on us — the fear which throttles spirit. It's thinking like they think — choo-choo — so we do their will without being told. Women, Sara, are natural mediums."

Chugging around the room, feet shuffling like the bars between the wheels of an engine, her voice booming, Elsie calls out: "Used to get burned for it, we did." She stops abruptly.

"I feel the fire." There is a slow urgency in Sara's voice. "The Salem witch trials were wrong."

"Yes, certainly, but in the school of fire we learn to read from the tablet of the invisible world. Practice alchemy. Fire is the crucible in which gold is fused from base metals. Love is the oven which warms those frozen in matter. The control you hold is fear. Let it go." She whispers: "Through love, suffering turns to joy. Let your heart transform the world."

Lighting a match, holding a cigarette to the flame, blowing a white stream into the room, she studies Sara then takes a seat beside her. "The 'control' is the iron fist of Patriarchs: Jehovah, the fire-spitter, and his servants, Abraham and Moses. Even the women are enlisted. Well ..."

Stubbing her cigarette out, Elsie stands. Feet spread, raising her arms to the heavens, defiant, she shouts: "I'm called de-moniac by those too simple for my complex cervix. They want service. Well, hell!" She stamps the floor. "The mountain is ours!"

"What do you mean?" Sara shifts in the chair.

"The mountain — stolen by the fire god who sacrificed intuition — belongs to us. The control you fear to lose is rational mind, frozen before the angel." Leaning forward, Elsie pulls Sara up and, swaying slightly, croons:

> "You're a natural girl so don't
> let the demon mind your home alone
> and don't let the demon drive
> the mother-mind out of you."

They face each other as if I'm not in the room.

"I don't understand ... " Sara starts.

"But you do. It's just demon mind that doesn't."

"What's demon mind?"

"That which fears the devil. Christians don't fear the devil. Love Christ. Open to the angels. Practice the presence. Only the minions of rationality fear the devil.

"It's the Christians who preach the devil," Sara says.

"Ah ... " Elsie's face lights up in wonderment then, dropping her voice: "But are they really Christians?"

Sitting and patting the empty chair for Sara to join her, in her normal voice, Elsie says: "You've bought the lie that only the rational mind knows. It's all lies, of course — fragments and splinters — but the female ones can give birth, produce miracles."

Sara continues to stand. Taking her arms and studying her, Elsie sing-songs:

"The rational mind can't know.
It only analyzes, dissects, controls.
The intuitive mind knows — but it
doesn't know it knows it knows."

Opening her eyes wide, like just waking up, Elsie says: "So we need both, not one afraid of the other. We should dance, Sara, both minds, not just de-moniac. Find the marriage. Don't let either drive the other out." Snapping to attention, saluting, she adds: "Got it?"

"But you said you don't know."

"I can't know what's coming through — whether it's right for me or you? Right?"

"Yes." Sara nods.

Clicking her heels, Elsie salutes the ceiling. "Weak or strong tidings, I've sacrificed the governor that the man-world teaches, true, but ..." She does a two-step sashay around the room as if she's dancing with an invisible partner:

"I raise children in us, so
don't you let
the little boy tell
the little girl
she doesn't matter when
matter is
the body of spirit and

what she is
is matter — got it?"

She backs up and bows, one arm in front and one in back. Cocking her head left then right, Elsie's face is like a clown's, joyous, uninhibited then profoundly sad as Sara nods, acknowledging that she understands something.

"I don't know what is right." Elsie places her finger on Sara's forehead. "But you do." She smiles warmly. "God it?"

"God it?" Sara reflects her smile.

"God-dess it. That's whole, that's truth. God-dess it, guard it, carry it home." Elsie salutes again, places her hand over her breast, sits down and lights a cigarette. Studying the smoke, then glancing out the window, she says:

"We're both male and female, Sara — princess in Egypt, covering for old Abraham — brother and sister but first it sure as hell was her land, well ... " She stamps her foot again and stands, "why do you think you're named that, Sara?"

Having taken a seat, Sara looks up. "I don't know."

"Rational and intuitive
Males in female bodies —
you and me are ... "

Scanning Sara, Elsie continues:

"sacred curves and proportions,
but the man in you says:
'It's not me, soft,
blue eyed, attractive.'"

Clucking and shaking her head, Elsie looks like a mother hen or girl scout troop-leader inspecting her daughter who is a tom-boy, who won't keep her dress straight, who just wants to run for the sun and crow like a rooster, and tumble in the dust — but approves, as well, saying:

"He's okay in you but don't forget beneath the female- denying-male there's a wild woman like me, a medium for black soil, fertility, miracles — running."

Grinning mischievously, Elsie brushes Sara's hair back behind her ear, then bobs down and up, spinning slowly along a vertical axis. Facing Sara, she says: "Rationality fixes this place — toot, toot ..."

She circles as if on a horse on a merry-go-round. "And as archaeologist, lawyer — I told you that, didn't I? — the man in me, the rational, likes that; but, toot-toot, I'm a dancer, too — with the spirit worlds that interpenetrate this one."

Slamming her palm down on the table, startling Sara, firm and decisive, Elsie declares:

"And so can, and should, you, too.
Toot-toot, doodle-doodle —
It's an irrational treat
But not always so sweet
It can be scary, so scary
That old-man demon
Clips our wings."

Holding her arms out, she sails around the room, singing:

"But we fly anyway, anyway, anyway ... "her voice trailing off like an echo. "Because," she stops and turns to Sara, "if you monitor at all with 'his right, her wrong, his left, her right,' you kill breath, life, Sara — inspiration."

Going back to where Sara is sitting, Elsie holds her face up, blue eyes on blue eyes. "Breathe because that's what we're born to and," she pauses, then emphasizes each word: "across the threshold of breath the angels pray."

I smell cotton candy. The room brightens. A breeze flutters in through the windows casting rainbows through crystals suspended against the light. Carousel music, or the suggestion of it, in the songs of birds, streams from the trees shifting gently outside.

"So," Elsie takes a deep breath and addresses me while Sara turns to the window, "you should contact Paladin. Just the type of help you need, Jay." It's as if the entire interlude with Sara had occurred in a parallel world, in an instant, or not in time at all. "He'll be very big. Writing for people. That's the key. You could work together."

"I barely know him." I follow her back into the kitchen area. Light floods through the windows now, mixed with gingerbread cooking, pies and oven smells, as if the two rooms are completely separate worlds.

"We've all worked together — lot's of times." Elsie lights her cigarette again. "Paladin knows it, or should."

"We talked a little — that's all." I pause while Sara enters and scans the room, reorienting.

"She's okay," Elsie whispers. "Watch this." She raises her voice: "He's doing a workshop. When you get back ..."

Sara interrupts: "We're coming back?"

"I think so." Elsie holds her arms up and shrugs. "Should be five of you. What do you want?" She takes a stick of incense from a clay vase, and holds it out to Sara.

Sitting at the table and striking a match, Sara hesitates, studies the flame. Moving behind her, Elsie places her hands on Sara's shoulders. "After it grows, blow on it."

Igniting the incense, waving it gently, Sara's eyes sparkle. Elsie leans forward from behind. They blow together. "Where does the flame go?" Elsie whispers.

"Into the smoke," Sara answers as Elsie kisses the back of her head, then turns to me. Shifting again, as if there is one world with Sara and another with me, she says:

"You could have attended his seminar but not now." She brings her fist down on the table. "We're on the oblique here. Gurdjieff geometry, the octave, shocks in the side. You know about that."

"What?" I ask, startled.

She opens the cupboard and hands Sara a carton of Salems saying: "You're both picking up a lot." She turns back to me. "Sacrificing the obvious to get to the real."

"So you think it's better I didn't attend?"

"Would we be here, if you had?" Elsie gives me a quizzical, innocent, little girl look. "Smoke teaches us, and," she points at the ash tray from which a spiraling ring of incense trails upward, "covers the real work. See?"

"The invisible?" I ask.

"I work with bubbles," Elsie goes on, "thin surfaces, spheric geometries. Embryos follow the same pattern. Everything in nature. Smoke covers the invisible, yes." She fixes me with a stare. "Helps us to center, hide, appear elsewhere — El See, you know — hide and seek. Good stuff, right?" She winks at Sara, then grins. "Better than see-gars, right?"

"Cigars? Right!" Sara laughs to herself. I see an image of her and my mother smoking a cigar after staying up late talking the first night we arrived here.

Elsie lights another cigarette, watches the flame then the smoke plume. "Have you seen anyone else, besides Jack?"

Glancing at me, Sara says: "Do you know Mike?"

Elsie's head swings back sharply. "Mike?"

"Yes." I slide into the seat opposite Sara.

Elsie opens the screen door and looks into the yard. As she turns back to us, the door claps shut behind her. "He might have seen the flags. Let's get some onions."

We follow toward the garden. "It's all mulched. Do you like it?" she asks casually. "Holds the water in, the weeds out, a special technique. Might help you." She turns to Sara. "You should garden, you know."

"My grandparents did, but we don't have much room."

"Doesn't take much," Elsie comments. "Bio-intensive. French technique, through Steiner — wonderful stuff. I can teach you. Brother Lawrence would be lost without his herbs."

"Brother Lawrence?" I ask.

"The Perpetual Practice of the Presence of God," she answers. "The CRC booklet, remember? About the monk?"

"The monk?" I respond.

"All of us."

"What flags?" Sara returns to her earlier reference.

"On the clothesline, see? Different colors for different possibilities. I learned all that from my husband. He was in the Pentagon for years. Used to go into the meetings, all these generals around a big table, and just rub his worry stone. Pretty soon, everyone was settled down and they could get the work done. I love the Navy, don't you?"

Turning back to the garden, Elsie reaches down into the layers of straw and pulls out several onions. Placing them in a white bucket, she leads us back into the house.

"I'm against the war, the entire military-industrial complex." I hold the door open for her.

"Men are trained by war," she comments, undisturbed.

"To slaughter each other," I respond.

"You'll never stop war." Elsie washes onions in the sink. "It's what you do with it that counts. In the Pentagon, Vern works for 'just' wars — symbol of white witches, you know?"

"War?" I'm astonished.

"The Pentagon — layers within layers." She peels back the onion skin. "Would you disband the scouts, too?"

"Boy scouts?" I'm confused, spinning.

"Best we have left of the old Indian orders." She lays the onions aside and lights a cigarette, studying me. "Invisible orders, yes. But in the visible — what one can see. Would you disband them?"

"I have no interest in them." I'm not sure I'm tracking. Looking over her shoulder, I see Sara putting a cutting board beside the sink.

"Well," Elsie stubs her cigarette out, "you're hurting your dad, and you're wrong about yourself. You've yearned for the forest, for the hunt, for the long dance — ever since you were a child — long before that, really."

Feeling pierced by a spear, I recall images of stalking game, sneaking up on enemy camps, climbing trees, dancing for hours around a fire, dreams and imaginings from my past.

Looking into my eyes, Elsie puts her hand on my shoulder. "You want to fight, because you are a fighter. Our boys must be initiated, must move through the rites of passage so their skills are honed, their craft made precise and beautiful. Only the master can be gentle. And ... "

She lifts her arms up. Clicking her fingers above her head like a flamenco dancer, warm spices in the air, she turns in a slow circle, and sings:

"I love the generals and the generals love me ...
I love the generals ... "

Her voice melodic, sassy, womanly, yet with the innocence of a little girl, she completes the line:

"and the generals love me ... "

She moves her arms back and forth as if pulling the ropes of a swing in order to sail higher, arching in suspense.

"And flying is fun for the innocent one
In the skies, above the ocean blue sea."

A coquette, impish, she does a little two step around her kitchen, then sings again, her voice deep and resonant now:

"Just don't stop at what you think you see."

Relighting her cigarette, she exhales:

"And don't believe me."

Turning from the sink, Sara asks: "Who should we believe, Elsie?"

Tilting her head sideways, crossing her hands over her chest, she bows slightly, then chants:

"I drop the guard to let the stuff in.
What you accept is what you win."

The scents of flowers, leaves, and grasses waft through the windows while Elsie bows deeply, arms out behind her, and shuffles backwards in the manner of an oriental servant before a potentate. A dog barks in the distance. The breeze rises.

Straightening, Elsie stamps and, shaking her finger at us, shouts:

"El See could guard the doors,
But that's the stuff of bores."

Stamping again, voice lowered, entreating, she continues:

"A dull guide I'd be
For the governor would decree
What should be said to you,
But who knows what's true?
 Choo, choo — I think I can — I can.
But what you accept is up to you."

"Who's speaking now?" I ask.

"Forces, intelligences, goblins and fairies
Creatures who bark, dark speckled berries
Wild fruit, to boot ..."

She kicks her bare foot across the wood floor, then stamps around in a circle. Stopping abruptly, she stands in Sara's face. "A supplement, a transformer, a facilitator — I don't abandon, I'm here." She points to herself. "But I don't monitor. I'm a receptor, a converter.

Most of what you get from me
comes from you."

"But," Sara hesitates, "what about protection?"

"These walls." Elsie moves her hands over her body then spins. Breathing hard, she wipes sweat beads from her forehead. "I have you. You are the prayer of the future. Our love protects us. And, Sara," she leans closer and whispers: "I have your poem."

Holding Sara's hand, Elsie opens it gently. Looking at her palm, touching it with her finger, each word measured, melodic, considered, she recites:

> "A butterfly comes
> and sits upon
> the golden lotus
> in my hand.
> I look at it.
> It looks at me.
> Am I real?
> Am I the butterfly?"

She closes Sara's fist then pulls one finger open. "Let it out." Sara's eyes fill with tears. "Protect yourself, yes — but, Sara, know that you are the butterfly."

Reflecting Sara's face, as master and student, hierophant and clown who can teach children to laugh, sing, cry and overcome tears — Elsie backs up and lights a match, studies the flame, inhales and blows white smoke into the room. A cat meows. Silence. Gingerbread baking. Elsie sings:

> "For I love you
> And I give what I am
> In trust for your keeping.
> Come out of your sleeping.
> Pain dissolves in love."

Head back, smiling at Sara, a tear in the corner of her eye, Elsie says: "Used to sing the National Anthem. Did you know that?"

"Did you?" Sara sniffs, eyes sparkling.

"Still can." Elsie returns to the sink. "Late night T.V., you know, when they go off the air. Just ghost singing, using someone else's name. They need my voice, the way this body's put together, to get the conviction. And I have it, too. I'm serious. All that stuff, about touching the face of God, is real. That's why I say Jay should fly."

Following her to the sink, starting to cut onions, female to female, Sara says: "He could be killed."

Elsie runs water, watches it, speaks as if to herself: "Some earlier, some later." Wiping her eyes, she looks at me. "He can jump if he has to."

"What?" I'm jolted by images of war.

"I made hamburgers for years, nothing else. Sara will, too. It's what boys want. But they must learn." She points at me. "You must learn."

"What?" I repeat myself.

"Before the bullet strikes." Sad again, something in her gesture makes my heart ache. "They got Robert."

"Who?" Sara asks, concerned.

"My son."

"Who got him?" Sara stands rigid.

"Black Hats." Elsie sits down, covers her face, then lights a cigarette, watches the flame. Exhaling and looking up, as if speaking to someone else, she says: "That's what we'll call them."

Returning to the sink, Elsie slides the onions Sara has chopped into a skillet, places it on the stove, then turns back to us. "The 'others' — the other side of all this," she points around the room with a butcher knife, "went after him. Silver bullet. All the special stuff."

"After your son?" Sara's asks, alarmed.

"Got away, though!" Elsie beams. "Jumped just in time — right out of his body." She opens her eyes wide, then swings her foot back and forth. "For a while I thought I'd find him."

"How?" Sara asks.

"Like Jack ... " Her voice low, Elsie seems tired now. "Some kids are so splattered we have to scrape them off the walls. He's a combination." She hunches her shoulders, tries to smile. "Put together from parts. We try to preserve the parts — for the genes." Looking at me, she sighs. "Reincarnation, sure — but what about the bloodline?"

"I don't know, Elsie." I feel her sadness. "War is terrible."

"Genes can't pass with the soul, can they?" Her face fills with questions, pain. "They have to be kept here, right?" She points to her heart. "I work on that. With Robert ... Well ... " She looks through her fingers at Sara. The little finger on her left hand is cut off at the joint. "We make certain sacrifices. Right?"

Sara holds her own hands up, little fingers together, the left one shorter than the other — cut off in an accident in a lawn chair when she was a child. I think about the unnatural shortness of my own little fingers.

Elsie says: "When you get back ..."

"Where are we going?" Sara interjects.

Looking up at the ceiling, her voice shifting, sounding more masculine, Elsie says: "Home and back." Then, a Chinese cleaver in her hand, looking like a Samurai, she points at the stack of fresh vegetables on the cutting board. "I'm having company for supper."

Struck by the smell of onions and bacon cooking, suddenly I realize that somehow, while we've been talking, Elsie has set the table for four. A steaming Creole casserole, on a hot tray, sits in the center. A gingerbread cake cools on the counter before the window, the aroma warm in the air.

"You've cooked, Jay." She rubs olive oil across the cleaver. "Properly handled, the sword slices through without disturbing a single molecule. Taoist magic. A Christian monk did the same, once, and was sainted."

Light reflecting in splendid rays off the cleaver's surface, she cuts the remaining vegetables in a series of movements which seem too rapid to be possible. Flipping the slices into the heavy black skillet containing the bacon pieces and onions, stir-frying the contents, humming and stamping side to side, I have the impression she is tromping happily up a wild mountain.

"A good mess, that's what I like." She winks at me, then turns the fire down. Rubbing her hands on her apron, suddenly looking like a grandmotherly cook, she turns to Sara. "I'm quite sure there are supposed to be five of you. Believe me on this." She chuckles. "I've done this all over the world."

Washing her hands in the sink, bending forward to view something out the window, then taking off her own apron, which I hadn't noticed she was wearing, and hanging it on the back of the door, Sara says: "Done what, Elsie?" as if she's been thinking about something else.

"Set stages, dear." Elsie lowers her voice. "Get the others ready. We each have parts to play."

"When?" A head taller than Elsie, Sara hugs her affectionately then takes her purse from the table.

"A week from Monday." Following us to the door, Elsie points at the clothesline. "Watch the flags. Jay is the driver, but you navigate. When you get back, there will be someone here greater than me. Someone to feed all of you."

The Team

"What in the world?" Sara stops on the path after leaving Elsie's. "I mean, what world was that?" Shaking her head, words tumble out: "How can she know so much about us? Not just what she says — her whole manner, her songs and gestures ... everything?"

The tumultuous sense of wonder experienced with Elsie has jerked to a confused halt in my own heart. My whole system is revved up, but with the brakes on. I'm anxious and expectant, skeptical and charmed, exhilarated and exhausted. Analyzing the experience, I say:

"She mixes humor, and mystery, and fear ... constantly switching the emotions — plus she has several levels going on in her conversation." We move back toward the rehab center. "She's more of an inter-dimensional being than Jack."

"She really scared me at times." Sara takes my hand. "But she's also very loving and motherly."

"And a cook, obviously," I laugh. "Probably a great one, from the looks, and smells, of what she was doing. I hardly realized what was going on until it was over."

"Me neither," Sara nods. "That's the strange part."

"It was like we just flipped in and out of different worlds. Some of the things she did felt so ..."

"Incredible ..." Sara breaks in. "But there aren't words, really."

"What do you think of her?" I ask.

"She's a teacher of some type," Sara glances into the woods, "who's inviting us to work with her." She squeezes my hand as something moves to our right.

"What did you feel when she urged you to channel?"

"I kept thinking of Karin — but we shouldn't be talking about this right now." She stops again, listening. "It's like there's an energy we have to hold just at the edge."

"And the thing about her son and the Black Magicians?" Glancing around, I'm suddenly apprehensive.

"Black Hats," Sara corrects me, lowering her voice. "They're a part of it, too. It's like she opens a window so you can see something, just a glimpse."

"And if she didn't shut it again, you'd see too much." I think out loud. "She knows just how much we can take."

"Right," Sara confirms. "And we're coming back."

"Yes," I acknowledge, still amazed. "But how?"

"I don't know." She moves forward. "I just feel everything is right."

In the silence, I breathe in the musty, deep scent of the forest floor and taste, in memory, the candy and gingerbread, the rainbow lights in Elsie's cabin. Following behind her, I ask: "Who do you think the five people are?"

"That's why we're going home, isn't it?" She leans into the incline.

"Larry and Kathy," I agree. "But who is the fifth?"

"Karin, maybe," Sara answers.

Deep in thought we move along the path. I know that Sara accepts and is connected to Elsie. I also feel it. But slowing down and trying to think rationally I can see that we blindly accepted her urging us to change everything and be back in a week — even though she more than hinted that there is real danger involved. We know that. It's all around us.

We ignored Elsie's insistence that we make our own judgments. Is she so charismatic that we aren't able to think straight or consider the consequences or alternatives? Or even raise questions when she stated that whomever or whatever speaks through her cannot be trusted — that she has no control, and we have to provide male discrimination?

But she also pushed Sara to hold the mountain for the female intelligence — saying that if Sara would drop her fear, she would know she is already a part of whatever craft Elsie teaches. Acutely sensitive to our thoughts and emotions and, obviously caring profoundly for us, she touched our hearts, tugging us from fear to acceptance.

Not everything she said could be true. We were not supposed to accept everything — but I can't remember the parts I rejected. Perhaps she is like a great magician who recognizes and tries to warn her audience against becoming fascinated by her power. She posits that everything she says is, or may be, based on illusion — but we are enthralled.

I'm not even sure what happened, but I am sure that the events which led us to her were objective. Perhaps she is caught in a wild fantasy based on improbable but dramatically convincing connections between mythic and everyday realities?

But what if she is a prisoner of the dark forces she claims to be fighting? I do believe that evil exists and that the divine confronts the human in ways which are potentially catastrophic, sometimes leaving us wounded or deranged. Yet I feel, at some deep, irrational level, Elsie is protecting us and that my time with her stretched and enlivened me.

More than anything else, my heart says I want to work with her to understand her vision, her pain, and her love — that she is the teacher I have waited for.

Clearing the bramble at the edge of the parking lot, we see that Jack's truck is gone. The door to the building still hangs open, windows blown out. Sara says: "It's really spooky how Jack showed up."

"The whole thing is spooky." I agree, anxious now to get back on the road. "I can't believe we left our car here."

Unlocking the door on the driver's side, Sara leans across to let me in. As she turns on the engine, I ask: "Do you really think Karin will be the fifth person?"

Looking both ways before pulling out on the road, she says: "I don't know, but we need to find her."

Sara turns in at the CRC lodge. The main room is empty. Hearing voices from the kitchen, we find Ned visiting with Karin. "Thought maybe you had left," I remark, surprised to see her.

"Jay's mom was sorry she missed you," Sara adds. "She wanted us to give you her love."

Karin smiles warmly. "Jayne is very special to me." She motions for us to sit. "I heard the last session was good."

"Excellent." I take a seat.

Looking at Sara, Ned says: "What've you kids been up to?"

"We took an I Ching reading." Sara hesitates, "and decided to stay longer."

"I love Kingsley's translation of the *Tao Te Ching*," Ned responds casually. "Do you know it?"

"Not that translation," I answer, "but I love Lao Tzu."

"And the practice of Crazy Wisdom," he adds. "So?"

"We met some extraordinary people." Sara glances at Karin.

"Who?" Ned seems troubled.

"This guy took us to meet a woman." He doesn't respond, so I add: "Down the road. Past the Hart Retreat."

"Mahdah Hart is interesting," Ned gets up and pours more coffee, "but you have to be careful around her cooks."

"Why?" I'm not sure what Elsie's connection, if any, to Mahdah Hart might be.

Stirring sugar, Ned thinks a moment before speaking: "One in particular, called L.C.B., is very strange."

"The woman we met recommends your publication on Brother Lawrence," I comment, avoiding his statement.

Putting his cup down and leaning toward me, Ned says: "Just watch yourselves."

Karin stands, ready to leave. "Have you kids eaten?"

Uncomfortable with the situation, I say: "I'm starved."

"Then let's go over to the Marina. I need to eat before I leave. Thanks, Ned," Karin adds, turning to shake his hand.

"Let me know if there's anything I can do." He walks us to the door, then stands on the deck, waving good-bye.

As soon as we've taken a table at the Marina, Karin lights a cigarette and, glancing around to make sure we can't be overheard, announces: "I'm interested in this L.C.B.."

"Elsie is the name of the woman we met," I offer. "I don't know if she's the same person."

"You're correct to be cautious." Karin pauses. "Last night my Teacher told me that the two of you would meet the person I'm supposed to work with. O'Riley warned you against her, but I think she's the one."

As she lays her cigarette in the ash tray, red lipstick around the filter, I notice she is smoking a Salem. We're alone except for two men at the counter. Walking to our table and filling our coffee cups, the waitress waits for our orders. Karin waves her off, then focuses on us.

"Do you want to know why I think this lady is the one?"

"She's the one," Sara confirms. "For us, everything just kept building. It's hard to explain." Karin nods. "We're sure you're involved," Sara volunteers. "But I want to clarify something. We call her Elsie. Ned said 'L.C.B.,' using the initials. We don't know Elsie's last name."

"Or what other people call her," I add, "but the Elsie we're talking about said she was a white witch."

"I'm sure she is powerful, regardless of what terms we use," Karin comments. "She wouldn't be the one I'm looking for if she weren't. Do you know anything about cell groups?"

"Not exactly," I respond.

"From the Tibetan and the Bailey Work?" Karin adds.

"I've read about Shambhala and the Ascended Masters who instructed the early Theosophists; is that it?" I ask.

"An extension of that." Karin glances around the room before continuing: "My thought is that your Elsie may be a part of a cell group or a battery, as it's sometimes called, by which adepts combine energies and boost 'The Work.' They may all work through the body of one person or there might be several different persons. They generally use code names. They may refer to her as L.C. Bee, as the mother of a hive.

"Let me tell you a story." Karin sips her coffee. "After my teacher started instructing me, even though no one else can see or hear him," she smiles and pats the table, "I start meeting these extraordinary people — synchronistically, as Jung would say — and they give me suggestions, books, metaphysical dictionaries, practical stuff.

"One night I went to a cafe after a lecture, with this older man who had been in the audience, and he encouraged me to listen to the voice, although I had to check everything out myself, of course. When he got up and excused himself, Aurobindo's *Mind of Light* was lying on the counter, certain passages marked."

Karin smiles infectiously, then glances at the waitress who is returning for our orders. "I didn't know his name and never saw him again, but I believe he was a part of a cell group which had been contacting me in various ways.

"Anyway, eventually I was told to come here. Since we talked, however, I've been told to go into Clayton and find a realtor. For now, maybe for the rest of this summer or longer, I'm going to stay."

"And work with CRC?" Sara pauses while we order.

"Jarvis was great, and all that," Karin picks it up again. "In fact I suspect that the workshop was important to raising our vibratory rate so that we're ready for the next stage; but, no, I don't have any sense of continuing work with CRC, except, perhaps, to just stay in contact, because I think it's a front for the other centers we talked about."

Taking a deep breath, Karin continues: "I hope to pull the rest of my manuscript, a hundred or so rough pages so far, together this summer — but I don't know."

"What about your son?" Sara asks.

"He's okay for the summer. And my boss says I can have an extended leave. What about the two of you?" she asks.

We both hunch our shoulders, uncertain what to say.

"Had you done much formal meditation before coming here?" Karin pauses while the waitress puts plates on the table, mine steaming with vegetables and Salisbury steak.

"We've been working with a South Asian professor," Sara answers, "but we're definitely not Maharishi types."

Karin laughs. "John has experimented with meditation, and drugs."

"Heavy drugs?" I ask.

"Some marijuana," she answers casually. "He's careful. Growing up in New York, he's seen drugs ruin a lot of lives."

"So he has his head on straight?" I comment.

"John wants to do something meaningful with his life." She takes a bite and chews slowly.

"Does he support you?" Sara asks.

"Knows I'm a bit cracked." Her face wrinkles into a pleased, self-reflective smile. "And he approves."

"What's he going to do next year?" Sara asks.

"Depends. I'm interested in what you said about your I Ching reading and meeting helpers because," Karin pauses, "I think John is supposed to be here, and I think you are, too."

Sara leans back. "You're going back to New York tonight?"

"That was my plan." She studies us. I'm wondering whether Sara is going to jump in or I should.

Sara crosses the threshold: "Elsie told us to be back here in a week — and there are to be five of us then."

Karin shudders as if that was a piece of information she had been waiting for. "Who are the others?"

"Larry and Kathy, our partners on the magazine." Sara searches her eyes. "I thought maybe you were the fifth."

Relaxing, Karin says: "I'm not the fifth. But I'm almost sure John is. Will your friends come?" Sara nods. "You can stay with me, if I can put all the pieces together."

"I think you're supposed to meet Elsie," Sara pauses.

"No question about it." Karin wipes her lips on the napkin and scoots back to get up. "Pretty obvious why I'm getting a house, isn't it?" She grins. "If we're to be back here in a week — I'll stay over and finalize things tonight."

"That's a lot to ask, Karin," Sara comments while I hold the door for them.

"Does it feel right?" Their eyes meet.

"If it does to you," Sara responds. "Why don't you follow us to Elsie's right now?" They walk ahead of me across the plank bridge toward our cars.

"Better yet," Karin puts her arm around Sara and, smiling back at me, says, "why don't we ride together and let Jay lead."

Karin's T-Bird following me, settled down by the food, I'm wondering how Sara can be so comfortable taking the initiative to return to Elsie's, from the front side now, with Karin. Elsie said we are to return a week from Monday; perhaps we're not supposed to, or don't have the right to, come before that.

Maybe we won't find any of the magic which we experienced this afternoon, because this time we aren't being led and we aren't following the rules? Maybe there will be other people there, and we will be intruding? Whom did she say would be there, greater than she, the next time we come?

In the Marina, the exchanges between Sara and Karin had been direct and conclusive. There had also been a familiarity and sureness between Sara and Elsie, which I didn't feel. I followed Elsie's references, but I didn't even know they were cooking supper together. It was female, or at least something I don't understand — by which, now, Sara knows what to do.

Maybe Sara does know the mountain is hers, that they're in this together. But if it's a sisterhood, how can I work with them when Elsie said that boys are born to war? I want to understand. I have been called. Elsie is the teacher but ... What's going to happen when we get back from Kansas?

Passing Dan Paladin's house, I notice him waving from the porch and remember Elsie's statement that he will make it big as a writer, and that we could work together; but that if I had gone to the work-shop, I couldn't have been with her — then entire interludes in which she had danced and sang, or gotten very serious, talking about Jack being blown up in Vietnam, about gardening, alchemy, and gene pools, about her son and a silver bullet ... whole sequences when it seemed dark, then light, rooms full of sounds and smells, a candy shop and a laboratory.

A gust of wind blows off the lake on my right, sending a chill up my spine. A young man, standing on a fallen tree extended over the water, is fishing. His float bobs on the rippling surface. Turning to-ward me, he smiles, toothy and freckled, then points. Following his hand, I see a white crane settled on the shore, the sun piercing its breast. Glancing left, my eye catches the purple flag fluttering above the Hart Retreat.

Forcing my eyes ahead, I concentrate on driving. Around the next curve, turning up the steep gravel incline, I park between the clothes-line and Elsie's house. Sitting at a picnic table, she is lighting a ciga-rette. A sunshade is closed behind her. There are four gold towels on the line. Someone is working in the garden, but when I look again there is no one there.

Getting out of the car, I stop, suddenly disoriented. Elsie ap-proaches: a black satin shawl draped over her shoulders, eyelids shaded dark blue, accentuating the liquid crystal of her eyes, a white flower circlet riding her forehead, at the center of which a triangle points upward. Her throat is encircled by a twisted gold torque, open at the center. Around her middle she wears a short Masonic apron over silk pants.

A carved staff, the top of which ends in a crystal skull, leans against the bench next to a large, black, conical hat with a floppy brim. Point-ing at it, Elsie bursts into delighted laughter. Clapping her stomach and stamping her bare feet on the ground, she beams: "You know what I think?"

"No," I answer in shock.

"You thought that was a witch's hat." Gleeful, Elsie points back to the bench then slaps me on the back. "It's the sunshade, you know."

Regaining my balance, catching my breath, I realize that the sunshade, over the table, is open now and the ornate staff is a simple walking cane.

Coming in front of me, smiling gently, her hands on the outside of my arms, she whispers: "When the shade is down and the sun is up — under my hat, I dance. Light skin and blue eyes, I surprise the watchers who aren't watching."

Elsie winks. Patting me affectionately, she leans up on tip-toe, and into my face: "Who's my friend? Why's she here?"

She glances toward Karin and Sara, then back to me, speaking louder: "Before she's left? She's right. Going or coming — I love you." Backing up, she looks at Sara: "And you."

Then, facing Karin, arms open, tremendous gold warmth streaming from her heart: "And you, my sister."

Bursting into tears, Karin embraces Elsie. Hugging each other, they tilt back and forth as Sara smiles appreciatively. Taking my hand, Sara looks at me. "We should leave now."

Laughing, they separate to face us. Her blue eyes sparkling with tears, mirthful, relieved, thankful, Karin says: "Do you have to go?"

"They've got assignments." Elsie slings her arm cheerfully around Karin's waist, turning them both in a circle like they're old and accomplished dancing partners, intimately familiar with each other's moves. "And so do you and I." Elsie sings, her voice deep, resonate:

"But tonight we play as sisters.
Tonight we dance and sing.
For the boys in the forest of learning
And the girls in the castle of the king
Need all the joy we are making,
Need all the cooks and the queen."

Approaching us, still arm in arm, Elsie grins. "Good surprise, isn't it, when sisters wheel out the cart and brother swallows the monster in his heart?"

Dropping her arm from around Karin, she stretches upward, kisses Sara on the forehead, and whispers: "Feed him for me, will you? But be careful not to freak him out." She bursts into gay laughter again, Sara hugging her, delighted.

"And you," Elsie turns to me, "guard her with all your love — drive carefully, be back sooner than the old heart could have known."

Chuckling, she pushes her finger into my chest then backs away. Sitting at the bench, lighting a cigarette, she holds up her left hand in farewell, waving her short little finger.

Coming forward, folding us in her arms, Karin whispers: "Thank you." Backing up, she seems to be looking deeply into Sara and then me. Crossing her hands over her heart, she breathes deeply, glancing at the sky before returning to us and taking our hands.

"There is much to learn, much to remember. We'll be waiting for you. Our love protects you. May the power of the one life pour through us as we undertake this work together."

The Recruits

We have accepted Karin without hesitation. Nothing about her strikes us as false or superficial or even foreign. Ned's warning about Elsie and my own hesitation seem irrelevant. Not that she might not be some type of sorceress, but that everything in our lives has brought us safely to this point and all of our instincts tell us to keep going.

Will Karin work something out? Will John join us? Will Larry and Kathy come?

Stopping at the same motel in northern Mississippi where we had stayed on the way down, we are no longer intimidated by the small towns, the dark passages through the rural South. We move in and out without drawing attention to ourselves. We've traveled here before; we're in familiar territory.

By late afternoon, the next day, we pass through Kansas City and drive the gray expanse of the Flint Hills, rolling patches of prairie cedar and hedge, beneath the dome of an endless sky — toward Manhattan.

"Hey, Guys! How you doing?" Surprised and pleased, teeth showing through a sandy-brown mustache, Larry rubs paste from his hands. Several collages lean against the wall on top of his work table.

"Welcome to Kate's Diner." Kathy calls from the kitchen behind us, her voice accompanied by the smell of oregano, the room warm with steam as we turn to greet her. Laying the big wooden spoon on the stove top, her long dark hair pulled back, twisted, and held by a leather clasp, smiling, full mouthed, a strand of hair dangling across her face, eyes laughing, she adds: "Want some world famous ghetto spaghetti?"

"Have we got a story for you!" Sara holds her arms out.

"Great," Larry exclaims, following us into the kitchen.

"We're going back." Sara hugs him.

"You are?" Kathy sounds incredulous. "When?"

"We all are." I give her a hug, appreciating her soft reserve, then Larry's hard, intense presence — our best friends. "All four of us."

"By next Monday," Sara adds, hugging Kathy.

"You can't be serious." Skeptical now, shaking her head, Kathy turns back to the stove.

"Come on, Kate," Larry urges, affectionately. "Where's your spirit of adventure?"

"Okay, let's hear about it ..." she relents slightly, filling four coffee cups while we gather around the table.

"We met this amazing woman." Sara starts right in. "Her name is Elsie and ..."

"It's a complicated story," I interject, knowing that essentially they'll have to accept it on faith, but must at least have some frame of reference.

"So," Kathy smiles, "start at the beginning."

"Well," Sara hangs a moment, sorting images, "we met Karin, who is a key to all this, at the workshop, then we picked up this kid, Mike, on the road who said we should stay — which was wild because ... "

"Sara was having hits on staying, anyway," I interrupt.

"He was really spacey — but tuned in, somehow."

"So we took an I Ching reading and it talked about treading on the tail of the tiger — which was the name of the town where we picked him up, and then we were told that we needed helpers, and to ask again, you know."

"If you have sublimity, constancy, and perseverance?" Larry acknowledges. "Did you?"

"It said that we would have great success, in spite of danger, if we got the right teacher," I simplify. "Then there was this strange synchronistic sequence where Mike showed up and directed us to this bombed out rehabilitation center which the rednecks had hit." I pause, vividly remembering the experience.

Hesitating slightly, Sara adds: "Then we were literally led by a spaceman, named Jack, to meet Elsie ... But we're going too fast, right?"

"Go on," Larry grins. "We'll get it."

By the end of supper, even though we've made virtually no sense of the experience and have rambled about Elsie, and none of us knows what to expect or how we will afford the trip — we're all committed to leaving on Saturday. Tired and eager to get home, but excited, we agree to meet later to fill them in and finalize our plans.

Wednesday evening, Larry and Kathy arrive. Soup simmers on our stove. We've just opened a letter from Karin:

"Dear Jay & Sara,

I'm in N.Y. now. I stayed another day and spent time with Elsie. What a blessing! She'll feed you. You can stay in the place I'm buying. I'll have possession by Sunday. John and I will meet you, Larry and Kathy that evening. I am enclosing a CRC flyer on the astrology workshop next week, and a map to my house.

Love, Karin"

"Wow." Larry stands. "She moves quick."

"Maybe you should do the workshop, Larry," I suggest.

"Esoteric Astrology?" He reads the brochure. "That would pull some things together. Fifty bucks, if I get the scholarship." He looks at Kathy. "Think I can get an advance on the project?"

"Maybe."

"I want to do charts. That's the part I need help with." He looks pleased.

"You could be our cover." I laugh, but am not sure what I meant, or where the thought came from.

"In what context?" Larry looks slightly startled.

"Elsie here, Elsie there, Elsie everywhere," I repeat the jingle Elsie used. "She talked about Gurdjieff."

"And everything else, too. " Sara jumps in. "It all made sense, even if it didn't. She called herself a 'Supplement,' which means that she has access to all this stuff which we already know but don't know we know."

"She's psychic but not a trance medium." I realize that, like a dam breaking, we're again rushing headlong into trying to explain Elsie, and just go with it. "She stamps around, recites poetry, sings songs, dances ... and somehow in the middle of it all she hits right to the core. A lot of it all at the same time. It's like she goes at full speed and you get it, but only get part of it, because there are other layers. It all kind of falls into place in bits and pieces."

"She acts as a transmitter," Sara explains, "for all kinds of information. She said she doesn't allow the 'governor' to control."

"'Government'? You like this, don't you, Doodle?" He lowers his voice, humorously: "Espionage work, Agent Uh Oh."

Sara laughs, always tickled by his favorite cover-name for her in their on going fantasy about spy groups and secret missions, how they could infiltrate and end the war. "Bottom line," she becomes serious, "we have to decide which parts of what she says are correct, like a puzzle. We have to put it together for ourselves. And some of it is pretty spooky."

Kathy, who has been listening quietly, goes to the window and looks out into the alleyway. Turning to us, she says: "And Karin is connected with some occult group?"

"Not exactly," Sara answers, "as far as we know. But she's writing about some future transformation."

"She says this is a transition period," I explain.

"And she works with an invisible teacher," Sara adds.

Kathy seems pensive as she returns to the table.

"If I've got it right," I pick it up, "Elsie is implying that we have to know there is danger. She talks about Black Hats — the forces who have their own agenda."

"Who want us to be automatons." Larry nods. "To stop us from becoming truly conscious." He looks to Kathy, who asks:

"Why did you relate Larry's class to the Gurdjieff work?"

Aware that much about my experience in Georgia is fading in and out, but that I am remembering more each time, I feel the need to talk about Ned's warning, and my own speculations and fears. Not sure where I'm going, but appreciating the fact that Kathy doesn't let comments drop, I respond:

"I'm not sure but," I look at Larry, "remember all that stuff about Crowley, Yeats, and Dion Fortune struggling to control the Golden Dawn?" He nods. "And the occult wars described in *The Morning of the Magicians*? And the Nazis destroying the Goetheanum? I don't know whether Elsie explained this, but there's some connection to all that."

"Making a shield." He thinks a moment. "You're suggesting my role would be to decoy the Black Hats." He shakes his finger at me. "Not sure I like that, old buddy."

"The idea," I want to phrase this correctly, "is that the other forces don't pay attention to us unless they think we're starting to act with true 'intention' to really wake up."

"If we're doing Gurdjieff," he grins, "we put just enough energy into a thought-form to deflect their attention. So," he whispers, "I'll run a fake so they won't know who has the ball." We all laugh, knowing he played football at K. State, but I sense that at some level he is serious.

The window air-conditioner puffs away against the late afternoon heat. Someone pulls along the alley, their radio blasting a Beatles song. Clearing the table, Sara adds: "Elsie did warn us to be careful about what we say."

"Since we don't understand what we're saying," Kathy remarks, "I can't imagine anyone else would either."

"The cosmic fliers strike again!" Larry exclaims as he settles into the back seat with Kathy. The sky, powder blue and vast with possibilities, stretches above us as we slide onto the highway toward Georgia.

Crossing the Missouri River at Kansas City, clouds form and the humidity increases. The sun, a golden disk barely visible behind white gauze, floats overhead. By evening the clouds are low and gray, the moon a thin crescent.

We stay at the Traveller's Inn. The proprietor, seeing us as repeat customers, turns on the lights over the pool and assures us we don't need to be out by 10:00, despite the sign.

The next morning, a mist falling, we lounge over a big breakfast at the truck stop. Looking up, like his thoughts have been far away, Larry says: "What about the boy, Mike? Is he connected?"

"I don't think Jack knew him," Sara speculates. "But Elsie said he might have read the flags ... the towels on her clothesline." She shrugs.

"You seem to remember more each time we talk," Kathy observes, then returns to the map she has been studying. "Are we taking the route through Chattanooga?"

Setting her coffee down, Sara nods: "It's like a tunnel winding toward Raven Lake. You'll love it."

"Wherever we're going," Kathy pats Larry on the shoulder, "I gather it's not on the map."

Rain clearing the path we follow into the South, the inhabitants are only vague images in the distance. Larry comments occasionally, but is mostly absorbed in his astrology books. Kathy and Sara visit quietly.

Reflecting on our time with Elsie, I know I can't convey an adequate expression of how paradoxical and stimulating she was and let the urge to talk about her pass.

At one point I hear Kathy saying that she just wants to get away from the rush and enjoy our time together, but has no other expectations. When Sara probes further, Kathy laughs gently. "Of course any time there's a wild goose chase, there's the chance we'll find the goose ..." She runs her fingers through Larry's curly hair.

"Who lays the golden egg." Larry closes his book. "And I have the feeling this is going to be a big one."

"So," I hover at a stop sign at the edge of Clayton, "how do we get there?"

Glancing up from Karin's note, Sara says: "Follow this road until you get to the Tiger turn-off, then back toward town. She's at the very end of Tiger Drive, in a new house."

Excited, we move up the street washed clean by rains, undeveloped lots on the east side opening into woodland, a cul-de-sac at the end beyond which a stream meanders — everything strangely familiar.

"That's got to be it." Sara points ahead to the last house on the right, Karin's T-Bird in the driveway, the houses in between unoccupied, the yards brought to rough grade but not seeded. "I can't believe we're back."

Blue eyes twinkling, Karin extends her hand, fingernails painted bright red, to Kathy then Larry. "Just in time." She smiles, looking back to me, self-possessed and efficient. "There's plenty of work to do."

The house smells of Pine-Sol. Dressed in old slacks, it's obvious Karin has been cleaning. Pieces of furniture are stacked in the center of the living room. In the slight haze of the sunset, I notice the last sliver of the old moon.

"Is John with you?" I ask.

"Getting unpacked." Karin turns to hug Sara. "Why don't you, Kathy, and I concentrate on the kitchen, while the guys handle the furniture? We'll talk later. This is pretty amazing, isn't it?"

Larry behind me in the hall, I knock on the door.

Opening it from inside, John smiles — small eyes framed by wire-rimmed glasses, long sandy-blond hair pulled into a ponytail, totally at ease, tall and lanky. A Richie Havens album plays on his portable stereo. He says: "I'm John."

"Jay and Larry." I slide onto the mattress. "Surprised to be here?"

"I'm adjusting." John sits cross-legged on the floor, his suitcase open in the center of the room.

"Are you taking the astrology workshop?" Larry asks.

"No." John runs a hand back through his hair. "I'm tired of school."

"Right." Larry glances sideways at me. "I'm the one taking the class." Turning back to John, he adds: "Ned O'Riley guaranteed me a scholarship."

"Mom says the teacher is top-flight," John replies.

"I'm sure," Larry comments, following us to the living room where Karin introduces John to Sara and Kathy.

An hour later, the furniture arranged, the dishes and utensils washed and put away, the beds made, we congregate at the glass-top table. It's dark and cooler outside. Karin pours coffee before addressing us:

"We're like a family. Consequently," she takes a seat at the head of the table, "we need rules." She looks at each of us in turn. "Elsie will feed you and you'll stay here at night. You are to be at her house by 10:00 each morning, but away from her house most afternoons, at least between 2:00 and 4:00. That's when she does her other work. Sound right?"

"Have you gotten to know her very well?" Sara asks.

"We're sisters," Karin answers matter-of-factly. "Other lives, perhaps, but also at another level. It has nothing to do with blood," she smiles at Larry, "and yet it does in a strange way. Are you familiar with group souls?"

As Larry nods that he is, she goes on: "I'd been told to come here and that I was looking for a teacher and a group I am to work with. After the conversation with Sara and Jay, when they said they were coming back with you and Kathy, I knew John was also involved."

"Did Elsie tell you to get this house?" Kathy asks.

"Elsie here, Elsie there." Karin laughs easily. "She doesn't tell you anything. She tells you everything."

"I know." Sara shakes her head in agreement.

"After you left, Elsie mentioned there was a house on Tiger Drive which she fancied I would like. That's how she put it. Within a couple hours, I had agreed to buy it."

"That's awfully fast, isn't it?" Kathy questions.

"The developer was willing to sell on contract. My boss said I can take a couple months off. If it doesn't work out, I shouldn't lose any money." Karin places her palms together and bows slightly. "So, I just did it."

Sun streaming through our windows, wakes us, Sara affectionate in my arms. We're in Georgia for the second time, for something we feel but can't describe.

Rolling off the mattress, I move towards hot coffee and join Larry at the table. "Any dreams?"

"Nothing spectacular," he looks up from his notebook, "but Kathy dreamt we were all in a boat, then Karin got off, then me, at different docks along a river, and both Karin and I held on to long ropes which were tied to each of you."

"What's your interpretation?" I refill his cup.

"Karin and I have different roles than the rest of you."

Noticing Karin, in a sleeveless dress, her hair back-combed, taking a seat on the patio, I ask about her plans.

"She's going into Atlanta." Larry lays his pen down. "We're on our own today."

Coming up behind us, Sara says: "Did we describe her accurately?"

"Doodle," Larry smiles at her, "I think Karin is elegant, organized to the eye teeth, and courageous." He holds up a strikingly accurate sketch of Karin.

"She certainly took a leap of faith," Kathy comments, having approached with a towel around her head.

"Spontaneous, but all business. Quite a combination," Larry adds.

"By the way, if you're going to drop me at CRC before going to Elsie's, we better wake John and get going."

Entering through the sliding doors, Karin suggests we fix cereal and put the trash in the barrel before leaving. We should follow the road through Tiger. "It's a beautiful drive," she assures us on the way out the front door.

"This is old country, isn't it?" Larry observes from behind me. Kathy sits between him and John. Sara is in front with me.

"Indian land," Sara comments.

"Can we put the top down?" John asks.

"Not until we know the route better." I ease up the river road, tall ancient forest on each side.

"We could see better," he suggests.

"And be seen," Larry says, surprising me.

"So what?" John asks. "We're free citizens."

Glancing at him, I let it drop for now.

"I think this was a battle field," Kathy observes.

Sara points into the trees. "Up there?"

"Long ago ..." Kathy's voice drops to a whisper.

The road curves through "Tiger, population 23." Turning right at the dead end, we pass Elsie's — Larry, Kathy, and John craning to look out the window — then the Hart Retreat and Paladin's before reaching CRC. Several people are milling around on the deck facing the lake.

"I'll walk back to Elsie's at noon." Larry scans the mountain behind the lodge. "Take care of yourselves." Carrying his shoulder-bag, he turns and mounts the steps. Pulling back onto the road, toward Elsie's now, I sense the excitement mounting in our car.

Storming the Temple

As we turn in at the Oasis sign, two young men and then a third emerge from the house, get into a car, and speed away. Suddenly, as if she appeared from nowhere, I notice Elsie in gray work clothes, carrying a black, broad-brimmed hat, barefoot, hurrying toward the porch stoop. "Run!" she beckons emphatically. "We need to retake the temple."

Tumbling out of the car, the others behind me, I reach the screen door first. Her voice profoundly familiar, with no preliminaries, her hand on my arm, Elsie says: "Watch your head," then tugs downward forcing me to duck. Pointing to the chair in the corner at the back of the dining table, she indicates I should sit and wait.

"And you, Sara, " Elsie gazes up into her eyes, "go to the garden for lettuce, carrots, onions, and potatoes. There's a bucket on the porch. Then we'll work together."

"John," Elsie pauses, "just like your mother. What a pleasure." She holds out her hands. "You're growing, too. Watch it now." She points to the door sill. "You sit here." She takes his arm and places him at the small table next to the front window.

"And Kathy, you're Indian, aren't you, dear. Yes, I can see it in your eyes, and you remember it, too. Another life. Southwest?" Elsie looks up at the ceiling, listening. "No, Southwest in this life; the one I'm seeing is around here."

She turns in a circle, her arms spread. "In a canyon. You're painting. You're having visions through your painting, for your people. Anyway, dear," Elsie stops abruptly, "if you will help Sara, I need to get the boys started. Have some tobacco, if you prefer. I'll be a few seconds."

Kathy, in jeans and sandals, her hair pulled back emphasizing high cheekbones and dark eyes, does look Indian. She stares a moment then follows Sara toward the garden. The sun streams through the screen door.

"Now, John," Elsie turns to him, "you're the musician of this group, so start by listening to this crystal." She hands him a large quartz crystal. "Just hold it in the sunlight, here, right above this water." She places a cut glass bowl on the shelf under the window. "When you feel a tingling and see a light reflected in the water, hold the stone to your ear. Try it at your forehead and throat, also. Just find the place where you can hear it's voice. Got it?"

"Sure." Fascinated, John bends forward to concentrate.

"Now, Jay." Elsie lights her cigarette and sends a puff over me. "There's not much time, so you must concentrate."

Opening the cupboard above the refrigerator, she takes down a carton of Salems. "Remember:

Wales, Wells, Jeru-Salem, witchcraft trials, trails of tears, tearing veils, tribulations and triumphs, mysteries and tunnels, sacred alphabets and codes — reversed, rearranged, suspended, implemented?"

"Yes." I accept the carton from her.

"Backwards and upside down — I teach patterns, messages within messages, air waves full of them. Chaos at one level is beautiful at another. The comic strips, for instance ..."

She pauses while I nod that I understand. "... are best for general news. No one thinks to look, unless they know." She giggles, girl-like. "An open secret."

Elsie stares at me, severe and serious, then laughs gently, patting my shoulder. "I'm teaching you where to look. So," she relights a cigarette, takes a puff, watches the smoke in the silence, "we'll start with cook books, shall we?"

"Sure, Elsie," I say. My mind is reeling. Sightly disoriented, I'm following her into a forest with no sign posts, her energy so direct that my heart has accelerated. Yet I'm confident there is a reason she has decided on this tactic.

"Some of us can get it through here." She points to her eyes, then to the unnaturally deep furrow in her forehead. "And bring it to here." She points to her heart, her finger touching her shirt just below a dark jade necklace.

"This necklace is a receiving station and a shield." She holds it. "We'll talk about one for you sometime, Jay. You're like me in this way." Moving behind me, she covers my eyes with her fingers. "You can't resist wanting to know. You're born to it. But all you really know is that you don't quite get it, right? So we need to encourage each other," she whispers. "We need each other's help."

Releasing me, she stretches on tiptoes to the shelf behind me. "I need your height. You need my depth. Pull that last bunch down, will you?"

Handing the books and catalogs to her, I'm vaguely aware that Sara and Kathy are moving through the garden, John is gazing into the crystal, Larry is at the CRC lodge. Elsie fills my immediate world. I'm where I ought to be. This is a lesson which somehow, a long time ago, was interrupted.

Blue eyes leaning toward me, Elsie chants:

"'Exhausted and life-giving
Worried reposeful
The single Rose
Is now the Garden
Where all loves end
Terminate torment
Of love unsatisfied
The greater torment
Of love satisfied
End of the endless
Journey to no end
Conclusion of all that
Is inconclusive
Speech without word and
Word of no speech
Grace to the Mother
For the Garden
Where all love ends.'

Lines of Eliot, do you recognize them?"

My heart fluttering, a lump in my throat, I can't speak.

Elsie kisses my forehead. Holding me a moment, she smells of garden roses. "Be encouraged," she whispers. "There's lots of work to do. Love is painful."

Releasing my arms, she hands me a Sears model 2100 Stove Operation and Maintenance Manual. "Wake-up!" she commands, voice strong and directive. "Start with this one. Upside down and back-wards. If we don't occupy it, the devil will."

"What ... "

"The temple."

"... is it for?" I finish the question, unnerved, turning the manual upside down, glancing at the schemata and graphs.

"I put kids back together, remember?"

"The soldiers in Vietnam?" My stomach tightens.

"Not just those kids." Elsie exhales deeply. I sense that she wants to laugh but can't. Slipping behind me, she digs into my shoulders and neck. "A group of us, Old Maids, they call us — I like that better than Witches, don't you? That's a laugh." She stamps her foot. "I've had kids — a son and a daughter." She presses her thumbs under my skull from behind. A searing light flashes up from the base of my spine. Bending me over the manual, her words precise, lance-like, she says: "We incubate gene plasma — prepare embryos. The windows have been cleaned. Now we open them.

"So, Jay," she pauses, as if we've passed some threshold, "you have to start somewhere." She points at the diagram, her other hand still on the back of my neck, warm now. "We're experimenting with laying information into familiar backgrounds. Like the Tarot, for instance, or the Pyramids."

I take a breath. "Who's it for?"

"Whoever can find it and read it. Just know it's here if you knead it, like bread," she digs into my shoulders again.

"And that it's here and it's clear
If you abandon ordinary judgment.
Find a new level where the bread
Of the witches is the nourishment
That the Order of Cooks have made
For the guests of the Divine Presence,
Gifts that are made with the pennies
Which seer the roebucks of our Fathers
While the Princess with her Unicorn
Waits in the woods near the pool —
If you're willing to play the fool ..."

Peels of gentle laughter sparkle about the room as Elsie leans close, tapping my head with her knuckle. "It's just record keeping, Jay — who needs what and who's got it. How we put the genes at the bottom of the wishing well. How the womb cooks the embryo for nine moons, the egg in the fountain, the spatula in the cook's hand — just a quick flip." Light rises from the manual spread before me on her table.

Processing information through channels which have nothing to do with English, I am nevertheless faintly aware of the girls pulling the screen door open and Elsie saying: "While the boys are busy, let's talk about cooking."

As they move toward the sink her voice and their images fade and my attention widens within the circuitry of the schematic diagrams. Progressing from the last page, upside down, I read a language in line and word which demonstrates the relationship between matter and consciousness, light and energy, totally unaware of time, time irrelevant ...

"The most important point in cooking is intent." I hear Elsie's voice. She, Sara, and Kathy are approaching the door from outside. Bringing myself back up to the surface, I lay the manual down and turn toward John. "What did you hear?"

"It wasn't music, I don't think." John straightens his glasses. "I need some fresh air." He shakes his head, then slides his chair back.

"Good idea." I reach out to steady him as Elsie pokes her head into the kitchen from the back room, startling me because I thought she was outside. Winking, she says:

"I'm showing the girls something, just for us." She giggles. "You boys run along, but don't be late or the snake will bite you."

Following John outside, I realize we're walking slowly, like sailors who have just come up onto the deck, into the sunlight, the ground swelling beneath us.

"How long were we in there?" John asks.

"Not long 'til we eat, boys," Elsie's voice rings behind us. She is putting a cigarette out in an ash tray on the picnic table. A white pole extends upward to the sunshade. She spins around, laughing, carefree. "I love it when we all visit like this."

Appreciating her, feeling normal now, I say: "I could see the things you talked about."

"Oh." She touches her finger to the top of her head. "I don't think so," she drawls, exaggerating her accent. "But you saw a lot." She nods seriously.

John looks around, orienting himself. "What was I supposed to hear, Elsie?"

Assuming the stance of a gunfighter, she inspects him. "Your mom's done right by you, son ..." She sounds like John Wayne. "But there ain't words for what you heard." She grins, then turns to me. "I teach archeology, too. Want to do some excavating?"

"Around here?" I move toward the picnic table, wanting to sit down.

"Careful." She pushes me gently towards the tree stump near the door, commenting to John: "Sometimes it's active, sometimes it's not. Scared Jay once. Looked like a hat." She winks at me. "They just turned it on."

"What?" John asks, obviously confused.

"The transmitter," Elsie whispers, pointing back to the sunshade. "This jewelry, for instance," she holds the jade necklace away from her chest, "links me through these earphones," she touches her earrings, "to a forest which hovers between this world and another. Which world? That's for you to discover." She holds a finger up to her lips, then brushes her hand down and toward the picnic table as she moves us toward the garden.

"All this was re-worked by the Atlanteans, then the ancestors of the Cherokees, Will's interest, you know?"

"At CRC?" I get a vivid image of Will going silent when Ned warned us about her. Studying me, she answers:

"His double brother,
Toil and trouble
Three witches in the woods
A stew, a bubble ...
Poison for some
Is soup for others.

"I'm telling you," her voice rises as she points past the garden to the forest:

"Shakespeare, you know, was a warrior
— with the good lady Macbeth.

Beautiful girl, really,
Scared to death
By blood on her hands
The snake baked in the stone
Sun sign of the moon crone
Blood beads at Jeru-Salem.
Know him? Blood circles
And Celtic witches:
Spot, get out, damn spot —
Bitch! they were screaming,
Stone then water, earth heaving,
Bone-fires melting."

She glares at me, then John.

"Shake a spear at that!"

Pouncing on the ground, barefooted, she rubs her hands vigorously and shakes her hips back and forth. John and I stare at her dumbfounded. Then pushing her palms down along her dress, seeming to regain self control, voice lowered, she points to the back of her house.

"Will is the gardener who lives there. He's been all over the world doing landscapes and rock gardens. He moves whole areas one stone at a time. Never uses heavy equipment. Reveals what's always been there, changed by time. Exquisite, quiet man. Anyway," she looks around, "you two go to the trees, and see what you see. Just don't question too much."

Placing one foot on one stone at a time, following a walkway through heavy mulch, behind John, vegetables pushing through on either side, I am aware of insects humming. About half way through the garden, without looking back, John asks: "Was she both here, and in there?"

"Don't try to understand, yet!" Elsie is immediately behind us. "Hear the silence. Feel the currents!" Startled, we shift back to face her. Smiling broadly, standing one-footed on a stone, she holds her arms out like a wind-vane. "I can be a gargoyle, too, and scare the crows. Or the crows can scare me. But keep going, mes amis, for answers depend on vocabulary. A tout a l'heure." Waving her hand as if dangling a delicate French handkerchief, she skips back across the stones like a young girl crossing a stream.

Chuckling, we turn back and move toward the wood line. At the edge, John crouches and stares at the base of a hackberry. I try to concentrate with him.

Walking forward then kneeling down, he runs his hands over the surface then turns to me. "An elf or something, was standing right here, watching us."

"You saw it?" I ask, startled.

"Something between seeing and hearing."

At that moment, Elsie calls us back, urging us to hurry.

Taking silverware from the drawer, glasses and plates from the shelf, we fall into rhythm setting the table while Sara and Kathy sip coffee at the front table, visiting like this is their break time, having completed the morning shift. Elsie has disappeared into the room beyond the workroom, or laboratory, where she grows the crystals.

The window over the front table, behind Sara and Kathy, is open wide. The breeze carries a new quality of light. Even though the temperature has climbed to 80 or 90 degrees outside, the interior is cool.

Elsie comes in from outside. I wonder how she went out without me seeing her. Carrying two bouquets of wild flowers, their aroma mingling with the air, she places them in vases with fresh water, crooning like they are conscious, and places one vase on each of the tables. "He's not been here, you know — not this time." She spreads her arms and turns in a full circle. "So we want it nice."

My eyes roving the shelves, walls and floor, everything sparkling, looking almost new, I conclude she must be anticipating a guest; perhaps the guest she referred to before we went back to Kansas.

"He knows the way, of course." Elsie looks at Kathy. "But each time, no matter where I do this, there is a chance for a mis-cue. What if one of us is lost?" She pulls a chair out to sit with the girls. "But then," she sighs, "he can jump, if he has to."

"Who are you waiting for?" Sara asks.

"Larry," Elsie answers. "He has other names, of course. David is my favorite. But let's call him Larry, or Mr. Lawrence, among ourselves."

"Hey," Larry walks through the door.

"At a boy!" Elsie spins around, pleased. "How's the workshop?"

"A bit serious." Larry swings his shoulder-bag onto the front table.

I'm amazed he acts so casual.

"Should be some good information, though," Elsie encourages him. While he leans over to kiss Kathy, she approaches and turns him to stand straight. Stretching above him, she runs her hands over his head, just an inch from his body, down his shoulders, sides, and legs then, moving to his side, repeats the process, her left hand in front.

"Do you hurt?" she asks, having finished her inspection.

"Just my hands." He glances down at her.

"We're going to fix that." Patting his back, she pushes him gently forward. "You don't eat right." Her fingers pressing on both sides of his spine, he leans against the counter. "You're carrying some old wounds, David," her voice drops at the name, "but we honor you."

Relighting her cigarette, she blows a puff toward the middle of his chest, then another above his head. "There's stuff in here. Stuff we're going to fix. Turn around." She puffs along his back. "A little sun. Clean water. Mountain streams. Less paint and glue. It will take time. You're still very strong," she adds approvingly. "Ever see a fire?"

"Yes." He turns back to her.

"Be some more, I think, before it's all cleaned out."

"Always leaving my work in the fire," he comments.

"Whatever's necessary," Elsie responds. "Just feed your body. Steady now. There's much to be learned." She turns to the rest of us who have, while she worked with Larry, taken our places at the big table. "With each meal, find the blessing, establish a platform and a progression. One, Two, Three ..." She pauses.

I realize she intends for us to complete a grace, or rhyme. Feeling awkward, I add: "God bless you and me."

"A beginning." She stands at the edge of the table. "Enjoy yourselves. Larry and I need a little fresh air."

She pushes him outside ahead of her. I go to the counter, with John, to make our sandwiches. None of us comment. As if nothing unusual is going on, we eat and visit, taking our time, Elsie's food alive with some energy which differs fundamentally from what we normally receive.

Eventually, Elsie and Larry come back in, visiting like old friends. Larry washes his hands and makes a sandwich. Elsie disappears into the back room.

While Kathy fills his glass, Larry pulls up to the table and, heaping his plate with salad, takes a deep breath.

"So how was your class?" she asks.

"Looks good." Glancing around the table at each of us, he adds. "Not the same as you're getting, but important."

After finishing his sandwich, Larry says it's about a ten minute walk to CRC and he wants to get a head start. As the screen door slams shut behind him, Elsie reappears from the workroom.

"Good man." She motions out the window toward Larry. "It's important we have a place for him. Now," she rubs her hands together, "you can have coffee before or after, but before you leave the table there's a simple rule you must remember, taught by my first incarnate Master, an old Chinaman with quite a temper."

Stamping her foot down and saluting, she pretends to have a pistol at her head, the trigger set to explode, then, relaxing, continues: "You never leave the table, unless you've cleaned the dishes. It's the same with life in general."

Relighting the cigarette she had left in the tray by the window, Elsie watches the smoke curl into the air, then moves to the door. "Just remember, rule number one is not optional." She sing-songs back to us:

"You do the dishes,
dry them, put them away,
or the bugs will eat
what I have to say."

Her voice trails off as she lowers the sunshade. "I'll be back later." She moves toward the garden. "Talk your heads off, if you want."

Pushing her chair back, Kathy says: "Let's clean up."

John laughs. "I heard the rule, but it sounds like one of my mother's."

"Elsie talked to us about the Order of the Cooks," Kathy explains. "She's the cook and we're the apprentices." She starts gathering the dishes.

"Coffee first, maybe?" John suggests. "Nah," he answers himself as Sara wrings a wash-rag and begins wiping the counter. While Kathy runs hot water into a plastic basin in the sink, John carries dishes to me and I scrape the remains into the compost bucket. We have moved into a new rhythm.

"What were you girls doing earlier?" John leans forward to look out the window. "I can't remember seeing you."

Taking a dish and drying it, Sara responds: "When we first came in with the vegetables, neither of you seemed to notice us. Then we went into the workroom and Elsie talked about growing crystals with no light, then just a little light and living water." She glances at Kathy. "And about the patterns on her work bench and the triangles and towers outside. Isn't that when she sent us back out to look at the garden?"

"Yes." Kathy confirms, but seems preoccupied. "When we came back in, you were gone."

"Did you see them?" I ask John.

"Only when Elsie sent us out." He seems confused. "I'm not sure."

"Well," Kathy straightens as Sara hangs her towel under the sink to dry, "she moves herself here and there, and us, too, apparently."

"I don't see how you or Elsie could have left or come back without us seeing you — unless she, or you, can go through walls." He looks at me.

"Maybe we were all outside at the same time," I suggest, but realize how out of sequence everything seems. "We went outside, and Elsie followed us, remember?"

"Several times." John turns toward the girls. "She showed up right behind us, talked about the gardener, or someone, and some witches who," he pauses, "were burned, I think."

"Yeah." I remember vividly. "And she followed us on the stone walkway. That was right before she called us back in to set the table for Larry."

"Why does she call him David?" Sara asks.

"David and Goliath, I think," Kathy answers.

"To fight the monster?" John shudders. "I better take this garbage out."

"How long were we outside?" I ask, still puzzled.

"We went out right before lunch," he pushes the screen door open, "just a few minutes."

"Longer than that." Elsie's chuckle follows her voice. Walking in as if John had opened the door for her, she surveys the room. "You do work well together. Now," she lights a cigarette, "if Sara will make some coffee, we'll have a little visit before the break. Karin told you about that, didn't she?"

"From two 'till four." Sara takes the coffee can down then runs water into the pot while John and Kathy take the compost out.

"Amazing boy." Elsie turns to me. "Seems like your brother. You're both Johns, aren't you?"

"John, Jr." I nod.

"Names run like that." She looks up, smiling. "Kind of a cover. Have you worked with limericks? I particularly like the dirty ones. Remember," she grins mischievously, "pseudonyms aren't jest for false prophets. I'm serious now. This one might be fine for Mr. Gurdjieff, but I wouldn't put my name to it in polite company."

She howls, tickled apparently, then recites in a slow, fierce, deliberate voice:

"Dog star yelping, tail wagging,
he bones the faery queen,
asshole crunching, the fire lighting
the naughty scene, chanting
the full moon bears the sun king."

"That's not a limerick, is it?" I ask, confused.

Swinging her head back, she guffaws heartily, and spreads her arms to hug me. "No." She laughs. "It's just a dirty poem about Sirius. I worked all night, with the other ladies, on that one." She pushes me back.

"What's it about?" I ask, trying to find the thread.

"The dog star, African prophecies, dark rites." She studies me. I know she's teasing the edges of real poetry, stretching me to respond, but I can't.

"You'll get it." She pokes me in the chest. "Try some limericks, really," she whispers. "Learn to laugh at your Serious-ness. Where can we start?" She grins.

"Let's see." She stares at the ceiling. "Look at the name. Study punning and permutations. Yes. See 'Emery' in Bremyer. Think universe-city, one point spinning, to paraphrase Eliot. Emory U. isn't in Athens." She looks at me, big eyed. "You thought Greece, didn't you? Well," she giggles playfully. "Pair a phrase with Eliot or Yeats. That's all we ever do. Start with a Limerick — Ireland. Roll from there. You've been to Cork, haven't you. Well, uncork it. Don't be frightened of Blake."

"I'm trying, Elsie." I see myself, three years earlier, hitchhiking along the Irish coast, catching a ride with tinkers in a horse-drawn Gypsy cart.

"We've been watching you." Elsie shakes her finger at me. "Build the connections, network to catch the spillage. Compost the garbage. But don't just keep gorging yourself on words — going round, fighting to not fight ... Sara."

"What?" Sara's attention is snapped back to Elsie.

"Do try to save him," she finishes the statement.

"Save Jay?" Sara asks while Elsie circles in the space between us, leaning inward as if on a staff, saying:

> "An old man limping in the woods
> his staff twisted with a snake."

She stops, and addresses me. "B R E M Y E R has a B for bloodline. Yours too, now, Sara." Almost growling, she starts circling again.

> "Blue gold, silver and diamonds —
> the forest deep, the running stream.
> You'll find the money
> But it's not what you dream."

She stops again. "Do well and you'll have it, but you won't own it. Use it or it uses you. What I'm saying," she acts like she's examining a staff, "is that 'Emery' goes back to the school of the Druids who trained Arthur. Acrostics reveal reincarnational connections."

"Acrostics?" I ask, trying to follow her.

"Cross-stitches," Elsie laughs. "Codes in names, names in poems, letters embedded in rhymes. Messages woven by the Mistresses in the mattresses. Find the still point. Do time," her head jerks back like she's been hit, "travel."

She spins out through the door as John and Kathy return. The screen bangs shut. Startled, we four look at each other. Before we can move, she returns, seats herself at the front table, and motions us to approach her.

"Don't worry about that sort of thing, if I don't fall down. Sometimes, wham!" She brings her palm up and slaps her forehead. "Something jams. The voices bounce off each other. There's a competition. I don't know what's coming through."

Relighting her cigarette, she thinks a moment. "There's a special guest here." She points around the room. "But this body doesn't always know who's speaking, when, or whether the bear's in the den, or the wolf's in the lair, or the mother hen's clucking, or the lion's in sheep's clothing, or who's the liar with pants on fire, but Elsie wears hot pants inside this body for you ... acting silly, maybe, but it's from the fire ... and it's for you that she does it."

Controlling her breath, no longer playful, she adds: "I need a few moments, a quick spin, to move out of the force-field, to touch earth. Understand?"

Looking worn now, her voice raspy, she signals to Kathy. "Show John the bead work, will you?" After they're gone, she takes Sara's hand and talks directly to her as if I'm outside their circle. "Jay has a work which will give him thirty pieces of joy stained with blood. You're frightened because you want to run and he wants to hold."

Turning to face her, Sara says: "I'm also afraid he'll let go, and I'll be left out."

She pats the chair for Sara to sit beside her, motherly now. "You're inside already. The question is whether you want to open the door. Jay's words are hammers. He's pounding to get in. Let him fight toward you."

"He knows more than I do."

"About what?" Elsie seems puzzled.

"Intellectual stuff. " Sara sniffs.

"Mind is his thing. You stick with experience." She relights her cigarette. "He's hard to live with, right?"

Wiping a tear from her cheek, Sara shakes her head.

"So is Vern." Elsie smiles. "And I don't even live with him. But I couldn't survive without him. All your fear comes from thinking that you need to be someone other than who you are. We need you as you are!"

Sara seems stunned. The chain of statements, which had flowed into her, breaks as Kathy and John re-enter the room. Turning to the rest of us, Elsie says:

"You've been together from the very first. You've worked the Egyptian temples. You've walked the earth with the Nazarene. You've faced tragedy after tragedy and learned to love. But it doesn't matter if you don't remember. You can't remember if you're not awake. So ...

"We light matches in the dark. And, if necessary," she snaps erect, "we'll goose you. Goose girls, you know?" She chuckles. "Unless I undress I'm grossly Miss Stakened," she thrusts against her chest as if driving a pike in, "even called vampire and old crone. But here's the heart: 'Shoo, shoo, shoo!' We spread the wings of young swans."

Slowing, Elsie takes a breath, and glances at Sara before continuing: "We're looking for reed pipes, the seven note scale. We're trying to feed you. This is special. Listen or you miss it. There's nothing easy," she stamps, "about eating with Elsie."

Stepping forward, her voice ricochetting around the room, she booms: "shoo, shoo, shoo ... We'll boost you if we can. We'll make it fun, if we can. We'll do what we can to keep the wolf out, if you care enough to listen and remember. The drums are your ears and I'm playing them."

Pointing for Kathy to stand beside her, she whispers: "The wolf eats those who are asleep. Sleepers don't feel it. Your danger is that if I succeed in waking you up, they will smell you. Real blood is what they crave. Instead of being random targets for their grazing, you become the feast they're looking for. You'll feel it, if they get you. Their teeth are silver blades, bullets ripping real flesh.

"Well," she returns to her natural voice, "don't worry, sweethearts," she extends the word out of the side of her mouth like making a joke, "because I'm crazy about you. See?" She points at the stove.

"Now, seriously," Elsie glances out the window, "you need a few herbs and spices for flavor." She walks over and shuts the door. "We're working with patterns of five, but there's much more than even five of us can keep track of.

"Attention!" We all straighten-up, Elsie's voice gleeful but military at the same time. "At ease," she adds, more gently, her eyes scanning the room. "Camouflage and defusion are part of the trick. To be honest, we need all the tricks and we need extra protection. We spook the spooks with inconsistency. The worlds are discontinuous. The universe periodic. We ride between bubbles. Terribly serious, we're full of jest. Got it? Not justice. Let it go, I say, because ... "

Elsie backs up and glances out the window before continuing: "I can't keep track, not consciously, of each of your needs. What comes from me, or through me, may be for one or more of you, or all of

Date 1-20

M

Address

Reg. No.	Clerk	Account Forward		
1	Chipped Cod		13	95
2				
3	men		4	—
4			4	50
5		2x	2	25
6			1	50
7			3	50
8				
9				
10				
11				
12			34	06
13				
14				
15		5409-10		

1200 Your Account Stated to Date - If Error is Found, Return at Once

you, and, right now, as the moon returns to earth," pausing, arms crossed, she taps her finger against her temple as if thinking, "or is it the other way? Is there any difference?

"Well," she shrugs like a clown, puffing her face out, "I'm not here to make it easy on you. Though I love you, things are going to be strange. If you're not frightened, you're asleep. If nothing else you'll know that time and space are not fixed, nor do they need fixing — they're simply for staging, and you will travel in time."

She raises her arms and spins slowly: "Things moved to different places because they're in different time-spaces."

She crouches. "You'll see people walking by you who can't see you, like right now, people see us whom you don't see. Well," she straightens up, "frankly, they're mostly friends and I intend that eventually you will see them."

Sara reaches for my hand. Glancing from her to me, Elsie says: "Everything is light and shadow, movement and stillness." She points around the room. "Hear light, touch light, smell light opening the crystal door in yourself."

"How is the stage formed?" Kathy asks.

"Good question." Elsie seems pleased. "If you don't ask, we can't answer." Looking upward, she taps her toe on the floor. "Space evolves from movement. Movement is time, duration — in the dome of your head, in your very bones." She stamps her foot. "Space-time depends on this consciousness." She taps her forehead. "Spreading them, we anchor them with false truths." Breathing deeply, quieter now, she adds: "May our counterfeits be fruitful."

"What about truth?" I ask.

Looking at me, then the others, sad again, Elsie says: "I sacrificed the governor so it all floats through — all that's good and bad, exquisite and dangerous, crazy and sublime, helpful and disastrous, a mistake and a stroke of genius."

"Spirits speak through you?" John asks.

"There are no barriers except those which you bring. What you hear will be the highest you can evoke through the vocabulary of my experiences — or the lowest, or the most subtly malignant, dressed in the glitter of a snake who is actually a fallen angel."

"How do we know the difference?" I ask. "How can we protect ourselves?"

Striking a match, she looks at us through its light. "Through the opening which is presented here between us, vast potentials heave toward expression. Value seeks to clothe itself through our lives. Carried by words, by movements, by smell, touch, by patterns nudging against each other, a dance occurs — the dance of the black and white swan.

"Hold up that which is within you against that which comes from me. If they match, then you should accept it — though that doesn't mean it is only good, or only right, or that you don't have to work on it to transform yourself through courage, through the fire of conscious experience, into greater love. Otherwise," she shakes the flame out then puts a finger on top of her head, "just leave it alone. Nothing can enter you unless you accept it."

"How much will we remember?" Kathy asks.

"Everything which matches what you bring to it." She sits. Silence permeates the room. Birds in the trees chatter at each other. A car drives by. "But much which you encounter here won't be remembered until the patterns in your futures match what's being laid in now."

Setting her coffee cup down, Kathy asks: "Did you say certain things are to be destroyed?"

"You have to decide what was said," Elsie answers. "There's bad stuff in here, too." She pats her chest. "Wickedness, black arts, magicians who want to control you. This isn't a perfect world. This world interpenetrates many worlds. But 'destroy'? I'm not sure who said that. Some voices come through which are not from, or for, any of us."

"So," Kathy observes, analytically, "we're totally in charge of what we get from you?"

"I'm available as a supplement. Those whom I work with, who love you, have no other desire. But they are not the only ones who mold words out of my bodies." Elsie winks. "I have several, you know. We all do."

"Then you don't know for sure, either?" Kathy questions.

"There isn't much time." Elsie backs up to the counter and glances out the window. "And there's more time than we can ever comprehend. My experiences have been good and bad, light and shadow. That's the way on this planet, in this world, in this heart.

"It has to do with so much: who we are, what we choose, who we are in this group." She pauses. "You're five with Larry. You're five with me. With Larry we're six. We're seven with Karin. Always, at least one is invisible, usually two. Decoys. Safe ducks on the water. We'll be nine, eventually. Jay and Sara will be four. I'm working on twelve. It's like my cigarettes."

"What?" I think I misunderstood.

"I get seven or more lights off each one," Elsie answers. "You get one." She looks at me severely, tapping her foot.

"Well?" She grins. "Hell!" she crouches, "would be a lonely place without the devil. Nothing is certain but

> God spelled backwards is dog.
> Sirius shit so watch your step in
> Egypt we worshiped the cat while
> Treading on the tail of ...
> Tiger everywhere and all we had was
> Old Lot's wife and Medusa's frizzy hair."

"Turned to salt?" I ask.

"Ladies' tears, for you, Jay." Elsie turns away. "But answering you, Kathy, what you accept is what you choose. But who are you? To what extent is this really a table?"

Kathy answers: "To the extent that we all agree."

"That's why there are real possibilities in this group." Elsie nods. "You're mostly kids, but none of us pretends to a false perfection. I light matches, watch my breath, ground, as I told you, Sara, because — do you know why?"

Sara takes a deep breath. "Otherwise you'd disappear?"

"Some of us are like that," Elsie confirms. "Kathy's tougher. She's an old Indian. She's been burned, too. You were with her." She re-lights her cigarette, watches the smoke, puts it out.

"In these woods, just after the Spanish came." She waves slowly, her fingers out. "They were still down south, but word had come up the coast. Your job," she looks at Kathy, "was to protect the sacred icons. You and Sara were sister- priestesses. John was your brother. You hid something around here. It's something you have to find."

"What happens if we don't?" Sara asks.

"Just do it later." Elsie chuckles. Holding her arms up, she squats, knees out to either side. I see her wearing a feathered headdress, embedded with precious metals and gems.

"But I don't make claims for you." Elsie slaps her legs, pushing upward, then sits facing us. "What did you see?"

"What you were talking about," John says, excitedly. "Kathy was a priestess. I was trying to help her."

"And you, Jay?" Elsie asks.

"You were wearing a headdress."

"Great!" Elsie slaps her leg. "And preposterous."

"It reminded me of the Mayan hieroglyphs," I add.

"You saw my Mother, maybe?" Elsie opens her eyes wide. "The Old One, the alien in the temple, wearing a crash helmet, long, pointed?"

Almost punchy, I say: "Your mother?"

"Got you there." Elsie laughs. "There are aliens, of course. Some good, some with black hats. But they're not my mother, right or left — they're just other, but Mom ran the temple and these girls were her servants. The Seven Sisters, you know. See six but know they're seven, not sex!" She stands again, glaring at me. "Not whores, not objects. They're dancers, sacred virgins."

Raising her arms to the ceiling and stamping in a circle, her voice deep, Elsie growls:

"Pleiades babies old Poseidon would claim
But we rose from the earth-fire and water.
Nobody proves our sire, or claims
Our daughters ... "

As Elsie sits again, winking at me, I say: "I saw feathers with metals and gemstones."

"The gemstones are communication devices." Elsie studies me a second. "The feathers act as shields and selectors. We might not have gotten it right."

"It's all a game, isn't it?" I suggest. "Ultimately, no right and wrong?"

"See what I mean, Sara?" she relights her cigarette, then puts it out at the counter. "He's an old chess player — driving you crazy. I'm sorry, but he just can't help it."

"Chess?" Sara asks.

"All the moves are right on one level, wrong on another. I'm up to twelve dimensions." She shrugs. "He's still struggling at two.

But," her whole face spreads in gentle affection as she leans close and whispers to me:

"We's loved you and still do."

Holding her hand up, calling for silence, Elsie says: "Listen ... " The ground shifts. A car drives by. "See yourselves here," she points at the floor, "at five."

Searching for the Pattern

Exhilarated but on overload, I pull away from the Oasis. Sara sits in the front, Kathy and John in the back seat. Hot stillness has settled over the entire area.

Leaning forward, John breaks the silence: "My head's spinning. Elsie said everything is different now. I'm sure she is right, but I'm not sure what happened, or ..."

"It was like this the first time, too," Sara responds. "You feel fired up and wrung out at the same time. She carries on several different conversations at once."

"Plus," I pause, remembering flashes, "sometimes what she says to one of us is really meant for someone else."

"Or," Sara interjects, "what she says means one thing to you but something different to someone else."

"I think she's primarily working at breaking down our preconceptions." I slow to go through Tiger.

"I didn't know what to expect," John pushes his glasses up, "but that was the wildest experience I've ever had. What's the deal with the sunshade?"

"She was concerned about someone overhearing us," I answer, not sure what to add. "It's a transmitter."

Kathy says: "This whole thing is like a masquerade ball, and we're the only ones not in costume. At times, I think she had us in some type of trance."

"Maybe," I glance back at Kathy, "it's the other way around, like Gurdjieff says. We're generally in trance, and she's trying to wake us up."

Everyone goes silent. Cruising toward Karin's, in awe of the number of subjects she covered, many of them bizarre, I reflect on our first group meeting with Elsie.

As we enter Karin's house, Sara turns to Kathy. "Elsie said that the clearest thoughts come while peeling potatoes. I need some of that."

"We all do." Kathy opens the closet and takes out cleaning supplies. "Let's start with the windows."

John and I outside, Sara and Kathy inside, we scrape with razor blades, spray Windex, and rub with newspaper. Anchored by the work, my mind floats. Did Elsie and Karin, knowing that we would have to ground ourselves, plan it this way?

Knocking on the glass and pointing to a smudge I had ignored, Sara is content and happy. We work as a team, knowing Karin will be pleased.

Arriving back at Elsie's, Sara reads a note pinned to the door: "I'm at the waterfall but will return soon. Please begin making a salad, so we're ready for our guest. LC - p.s. And change the flags, Jay."

Windows open, light inside, a stick of incense burning in the windowsill, crystals submerged in water — her house is breathing. "At least the shade is down." John points out the window at the picnic table.

Sara works at the sink while Kathy and John go to the garden. Not sure how I am to know which ones to put out, I wander into the workroom to look for towels. The walls are lined with tables and shelves, stacks of baskets with stones, trays of beads, a glass container next to a Bunsen burner, piles of magazines, a small drum, a very old obsidian knife, a set of antlers, a basket of folded towels.

Bending over the basket, I glance into the back room. Elsie, or someone, is lying on the bed in the shadows. Backing away, I pull out a blue and a gold towel.

"The new flags?" Sara asks as I re-enter the kitchen.

"For Larry." I nod, not wanting to say anything further, then push the door open to let John and Kathy through.

Moving past the picnic table, I hear the backfire of a muffler against the hush of woodland. The sunshade has been opened. A shadow covers the picnic bench and stretches toward the lake. I hurry to the line and replace the towels, securing the new ones with wooden clips from the canvas bag.

Wrapping the other towels in a ball, I hear Elsie talking about running water and relaying stones. Her voice seems to come from the sunshade, yet I catch a glimpse of her and a man at the edge of the cottage, moving around to the back side. Rounding the corner, I discover a rock garden, a small stone monument in the center, bells jingling — but see no one.

Unnerved, I start down a stone pathway into the woods, but then hear Elsie in front of the cottage. Hurrying towards the voice, I see that the sunshade is folded down again and assume she has gone inside. Sara and Kathy are finishing the salad. Not knowing what to say, I help John set the table then follow them back out into the sunlight.

"When do you think Elsie will be back?" Sara asks while John and Kathy move toward the picnic table.

"Didn't she come through while I was outside?"

"No." Sara looks at me like I'm batty.

Suddenly I am apprehensive about the sunshade. Before I can say anything, Elsie emerges from the door behind us. Moving slowly, she is wearing a scrub lady's dress, her head in a dirty bandanna. Almost groggy, focusing on us, she says: "Ask John to open the parasol, would you? Then take a walk."

John and Kathy turn toward us, startled. John says: "Now?"

"Yes, please," Elsie responds, sounding exhausted.

While John hurriedly cranks the sunshade out, Sara starts toward them, saying: "Let's check the woods out."

Turning to Elsie, I say: "Why?"

"The others, you know." She lights a cigarette and blinks, looking around, checking the clothesline. "Blue and gold — good choice. And you're right, the shade is a transmitter. But energy goes both ways. Has to. Anyway," she points to the picnic table, "we'd all disappear if this were paradise, wouldn't we?"

Elsie hobbles back into the house as I hurry to join the others moving toward the woods. Kathy stops at the tree line. "That didn't even look like Elsie."

"She was really groggy," I make an effort at explaining. "I guess she had been asleep."

"While you were outside," Kathy looks at me, dark eyes, serious, "Elsie glided through the kitchen wearing silk slacks and a jewelled jacket. Her hair was fixed in a tight bun on top of her head ... which was impossible, I know."

"I didn't see her," Sara interjects.

Glancing at John, who shakes his head, then back at me, Kathy says: "I thought she was going to talk to you. You were out there a long time. Didn't you see her?"

"No, not exactly. But I heard her talking to the guy who lives around here." I hesitate, uncertain. "Who works with rocks and waterways."

"She talked about that." John glances toward the cabin. "That whole thing about William Shakespeare ... and the witches ... Right?" he questions himself.

"You're cooking now." Elsie laughs, then pushes the screen door open to us. She's wearing a cotton sun-dress, looking fresh. "Our guest is coming." She smiles. "Let's act like nothing strange has happened." She winks and spins back into the kitchen. Kathy follows her in.

At that moment, Larry, whistling, strolls up the drive. "Have a good afternoon?"

"Washing windows. How about you?" Sara questions.

"This gal knows her stuff." He swings his bag down onto the tree stump. "I've actually got homework."

"Mr. Lawrence," Elsie announces as we enter together.

"Miss Elsie." Larry bows slightly. She beams at him. Turning to Kathy, he nods: "Hi there, Doctor Potatoes," then washes his hands and joins us at the table.

Standing over us, Elsie claps: "One ... two ... three."

Remembering the little prayer exchange from the noon meal, I say: "Blessings from the ... "

Elsie adds: "Lord of the land, Mistress of the sea."

As she backs away, we make a play at being casual, but I feel an uncertainty on the part of all of us. We want to tell Larry what has happened, but we all conspire to keep the conversation light. At one point I hear Elsie talking on a phone in the workroom, but know there is no phone.

Sara simulates conversation by asking questions about Larry's astrology class. He obliges with long explanations, none of which are of interest, under the circumstances, but we pretend — giving the impression that everything is normal. We tell him about working in the garden, but never mention Elsie's comings and goings, some of which seemed totally discontinuous.

"You know?" Elsie reappears from the workroom. Sara and Kathy are washing dishes.

"What, Elsie?" John turns to her.

"It's just that there's so much going on that I'm never quite sure. You know?" She lets the question hang, almost like a sad little girl. None of us respond.

"So it might be best," she turns to me, her mouth turned in a sad smile, "if we call it a night." She checks her wrist as if looking for a watch. "How about tomorrow at ten? That's whole enough — although thirteen has one foot in the mud and the other in heaven." She spreads her arms. "Learn what the others are learning."

"If we can get five for one, that's cheap." Larry nods like they're having a private conversation then points to the door, indicating it's time for us to leave.

After driving back to Karin's, still uncertain how to get into a real conversation, Larry and Kathy take a walk by the stream. Sara and I make coffee, anxious for their return. When they come in, Kathy seems upset. Larry purposefully spreads his books on the dining room table.

"Are you going to study?" I ask, surprised.

"Look at this bibliography." He hands me a list citing Aurobindo, Bailey, Blavatsky, Leadbeater, Gurdjieff and Steiner. "It turns out that I've got the ball." He pats the books. "I have to concentrate on the class or I'll miss what I came to do." I sense that he's acting, making a point.

"All I know is that I need a break." John grabs a soda from the fridge. "I'll be in my room, okay?"

"Your mother should be home soon, shouldn't she?"

"Don't know," he answers Sara then moves away.

"Anyway," Larry leans back, "I have a couple hours of reading, and some calculations to master, and ..."

"You may enjoy subterfuge," Kathy interrupts, "but I don't, and I'm certain that the four of us need to talk."

"At least tell us," Sara interposes, "what Elsie meant about you teaching us?"

"When did she say that?" Kathy looks surprised.

"She whispered it to me before supper."

"It's not what you think." Larry holds his hand up. "Outside, this noon ... "

"I want to hear about that," I say and take a seat, eager for context. "Larry, you were a different person when you came back in."

"It was extraordinary, but basically," Larry shakes his head, "she told me to act like I know what is going on, like I'm a scholar and a special guest."

"Tell them the rest." Kathy is insistent.

"I told you I'm not sure how much we can say or where it's safe to talk." Seeming uncomfortable, he glances out the window. "All I know for sure is that we're on a tight-rope and have to walk carefully, sticking with our own business and not wandering off into other things."

Kathy glares at him, her arms folded across her chest.

"Anyway," he looks to Sara and me, "Elsie talked about life streams native to earth, but also how we're influenced by aliens. She said I'm tied in with the old Enochian line, blue eyes and all — particularly Jesse, David, and Solomon, but for now I'm supposed to just play along, keep it light, and laugh at the devil." He forces a grin.

The world is spinning. All of a sudden I see that the shifts Elsie has put us through all day are like different rooms and that when I'm in one I forget the others. Trying to focus, I remember being concerned about aliens, but had dismissed it. Wanting to see a bigger picture, I ask whether she talked about the sun-shade?

"Just that the Black Hats listen through it, not to say too much around it, and that John is in charge of it." He takes a drink of water. Voice raspy, he starts again. "I'm not sure what we're hiding from them, but she said we have our roles and they have theirs."

"Aliens or Black Hats?" Kathy is unnerved. "Don't you think we have to consider what she's talking about?"

"Some of them are both, apparently." Larry studies Kathy before continuing. "She said we can't understand their roles unless we get a hold of it right, like a priestess holds a poisonous snake." He reflects on something. "She did this incredible movement when she told me that."

"It's unnatural how she moves." Kathy pauses, thinking.

"So we're supposed to play off you? Is that it?"

"I'm supposed to make it seem that the class is the main reason we're here and model a pattern to keep us fixed. And she said I have to learn to sense when the Others are watching or listening, and use their energy for 'our' purposes — something like the Gurdjieff stuff we talked about."

"And what are 'our' purposes?" Kathy is angry. "That's my point. She's pulling us into something we know nothing about. She's saying how we relate to you will anchor us. Great! That also deflects us from comprehending what she is doing. It's a distraction."

"It is," Larry agrees, "but that's to take you out of the immediate intensity of relating to her. She's working on a lot of levels and she said that by creating the illusion of one event, which we intend, she can input an extraordinary amount of information on another wavelength which is at that point unattended and ..."

"I have a whole list of questions," Kathy interrupts, "which need to be answered objectively. First, we have to decide what we're willing to go along with."

"Is there any such thing as objectivity?" Larry asks. "Whether the danger is objective or subjective ... "

"It's still danger," Kathy insists. "What if we're going to lose track of who we are? I've worked too hard to gain some stability. I'm not ready to let it go."

"I don't think you will, Kathy." Larry is conciliatory. "In any event, we don't know enough yet and," he pauses, "at some level, all this is real and, it seems to me that, for whatever reason, we're ready for this experience."

"I'm not questioning the fact that Elsie is fascinating and at times intensely loving, but I believe these are questions we must ask." Kathy shakes her head. "And I am sincerely worried about you."

"I know." He shifts in his chair. "But Elsie said she would set a back-fire to cover me so that, when I'm really learning something, she'll be drawing their attention away."

"It's so bizarre!" Kathy protests.

"Yes," Larry agrees. "But she's so extraordinary. We have to accept a lot, for now. It's like art, when you first encounter it. You can kill it by too much rational analysis."

"What's the connection between Elsie and Karin?" Kathy refuses to let it go.

Taking a deep breath, Larry says: "Karin is acting as a diversion, like me, only in her case taking the attention toward Atlanta." He glances outside. "I do need to study."

"Let me get this straight," Sara interjects. "We're supposed to treat you like a guest when we're at Elsie's. That anchors us?"

"Exactly, Doodle." He grins. "You guys are taking care of me and, according to Elsie, I'm taking care of you by drawing attention away from what she's teaching you. Then we're supposed to exchange; but only when we understand how it can be done without undoing the illusion that we don't understand. Does that make any sense?"

"No." Kathy stands. "Either you buy it or you don't. And if you do, you should be scared shitless."

"I am." Sara glances at me. "Elsie said if we're not, then we're asleep."

"Hold on, Kate." Larry reaches for Kathy's arm. "You don't have to buy it to play along."

"Bullshit, Larry." She pulls away. "Elsie gives us this stuff then you give us another layer. This isn't a game."

"I just want to understand the rules," I intervene.

"You can try." Kathy turns to me. "But," she softens, "I'm tired. Maybe I'll feel differently in the morning. Are you coming?" She glances back to Larry who pats his books. Turning toward their room, she shakes her head before disappearing down the hallway.

Emotionally drained yet somehow still exhilarated, I suggest Sara and I move outside for some fresh air, leaving Larry to his assignments. Standing in the front yard, I ask how long she thinks we will stay.

"Through the week, because of Larry's workshop."

"We could stay indefinitely," I suggest.

"No." Sara sits on the front stoop. "We're here for something special. Then we're going home."

"We really have no reason to go back to Kansas," I comment tentatively, sensing that in spite of seeming so natural with Elsie, Sara is already withdrawing. Like Kathy, something deep down is bothering her, something which I am reluctant to discuss. I just want to hang on and find out to what extent I can function in Elsie's world. "We could put all our stuff in a trailer," I open it up slightly.

"You're going too fast." She stands up. "I'm not ready for that."

I protest, softly: "But I feel like my whole life has been leading up to this."

"I know." Opening the door, she moves toward our room. Waving at Larry, concentrating under the light, I follow her knowing that, like Larry, I'm already emotionally committed to whatever Elsie has in store for us.

Pale light falling through the windows, unable to find further words, I lie on the mattress staring at the ceiling. All the questions Kathy is raising are valid. Why did Elsie, and how could she, set all this up? How much is real? Is she pulling this out of our minds? How much danger is there? What am I not understanding?

But regardless of the risks, my heart is being extended and I feel certain that I can trust Elsie, and that whatever it is that she is giving me has already opened me up, and that I am committed to seeing it through.

Knowledge and Heart

Larry laughs as I stumble out our bedroom door, shaking off a dream, and move with him toward the kitchen.

"What time is it?"

"Almost 8:00," he answers. "Karin just left."

"Did you knock on our door?"

"No." He turns to me, a quizzical expression on his face. "I was just walking by."

The dream comes back: Larry, or some aspect of him, wearing a three pointed harlequin's cap, dressed in a striped and polka dot body-suit, is juggling a set of knives in the hallway outside our bedroom — trying to get my attention. A midget, riding a huge tiger, pulling a red wagon, is coming down the hallway toward him.

The opposite wall opens to a forest clearing. Hundreds of court damsels, with black ribbons floating out behind them from long conical hats, are riding dolphins in a moat which encircles the clearing.

Larry steps back. His knives tumble to the floor, four of them sticking upright in a row, sounding like knocks against our door. The fifth, landing horizontally across the others, drives them into place — waking me.

"You look shocked," Larry observes.

"I'm just remembering this series of images." I let myself out through the sliding glass door. Outside, the sun hovers in a bright blue sky.

"I had some wild dreams, too." Larry slides the door shut behind me and returns to the table where his books are spread out, like he has worked all night.

Eventually everyone is up and involved in their own morning ritual. Piling into the car, we head for CRC, drop Larry off and return to Elsie's by 10:00.

"They've just landed." Elsie holds the door open for us. "Some of the people over at Mahdah's have been tracking them."

I glance back at the picnic table. The parasol casts a slight shadow. Three green towels are on the line.

"Who's landed?" John asks.

"Apollo's Missionaries." Elsie looks up. "I'm concerned, of course. The man IN the moon," she exaggerates, "— not sure he wants them walking on him. First time for anything, I guess."

Wearing baggy gray pants with a light jacket, looking like a Chinese communal farmer, Elsie moves into her workroom. "You've seen the picture of Vern, haven't you?" She points.

Crowding around for closer inspection, I am shocked by the photograph. A flame explodes from the end of his finger — which he is using to light a cigarette.

"Remember that I told you Vern could control a meeting just by rubbing his stone?" Elsie asks. "That was subtle, but ... " She shakes her head disapprovingly, then dipping and swaying, pleased, announces: "He's here, now." Sliding her feet around in what looks like a waltz, I glimpse a long conical hat and black ribbons streaming behind her.

"But we have our separate work." She stops, her eyes deepening, burning into me. "We're all in and out of the pentagon depending ..." She puts her finger on top of her head and pulls upward, spinning gracefully. When she stops, the room seems to spin as she says: "Some of his tricks get him into trouble. We can all throw fire, but Vern can control it. Normally he hides the picture."

"You mean if people knew they would ... " John stops.

"Lock him up if they could," Elsie continues. "And he'd have to stay there, you know. At least until we found some explanation. The C.I.A. is based on explanations."

"Natural laws?" I ask.

"Cartesian laws." Elsie leads us back to the other room. "It's not just what you can read, by reconstructing the letters. It's what you can sound out. Descartes said there is an unbridgeable gulf between what's inside and outside — what's here," she points to herself, "and what's out there." She points out the window.

"Descartes was a great brain, but he got it wrong. Maybe he meant to. Either way, he provided a platform on which machines could be built. Even Kant, you know, 'Can't' ... " she breaks off, laughing.

"What is poetry?" Elsie leans over the table looking at me. "What are the symptoms of good poetry?"

"When you bring the two sides together," I suggest.

"Not good enough!" She walks to the window. "It's when you break the false borders. It's when the truth is secreted and explodes into our lives — utterly changing everything. Ultimately it's the living crystallization of the essence of an emotional experience."

"'Crystallization'?" I try to see the image.

"Steiner maintained that certain thought forms, based on false premises, have dominated the intellectual mind." She lights a cigarette. "In terms of the evolution of consciousness, those ideas were helpful. But the forces of Ahriman defeated Goethe, whose spiritual science would have re-balanced the thought forms. Using the artifacts of our own secretions, Ahriman attempts to encase us in matter — to stop Lucifer, Fire-Bearer, whose forces would keep the slime alive, would keep us growing.

"Lucifer withdraws from gross matter. He doesn't want to get dirty." Stubbing her cigarette out, she leans forward, swings her arms, and screws her mouth sideways, grimacing, like something is terribly distasteful. "So you see?"

"What?" I ask, uncertain.

"Every creature, at a fundamental level, all the way down to its cells — every cell, in fact ... " She straightens, then holds her hands out like claws, looking for a moment like the dragon monsters which guard the gates to Chinese temples.

Relaxing, Elsie moves to the table near the window. "Every cell, every living thing, feels justified in defending itself — even though it may not be under attack." She chops her hand sideways into the air, stepping with it. "We hold our identity by aggressive behavior. Perhaps it's necessary. Sometimes it is. Ahriman by death. Lucifer by light. Either way, poetry is dangerous. It's ecstatic, crystalline, loving — but loving what? Why? It fights for the perfect, which is dying. It fights to live."

Elsie marches at me, wholly concentrated, aggressive. "Write a poem which demonstrates that, Jay. You have the impression it isn't work, but it's more hell than you have yet dreamed. You're going to have to take over some day — each of you." She points at Sara,

Kathy, then John, who have been watching her back me around the room. Drawing back, her eyes blazing into me, she screams: "You think I can't talk when the sunshade is spread? When the shadow creeps over the ground?" — then collapses to the floor.

Absolutely disoriented, I jump backward. John's mouth has dropped open.

Sara and Kathy hurry forward and kneel. As Sara's hand touches Elsie's shoulder, her eyes flip open. "Got you!" she exclaims, delighted. Then, voice lowered, just loud enough so John and I can also hear, she whispers: "Larry was right, you know. But we can't let them know I told you so. We're using their energy to feed the giants, scare the crows. Everything is heightened exchange."

Getting up, reciting, she swings her finger as if conducting a chorus:

"You give me pennies, I give you dimes.
Give me dimes, I give you quarters.
Five we are — pentagram's the star ...
But little boy blue ... he knew
Emotion rouses attention ...
Not too much; not too little.
In the crunch, just don't piddle."

Laughing, Elsie glances at me, winks, then backs to the window. Holding her jade necklace, she points at the picnic table. "Everyone has a role: dog bones, crystal skulls, and all that rot." She tip-toes to the door, then slips out and lowers the sunshade.

Re-entering, Elsie allows the silence to hover over us.

Seeming to become larger, extremely powerful, ominous, she looks to Sara, Kathy, then John and me, before speaking:

"We've been carrying the fire which burns, here." She thumps her chest. "And here." She points to her forehead. "Our bodies are on fire."

She turns and walks back to her chair. Sitting, then relighting her cigarette, she concentrates on the flame. Taking a deep breath, she watches the vapor curl into the air and disappear, then looks at us. "You have to learn how to burn. Your bodies must stretch between Ahriman and Lucifer. You are the bridge." She looks specifically at me. "The crystallization of the essence of an emotional experience."

Not sure I have followed her, I shake my head.

"Take the steps," she adds, insistently. "Cross the bridge."

"Through poems ... " I falter.

"Limericks are fine, but you don't even get them." She stands. "If you'll listen, you'll see we're practicing all the time. But the real stuff, which still breathes after a hundred years, that's tougher, that's something we really have to work on. I'll work with you," her voice softens, "but you have to master the form."

"A form which can breathe?" I ask.

"Study the geometry of crystals — of war, courage, hope, love. Understand that you are defending yourself — forming a separate life. You're holding identity in place and time — tied together in a donut, a Moebius strip, circling a center which doesn't exist.

"See my hand. Follow the surface until you find you are inside, that there is no difference. You apprehend the center, the void. You try not to disappear. You secrete a poem so close to perfection that it is the essence of what makes all of us, all that is manifest — just defective enough that it will last, that you can hold to it by fighting off both light and darkness, disintegration in either extreme."

She stands, fists on her hips, legs spread, looking at us as if she were a sergeant in the military getting ready to send her troops into battle. "At ease. Smoke if you wish. I'll be back later."

Uncertain what to do, finally we settle at the table. Scratching his head, seeming totally bewildered, John clears his throat. "Who did she say is landing today?"

"The astronauts, boy." Elsie intones, her voice husky as she pushes back in through the door. "The pictures of them walking on the moon, and of the earth hanging in space — the water planet — will change the world. I've been to the dark side many times, but they won't show that now. The world's not ready for that."

"The dark side of the moon?" Kathy asks, disbelievingly.

"The guys down at Mahdah's have been tracing them, body readings with eloptic energy, the whole thing, even on the dark side where NASA loses them. What the astronauts are seeing there won't be projected back to earth."

"What are they seeing, Elsie?" I ask.

"An alien outpost for one thing. When the moon broke off from the earth, they made a base there. We don't admit they have to have someplace to live. They chose the back side."

"But don't they influence us?" I ask.

"They're here, alright," Elsie says. "But we don't recognize them. They have their role, but we call it other names — lie to ourselves. We deny who we are. We claim we're the point of evolution, the very ... " she squeezes the word, raising her voice, "tip."

"What are the people at Mahdah's doing?" Sara asks.

"Honigberger keeps a full-body picture of the astronauts, all their functions, just as if they were in an intensive care unit — uninterrupted. The C.I.A., even Vern's Navy boys, don't want it known, because they are unable to know, and therefore they will attack Honigberger and his machines. I'll stop singing for them, if they do. That will be my protest, because I think the world must know."

"You're saying," I ask, "that the world must know about the colony on the back side of the moon?"

Moving to the little table next to the window, Elsie sits quietly. The world washes around the cabin from the outside. A vehicle approaches, sounds like it pulls into the drive, idles a moment, then backs out and goes on.

Elsie stands. "Anyway," she turns to Sara, "I'm against tromping on alien territory, then denying it. The extraterrestrials can take care of themselves, of course. But I build confusion by refusing to behave."

"You confused me." Kathy lights her own cigarette.

Putting her hands on our table, leaning forward, grinning playfully, her blue eyes sparkling, Elsie says: "If there were no confusion, we wouldn't be here, would we?"

As if she doesn't want to be engaged, Kathy stands and goes to the window. Turning back, she says: "Is there a landing site in the woods, connected with the Hart Retreat?"

"There are several different civilizations with interests in our planet. Some we would call good, generally." Elsie gets herself a cup of coffee, then sits at the little table. "Some are just curious." She shrugs. "Some want to use us for their own purpose, like our scientists use other species. They have to be resisted. Some are here, testing us, but careful, like you Kathy. Your skepticism is healthy — desperately needed, in fact. Keep asking your questions. They juice me, while the others fog out." She laughs then salutes Kathy, who nods in return.

As if he didn't hear that exchange, John asks: "Are they from other planets?"

"Some are humanoid, essentially," she turns to him, "with home planets similar to ours — carbon based, oxygen breathers. The colonists on the moon, aren't. Their chemistry is quite different. But they're somewhat physical. They can, for brief periods, exist here. It's an outpost. Some think they want to modify our atmosphere, more sulfurs, mostly, so they can breath without converters. Part of the industrial impulse was their work — a determination to move part of our mantle into the sky."

Elsie pauses, listening. Another vehicle approaches, then pulls out again. I sense a pressure, by some outside force, to spread the sunshade, and that somehow her manipulations, the timing of what she says and does, are keeping our enclave secure from encroachment.

"It's been weeks since we've seen the news," I volunteer, tentatively. "Are you saying that the Apollo Mission has gotten to the moon?"

Elsie nods.

"What do you think of the space program?" John asks.

"I told Jay, the first day he was here." Elsie looks at me, suddenly intense. "I'm all for boys flying. Builds character."

"But if there are other forces," Sara says, "forces which we can't control?"

"We're not here to control," Elsie addresses Sara. "We're here to care. The table was already set. We're not in charge. We're servants. So," Elsie bends over and claps her hands between her legs then, standing, puts on a straw hat with a large brim, "it's time to weed the garden."

Glad to get outside, we follow her through the door. The sun is shining now, radiant, touching everything.

"Girls at the far end, boys here," Elsie instructs.

"Start at the corners and move toward each other. Shouldn't take long. Meanwhile, I have an errand. Check the site, you know. Make sure nobody's around."

Already on my knees, I turn back to her. She looks just like a southern lady dressed to work around the plantation, who's giving the morning assignments before undertaking her own chores. It's like everything is back to normal; yet nothing is normal. We're 1000 miles from home, with a woman we barely know, and she's going to a spaceship landing site, leaving us to anchor some illusion which she has orchestrated.

Bending forward, fingers in the loose earth, digging into the mulch, pulling weeds out, breathing fresh, moist, luminous energy which hovers between soil and gardener, knowing Kathy, Sara, John and I are starting at the four corners, moving toward each other, I have the distinct impression of ourselves from a perspective in the sky. We are working a grid, showing how it is done. This is a portrait of what's good about humans, our proper, harmonious relationship to the earth.

"What did you think of all that spaceship stuff?" Sara asks once we're close enough to talk. Gradually refocusing, I realize that the string of thoughts, which had given me glimpses of what Elsie was talking about, has dissolved into the peace and assurance of the work.

Nearing the center of the garden, I say: "We have to decide what each aspect means to us."

"I think we have to focus on our own business." Kathy sits back on her haunches, looking around.

"Maybe so." John points toward the picnic table and shade. "But how do we know for sure?"

I have another flash of us in the garden, like from a satellite shot which is being magnified billions of times, with sound enhancement, but feel that by moving into the center from the four corners we've earned the right to say whatever we want, that we're in a supportive and safe environment. Looking from Sara, to Kathy, to John, I see that we are relaxing now.

"We should have a salad again." Elsie stands at the edge of the garden. "Something to lighten Mr. Lawrence up." She laughs, slapping her side, head back toward the sky. "He's healthy as he can be, being so serious."

"Larry?" Sara glances at me as I move toward Elsie.

"He has seemed awfully serious," I comment, intending to play along, glad Larry gave us the extra insight last night, aware that at moments Elsie talks to us like we know things and at others — I glance over and see that the sunshade is still shut — she acts as if we're without a clue.

"Now we prepare for the guest," Sara whispers.

"Apparently." I grin back at her.

"If Jay and John, or is it John Jay?" Elsie pauses, putting her finger to her ear as if listening. "There's an old justice here," she announces. "Yes ... Yes ... Okay," she says, like she's having a telephone
conversation. "Certainly ... Then we'll let him ... All right ... "

I'm standing in front of her but she seems absorbed in the conversation. Turning to me, she says: "You're like me. Know the law,
right?"

"I have a lot of lawyers in my family," I respond.

"They say if you get the structure right the rest falls into place.
Look into it."

"Mr. Lawrence." Elsie holds the door open like a delighted hostess. "Please come in and relax."

"Thank you." Larry nods respectfully.

"We are so pleased to have you with us again." Elsie waves her
hand toward the table — cabbage and cornbeef steaming on a serving platter next to a big bowl of salad, homemade bread, butter, jam
and a glass of milk, which she hands to Larry to drink before he sits.

Standing to the side, Elsie says: "It's all blessed. But if you want
to add something ... "

The five of us reach around the table. Holding hands, bowing our
heads, we breathe together in silence. A moment later, squeezing
hands, we all raise our heads, smiling, eyes flowing around the table.
Elsie is gone.

The lunch seems to be a time to anchor back to normal reality, like
taking on nourishment, accompanied by an unstated insistence that
the world is in order and we're doing what we always do.

Larry eats voraciously and goes into long explanations of the
workshop, offering at one point to get his diagrams out and plot
various astrophysical vectors. "It's nothing new." He starts to get
up. "But knowing how to do it, the mechanics — that's new to me.
I can see all kinds of applications."

"Imagine that," Kathy comments, but does seem more relaxed
than last night when she was ready to insist we all leave. Watching
her, I sense that she is as strongly drawn to Elsie as Larry and I are.

Elsie crosses the floor and puts her hands on Larry's shoulders from behind, thumbs at his neck. Watching him, I understand that his jovial exterior is a mask, and that he is struggling with something he is carrying for us.

Kissing the top of his head, her hands thumping him on the chest, Elsie says: "Your cap, Master Larry. Wear your cap while you're walking. Keeps the sun out, you know. We're on a new moon now. The energies require some stepping down."

Getting up, Larry opens his bag and models a black baseball cap — "CRC" written across the front in white letters. "Ned gave it to me."

"That's one approach." Elsie reaches up and outlines the letters with her finger. "But extreme, don't you think?"

"I guess so." Larry glances at me like he is uncertain.

"But it works if you understand," she relights her cigarette and puffs white smoke toward him, "that the charts are games, the positions are roles measured by rulers, straight lines which are temporary ... Aren't they?"

Elsie glances at me, then back to Larry. Suddenly I understand this is a coded exchange and she is testing to see if he is playing on more than one level. "Black hats with white letters are illusory, David," she whispers, "but useful in climbing the ladder, learning the new astrology."

"We're dealing with preliminary calculations here?" he responds, as if he's just received a new insight, and agrees.

"Indeed." Elsie sighs, looking tired now. "But we want so much for everything to go well."

"I'll be fine, Elsie." Larry smiles warmly, then hoisting his bag and securing his cap, turns to us and nods before leaving for the afternoon class.

After we clean the dishes, John and Kathy go outside. Thinking it's time to leave Elsie to her afternoon work, Sara and I start to follow but are startled by Elsie's voice: "Would you come here a second?" Turning back, we see she is sitting at the table near the window.

Signaling Sara to sit, Elsie says: "You're frightened because the words don't make sense and you feel like you'll be left behind."

Sara shakes her head in agreement. "The words cloak sense, Sara, they don't make it."

Putting my hands on Sara's shoulders, I am helpless to reach whatever aches inside of her.

"You're a young soul." Elsie leans back studying Sara. "Younger than you were in the beginning. Do you accept that?"

"I don't know." Sara whispers.

"Our school teaches the acceptance of pain, the carrying of burdens, becoming younger instead of, like most humans, growing older, coarsening their shells. Yours is already younger, more permeable. I'm so young I lost mine altogether." She laughs gently. "I'm young and dumb, and don't make any sense at all, but ..." She stands.

"I understand so much, in my body, not in words, that it passes knowledge." She holds Sara's gaze. "Reborn in the School of Mary, we're empathic and vulnerable. You understand everything but know nothing."

"Jay understands," Sara whispers, "but I don't."

"Or thinks he does." Elsie laughs. "He ages while you get younger — that's the heartache, the bridge between you. And I'm there waiting," she chuckles, "the match girl, herding the geese, pointing at the duckling who's beautiful."

Sara straightens up, smiling.

"He's virtually impenetrable, Sara," Elsie taps the table, "to the intelligences who hover around us. Thinking with skull mountain, he gathers details but sacrifices understanding in favor of accumulation, growing older while we grow others. That is the business of crones, mothers, and maidens." Sitting down again, Elsie pats her stomach.

"He's older than he was in the beginning, but he aches for our understanding while you wonder at his thinking. You are his entry to an old and sacred forest — full of witches." She nods at the ceiling then looks back to Sara."And you will grow older in knowledge as he grows younger in understanding. You must unite these two in each other."

Elsie glances up at me then turning back to Sara, adds: "It's a rope taut with pressure — pulled tight in growing older and younger — a path across which the two of you must walk, meeting in the middle."

"A path?" Sara asks.

"Being born again we die, then
in the ending, time begins again.
We return younger and older when
all time-bound divisions end,"

Elsie riddles.

"So don't let go of his hand,
But do let go when
She who knows understands
The fear of letting go ends
In the knowledge of your hearts."

A shiver goes through Sara's body.

Elsie stands and points at me. "He is not young enough to fear true knowledge. Although he is frightened, he doesn't know why." Looking to Sara again, her voice lowered, she adds: "But he will know as you understand."

Smiling, she pats Sara on the back. "The School of Mary leads from empathic pain, through understanding, to knowledge. He will gain understanding while growing younger." Elsie grins. "That's the trick, Sara." She seems delighted, like she has just discovered something. Handing a cigarette to Sara, she holds a light out.

"Watch the fire." Her voice is gentle, reassuring. "Even on the blackest night each time you strike a match, something of me and something of you coincides."

"Yes," Sara responds, eyes on the flame.

Glancing at me, Elsie says: "Do you understand?"

"Yes."

Standing before us, she whispers: "By this bond you will grow each other."

I join Kathy and John outside, warm and enthused by Elsie's gesture, almost a consecration, while Sara lingers. Within ten minutes, Sara waves to us: "Elsie said to change the flags, Jay. John," she pauses in the doorway, "you're in charge of the parasol from now on. We'll wait in the car." She smiles as I pass her on the way back to the workroom for towels where, re-examining the picture of Vern, I'm struck again by the fire coming out of his finger.

"That's me." I jump. I hadn't seen Elsie when I came through the kitchen. Carrying a mop and feather duster, she's wearing work clothes and a headband.

"I thought that was your husband," I respond.

"I'm the fire between the cigarette and his finger." She points at the flame. "He's been talking to you, you know?"

"A lot of voices have been talking to me."

"You have to watch out for her."

"Who?" I ask, thinking she's referring to herself.

"Sara." Taking my hands, swinging them back and forth between us, she looks up into my eyes.

"Why?" I ask, my heart aching.

"She's saved you. But she can't just keep doing it. You have to do your part."

"How?" I feel like it's all slipping away, and there's just Elsie and me, holding hands. We're on a swinging bridge between two cliffs. The only things I see are her eyes, and they are Sara's eyes, and I'm going to let go.

"Don't let go," she separates each word, "until she does
because you don't understand
and she doesn't know.
When you let go, that's when
you'll hold each other best."

Elsie drops my hands and turns abruptly. Her back to me, she says: "Don't close the door."

Allies and Adversaries

"Change the flags." Sara reminds me. Returning from our afternoon break at Karin's, we get out of the car and head toward the cabin. A yellow towel, with a red circle, is displayed on the clothesline.

Realizing that I don't want to leave the line bare, I go inside to get more towels and pick a green towel from the shelf in the workroom, then a purple one, thinking of Mahdah Hart's flag. Passing through the kitchen again, Elsie whispers to me: "I'm a little concerned about Larry." She has a scarf wrapped around her head, her pant-legs rolled up. The floor has been scrubbed. Incense is burning in the window. A mop leans against the wall.

Her eyes following me, I feel an urgent need to make certain that the pattern is correct. Hurrying to the line, I hang the purple then the green towel before removing the yellow one with the red circle. The flags hang stark still, the wind hushed.

A truck approaches, pulls into the drive and hovers. Two men, wearing suits and felt hats, stare at me before pulling out and driving on toward Mahdah's. A big red shiny tool box stretches across the bed. The truck is yellow, brand-new.

Elsie comes through the door and claps her hands toward the drive. Humming to herself, she takes a big broom and sweeps a path from her door to the road then sprinkles a bird seed trail back to her house, clucking like a lady feeding chickens, then singing:

> "A path to the gingerbread cottage?
> Like the moon, is it made of cheese?
> Where's the oven? Who's for supper?"

She laughs and winks at me.

> "If we can get Gretel in, what of Hansel?
> What of the wolf? What of the devil?"

Leaning her broom against the wall, she shuffles past me while I hold the door open, cackling to herself:

"He's a bright boy and tender.
Follow the cook and he'll be splendid.
Rough on the edges. Hungry in the center."

"You're talking about Larry?" I follow her in.

Staring at me, intense, she says: "We mingle with this place. Inhaling, we take in this place." She lights a cigarette and watches the smoke, thinking.

"No way to avoid it.
Consciousness rides the smoke, gives form
to the vision, instills hope or fear, informs
memory, casts the glamour, honors
the monster, shows the dragon
the hollow, knows that force
rides the vacuum.
Play the game.
Don't be frightened."

Her last words harsh, Elsie stubs her cigarette out, then, seeming to hover just above the floor, glides quickly behind Sara, John, and Kathy, busy at the counter, and disappears into the workroom.

Turning to me, Kathy says: "Larry should be here by now." Moving to the fridge, she takes the ham out, hesitates, then replaces it on the shelf, before returning to the counter. "It's after six."

Changed to a purple shift, with her green jade necklace and earrings, Elsie opens the screen door and scans the room. "You might put the shade down." She looks at John. Taking a seat with me at the little table under the front window, she adds: "And bring me some coffee, would you, Sara?"

"I wonder where he is," Sara comments, setting the cup down in front of Elsie and glancing at me before joining Kathy at the sink.

"Time is relatively relevant, isn't it?" Elsie nods. "For now, it's best to be patient." Turning toward the window, she watches John manipulate the parasol. The wind is starting to pick up. It's so dark that a cloud burst, at a minimum, seems imminent.

"He might be having his own adventure." Elsie turns her attention back to me, her eyes clear, almost sparkling. "We just need to relax, enjoy ourselves. That's the secret." She stretches to turn the lights on, but the electricity is off, probably due to the storm. John secures the door and pulls down the windows against the wind, then moves across the room.

"Elsie," I lean forward, trying to be casual but increasingly concerned about Larry, "is he okay?"

"Do you hear a ringing?" Without waiting for a response, she puts her coffee cup to her ear and gazes at the ceiling. "Uh huh," she nods. "Hell of a deal. That will be fun. Yes." She puts her cup down.

Focused on me, she raises her fist then lowers it rapidly, with controlled intensity, toward her coffee cup. I flinch; but instead of hitting the cup, her hand passes through it, through the table, then folds gently into her lap.

"Did you see that?" She stares at her hand while, in a squeaky voice, like a puppet, her hand says: "Bring the others to see El-see so we see what they see and what they can't."

Then, like a circus master of ceremonies, startling the others, she booms: "Let's have a demonstration!" Grinning, she raises a finger to touch the brim of an invisible top hat, and whispers: "Now we'll see about the cat's meow."

Responding to the voice, Sara, John, and Kathy pull chairs over to sit in a semi-circle facing Elsie. Her back to the window, she separates us from the dark rattle of the wind. Our reflections are ghosts against the glass.

Lighting a cigarette, she says: "The practice of invisibility is a preferred art when dealing with Black Hats and scalawags." Shaking a finger at each of us, I realize she has slipped on white gloves. "This is practical magic." She reaches back and taps the window. "Do you see this?"

"What?" John asks.

"That the pane's invisible," she responds. Inhaling on her cigarette again, she exhales, propelling smoke along her arm, cumulating at the point of her right index finger against the window. Holding our attention there, Elsie says:

> "My shadow meets me at the looking glass.
> My breath glows white in curling mist.
> Shadow do what shadow knows best.
> Here's the ring, where's the test?"

Rising to look more closely, John says: "Isn't that a reflection?"
"The smoke's real," Elsie hisses:

"Break it and fix it,
so they don't know what is isn't.
Believing what's fusion is fission
with alchemically crazy precision
use action as distraction —
the Cheshire cat playing
in the dark woods with
only his mouth remaining."

Clapping her hands, Elsie throws her head back in easy laughter.
Lowering her eyes to us while lightning streaks through black skies
behind her, she whispers:

"It's getting too dark
For just fire and water."

Smacking her lips, thunder hits the outside of the cabin, sending
a shudder through the room. "Lewis Carroll got it right. The cat
can't catch you 'till you're ready, unless you're greedy; but never-
the-less take the chance at heightened vigilance. First you see him,
then you don't. He sees you, though."
Extending her tongue, she licks her mouth.

"I'm eating your shadows
for de-light of it,
giving back more
than I take in
if I'm right about it
because I love you ...
toot - toot ... tout d'suite,
I do love to eat."

Breath rushing from her puckered mouth, sliding her feet, Elsie
circles the room, pushing her arms forward then pulling back —
rowing a boat. "What separates us doesn't exist." She reaches
through the window. A gust of chilled wind hits my face. Lightning
flickers. Clouds collide and unfurl above the mountain. The parasol
creeks, as if someone is opening it. I take Sara's hand. Kathy peers
into the darkness.
Turning back to us, the window shut behind her, our room illumined by lightning, Elsie holds her hands up: "You see what I see?"

No one responds. "Anything strange about the window?" she asks as thunder hits the glass. "Energy."

Spreading her arms, she inhales; then, fist on her hip, cocking her head, stomps petulantly. "Can't a girl have some fun?" Pointing at Kathy, she coaxes: "Relax ... really. This is technique. If we get on the phone, we could call him. But we have to clear the lines — first fear, then laughter. The one thing the spooks can't stand is ... " She slams her fist down but stops inches above the table. Clowning, she limps around dangling her fist, then howls in squalls of laughter. "Got it!" She is abruptly serious: "What's visible depends on mind-set. We bring him home." She points at Kathy.

"Not visible now, because you can't see him, right?" Tentatively, Kathy shakes her head. Sipping her coffee, Elsie scowls with exaggerated distaste, muttering: "Tepid leads to distemper," then holds her finger up as a thunderbolt hits outside. Her whole hand, gloveless now, glows red. Stirring the coffee with her finger, she takes another sip. Leaning back, she exhales, deeply satisfied.

"Heat is good, isn't it? Add the 'r' ..." She trills her tongue, a gurgle rising from deep within her chest, "and ..." Wind hits the window, shaking the house.

Alarmed, John interrupts: "Is Larry okay?"

She looks at him, blank, as if dumbfounded.

"Heat?" I say, trying to get back on track.

"We must turn 'heat' into 'heart' to serve Brother Lawrence." She slams her fist down. "I've told you lunatics often enough, haven't I?" She rages: "Unless we raise hell the bad guys will get him." Steam rising from her coffee cup, she leans forward and whispers: "He's fine, just invisible."

"Could we see him if he were here?" Kathy also whispers.

Leaning back, eyes full of tears, looking at each of us one at a time, Elsie says:

"Who sent him against the giant?
Who gave him a harp to sling stones?"

Utter silence.

After a long moment, I ask: "Can we learn invisibility?"

"Sure." Elsie brightens. "That's how we'll find him." She grins and gets up. Taking her feather duster she works over each of us.

"Now," she lights a cigarette, "the first question is whether you can still see each other."

"Yes," I say, fairly certain, although it seems darker now. Elsie is laughing, her voice fading into the distance. I'm flowing backwards, getting smaller, going down a tube away from her. She and the others are disappearing. "Find him, then." Elsie's voice is a precise ringing in my ear.

I'm under a monument, on a mountain, sensing other bodies around me — then hear Larry. He's chanting. I see an outline of him hunched over, pounding his stomach, stamping his right foot. Huge shadowy figures are trying to stick things into him, but his chanting is keeping them back — making him impermeable.

Reaching to put my arms around Larry, I'm hit by an explosion flinging me backwards. Rolling through a tunnel, laughter wailing around me, claws stretching in my direction, the pressure in my ear becomes words, Elsie's voice:

"Pound your stomach and stamp!" She's very precise, calm. "Pound your stomach and stamp. We're bringing you back. Protect your middle. Close your mind to their enchantment. See my eyes."

Exhausted, sweating and chilled, I open my eyes. Elsie is running her hand up and down my stomach, heat flowing into me, then straightening me up in the chair. Looking around, I see Kathy and John are at the sink. Relighting her cigarette, Elsie moves to the workroom door.

A car passes outside. Everything is still. Large raindrops are falling, splattering against the ground, sliding down the window. Sara, her arms around me, is whispering: "Are you okay?" I shake my head, still dazed, unable to talk. "Elsie said to keep busy. Are you sure you're okay?"

"Yes," I assure her, patting my middle, deep breaths struggling to get in and out.

"The moon is doing that, you know?" Elsie's voice floats toward us as John and Kathy join Sara and me at the window watching the rain. "The power is greatest just when it turns back from empty — has to be to turn it. Everything would disappear otherwise.

Hathor's horns, you remember?
We all were in Egypt together

At the Great Temple ...
When the sky was crying and
We thought he wouldn't come back."

"Who?" Kathy turns to Elsie.

"David ... We were all there. Just like tonight. David had gone off on a mission. Sometimes people get lost — even great adepts." She pauses. "The higher we climb the harder we fall, if we fall."

Kathy lifts her coffee cup, watching Elsie over the rim, then asks: "Was he, is he, in danger?"

"We all are. Always ... But we never face anything we're not ready for. We can't."

"Why not?"

"Because we can't experience anything beyond our own power. Not consciously." She puts her cigarette out. "And conscious activity is all that matters. It's all that fuses spirit to ground. All that is permanent. All that remains from incarnation to incarnation. Sometimes it's just a shadow. Our job is to cast the light, find the pattern."

It's stopped raining, seems lighter outside.

"Maybe we could go look for Larry now?" Kathy suggests.

"Do it by finishing the table." Elsie walks over and taps on it. "Seems solid enough." She winks. "Honestly," she shrugs, "there's no better technique for bringing the boys home — from," she shakes her finger at Kathy, "invisible to visible. That's what food is for — real food and good cooks!"

"Listen," she pronounces it like a command and points at the chairs, indicating we should all sit. "There are just a few simple rules. First and foremost, the human mind can only be occupied by one thing at a time. Set the table. Really." She exaggerates the word, twisting her mouth. "Put a candle in the window. Don't drive him away with your fear."

Kathy immediately gets up, takes a candle from the shelf, lights it, and sets it in the window.

"Keep laughing, breathe consciously, be busy ... remember ... we used to sing the sheep home by singing the shepherds home, and ..." she puts her arms around Sara and Kathy, "now we sing to keep the ghosts out. That's what Jiminy Cricket's all about. Study Disney if you're uncertain. "And understand that one of our projects," she squeezes their shoulders, "even after I'm gone, is to rewrite the fairytales. I say, twist the tails on the fairies ... but ...

Scream for ice cream not gore,
a dog in sheep's clothing, a wolf
at the door. Little red robin hood
guarding the pigs, there's plenty of food
for all the kids. Well or ill there's
truth in it still. The point is
we're cooking the rules ... Right!

Not wronging them!" She pauses, her volume having risen steadily, then releases the girls and turns to me.

"Brother Lawrence has the first rule. I told you that, didn't I? Remember? *The God Illumined Cook* book: the perpetual practice of the presence. William James taught the other: 'act as if,' even if you haven't got it. Stop thinking the opposite. Be positive." She presses her finger against my chest. "Act on the presence. Call home the friend who fights in the woods."

Stepping back, I have a vivid flash of Larry hunched over at the end of a tunnel.

"Set the table — create the visible in the space of the invisible — draw him in." She rattles it off like a commando. Using her finger, she traces a shape in the air. "See this?" She winks at John. "This magic is playful and crazy ... just a simple fact. I'm crazy about all of you, but, really, you need to know and understand, practice and act, believing in the force of it." Lowering her voice, she adds: "See him here."

Back to me, raising her voice, she says: "Dismiss thought, Smart Guy. Feel his presence." She touches my forehead then chest. "And enjoy yourself." She grins. "If there's no joy in it, well, you know," she makes a face like a baby who doesn't like something, "it gets old fast ... and," she grimaces, "you have to get younger."

Rotating slowly, she smiles at Sara and winks, then stops at Kathy, adding: "Don't worry. You've done your part. He's here already," then turns on around to face the door as Larry, soaked, looking disoriented, peers in.

"Your seat," she points to the table, "is warm, your belly empty."

"I'm starved. What time is it?" Larry glances at me.

Intending to model for him, I turn back to the sink to wash my hands, not certain what to say. Glancing through the window, I see the sky opening in blue patches, leaving a few dark clouds — not enough, I hope, to storm again.

Dropping his back-pack to the floor, Larry rolls his sleeves up, and waits to wash, silent. After putting ham and a salad on the table, with fresh bread, Elsie sing-chants, clapping her hands slowly as we take our seats:

"One, two, and three ...
The bum put out to sea.
As Noah rode the ark
Jonah fought the shark.
One, two, then three,
The Master rode the tree.
The Mistress came to see.
The bread is warm.
The ham is torn.
The greens are full of blood."

She indicates we should join hands.

"So say we now the sacred cow
Has turned her horns again.
The moon is cheese
But if we please
The earth begins in sin
But ends within
Where silence breathes.
One, two and three.

Holding her arms out, standing above us, she whispers: "It's a blessing ..." then smiles reassuringly, "that he's back."

Dropping our hands, we dig in — obviously hungry even though, up to that moment, food had seemed irrelevant, at most a prop to bring Larry home. Nodding approval, Elsie backs into her work-room.

After several bites, Larry looks up and speaks through a full mouth: "I got caught in the storm. Man," he exclaims, "it was really strange." He pauses, thinking. "Anyway," he looks around, "I'm here now."

"What happened?" Kathy puts her hand on his shoulder, but he seems puzzled. "Larry ...?" she probes gently.

"Well," he chews slowly, "I was leaving CRC on my way here, you know?" He takes another bite. "Then the storm started and I went up a road to get out of the rain. There was all kinds of traffic, and lightning ... In fact," he hesitates, "someone was driving back and forth." An urgency enters his voice. "I was trying to hide."

Elsie reappears. "What were they driving?"

"A pick-up." He looks up like remembering something. "Apollo reached the moon, today, did you know that?"

Staring at her, Larry responds: "Our teacher said they broke an old boundary."

"A new channel is opened." Elsie gestures: "There to here, here to there — and tomorrow," she comes and stands behind him, her hands on his shoulders, "we're going to talk about time warps — based on triangles, following the signs and figures. Some danger, of course," she moves in slow, tight circles, "but while they walk, we'll walk."

"Who?" Kathy glances from Larry to Elsie.

"The Argonauts." She grins.

"Who are the men in black?" Larry is abrupt now.

"They followed you?" Elsie seems surprised.

"Yes." Larry is quite serious.

"There are different types here." She lights her cigarette, then backs up so she is facing all of us — solid, her jade necklace rising and falling with her breath.

"Why were they following me?" Larry looks squarely at her, insistent.

"You are safe now, Larry." Her voice is soft, instructive. "Let it drop."

Seeming far away, Larry remains seated. No one has spoken since Elsie left us alone to finish eating. Glancing through the door, I see a figure standing within the shadow. Larry goes in. Out of the corner of my eye, I see a match being lit. Larry and Elsie are standing in the far corner. The food has changed everything. The apprehension has disappeared. The breeze is light, the air crisp and clean after the storm. The electricity has been on since Larry returned.

"We ought to get going," Larry announces from the workroom door. "I have some reading to do."

On the way back to Karin's, Larry insists on talking about his esoteric astrology class, then about his teacher's lineage. I realize that Elsie must have told him to act as if nothing happened. His conversation seems like a radio program in the background while I concentrate on the road.

Wearing a dress-suit and white-gold jewelry, which matches her hair, smelling of perfume, Karin greets us at the door, looking like she has just come from a dinner engagement. "How was your day?" She inspects us as we pass before her.

"Wild," John announces. "How about yours, Mom?"

"Good enough." Karin looks tired. Offering nothing further, she excuses herself. A few minutes later, she returns in pajamas and a robe and puts a bowl of ice cream on the table in front of Larry. Her hands on his shoulders, she says: "Elsie wants you to have milk products."

"I know." The skin on his hands is red and peeling.

"We're fixing you up, old boy." Karin smiles. "Just follow instructions. Everything will be fine."

"We had quite an experience at Elsie's," I volunteer, uncertain how explicit to be, but sensing she already knows.

Karin nods, her blue eyes reminding me of Elsie. "If you think that's weird, you should be with me in Atlanta."

"What are you doing there?" John asks.

"It's complicated." She glances at him.

"Are you okay, Mom?" There is an edge in his voice.

"Yes." She gives him a hug. "But tonight, Larry has work to do. We're all tired." She yawns, then smiles, turning to the rest of us. "So we'll leave Mr. Lawrence alone; so he can get to bed early, too."

When we are alone, Sara says, "You scared me." She closes our door before folding her arms around me. "I thought you had passed out at Elsie's."

"I'm fine now." I hold her, wanting to stay, but need to find out what Larry went through. "How are you doing?"

"I'm okay, if you're okay." She squeezes tighter.

"Do you want to talk about it?" I ask, but know I'm hesitant to share with her what happened to me.

"Isn't it pretty clear we're not supposed to talk?" She looks up into my face.

"I want to ask Larry one thing." I reach for the door.

"I'm hitting the sack." She stretches, then leans up for a kiss.

Returning to the kitchen, I find him bent over his note pad. "Writing?" I try to sound casual.

"It's the dark of the moon." He lays his pencil down.

"Can we talk?" I hesitate.

"Not directly." He seems alert yet very tired.

Leaning forward, I whisper: "I saw shadowy figures around you."

He moves his head purposefully toward the sliding glass door. The yard is utterly black now, except for the spray of light through the glass. At the edge of the shadow, something moves. A chill goes up my spine, with an image of crab-like hands reaching for me and Elsie's voice saying she's bringing me back.

Steadying myself, I take Larry's cup and fill it. Glancing out of the window by the sink, it seems that the dark perimeter has receded slightly. I realize he is not willing, or able, to talk about what happened, and that some one or some thing is watching us. A fist tightens in my stomach.

Returning to the table, I say: "How's the scholar?"

"Elsie showed me a book." He looks up from his notes. "She said it contained more truth than most people can stand."

"What's it about?" I follow his lead.

"A call for 'initiates' to take the next step."

"What did you think of it?" I assume he's using some type of code.

"With Elsie," he lights a cigarette, "there are moments when I feel I've known it all before." He shakes the match out. "But some of it bothered me — things about adepts having the right to mislead disciples. That sort of thing."

"Maybe she gave it to you to show what can go wrong." I pause. "She told me that the occult is the biggest con game in the world."

"Do you think she's conning us?" He sips his coffee.

"No." I shake my head. "We've been told not to accept anything on faith. She's teaching us to read the patterns. That's all. And I know she loves us."

"The book said that the negative forces encourage mental masturbation, so they can suck the juice out of us. To grow, ideas have to be incubated, left in silence. If aspirants talk too much, all that remains is an empty shell."

"Are you okay?" I lean forward, concerned, uncertain where he's leading.

"That's all I can say." He nods. "Except that I have assignments." He lays his hand on his book.

Unwilling to let it drop, but knowing he's asking me to, I lower my voice: "How are you dealing with all this?"

Standing, then backing into the kitchen so I follow, he whispers: "You saved my ass but we can't talk about it now."

"How?" I'm startled.

"By distraction." He tilts his head towards the outside. "That's when I got away."

"From?" I whisper.

"An energy, or Black Hats, whatever it was. I'm just starting to remember. Elsie said I have to keep my mind occupied — you, too — with other things. We're targets now. Once they have the smell of you, it's dangerous."

"But I can't think about anything else," I protest.

"All I know is that it had something to do with Jack. Anyway," he pauses, "please just accept this for now." He walks back and faces the sliding glass door and raises his voice: "With all this studying, I'm learning a lot. Thanks for asking." He turns to me. "See you in the morning, okay?"

Nodding acknowledgement, I trudge toward our room. Suddenly I feel the attention of the world focusing on the sky. Then I hear Elsie saying that the moon walk will change everything, or remember her saying that. Deciding to dismiss the thought, let it settle, feeling the need to act as if nothing were out of the ordinary, I know, without putting it into words, that portraying the ordinary provides a type of shield against intermeddling forces.

Lying flat on my back, heart aching, I catch threads of last night's dream. Elsie, or someone, in a black hat. Larry as a harlequin. Knives striking the floor.

Larry's books and papers are spread on the table. The coffee is hot. Karin has left a note on the refrigerator:

"I'll be back late again. Hope we can visit then. Keep your eyes to the sky and your hearts to the ground. Love, Karin"

"How did you sleep?" Larry approaches from the shower.

"Lot's of action, but I can't remember what." I point to his stack of papers. "How about you?

"Surprisingly well, actually." He glances around. Seeing that we're alone, he says: "Kathy had another dream."

"Like the one where you and Karin were anchoring us?"

"Maybe Kathy will go into the details later, but," he lowers his voice, "this one was more real, like she wasn't really dreaming. She's convinced that Elsie projected herself and was pushing her to get involved with some group."

"How did she feel about that?"

"It bothered her. And she's still concerned about what happened last night."

"Me, too." I remember the tunnel. "Did you tell her?"

"Not much. I don't know much. But we're okay, right?"

"Right," I agree, "but we're not supposed to be pushed."

"If we aren't pushed," he looks directly into my eyes, "we go to sleep."

The others join us in the kitchen. Reading the note, Sara comments: "It's strange how little we're seeing Karin. What do you suppose she's doing?"

"I don't know." John opens the refrigerator. "But I didn't like what she said about Atlanta."

"She's fine," Larry assures him.

Drawing me to the side, Sara asks how I'm doing. "Pretty well." I hug her.

"This is like a roller-coaster, isn't it?" She kisses me. "Anyway, I feel good this morning."

After we've finished breakfast, Larry stacks books into his shoulder bag and announces: "I'm having lunch with the other students, so you won't have a guest this noon. What's your schedule?"

"Space and time, if I heard right," I answer.

"You be careful, Larry." Kathy approaches from behind.

"You, too, Potatoes." He hugs her. As they head for the door, Sara, John, and I hurry to catch up.

The Back Side of Space and Time

"The house is closed up." Sara points to the line. "And the flags are gone."

"The sunshade's been moved," John adds.

Elsie, wearing a white straw hat, a baggy country-lady dress, carrying a black purse, walks up to the car from behind us. "You're my nieces and nephews, got it?" She winks. "If any of them grab us, I'll whack them with this." She slings her purse around like a club. "I think we're ready."

"Where are we going?" I slide into the driver's seat. Sara holds the door on the other side. Elsie settles in the back between John and Kathy.

"While all the attention's up there," she points skyward, "we'll have our own little adventure. It's a good day for triangles, space and time warps, the Grail Quest, you know — got to make tracks in the unformed forest."

"Which way?" I turn the engine on.

"The way you always do it." Her purse on her knees, feet on the hump down the middle of the car, Elsie leans forward.

"Left or right?" I ask.

"Full of attention, start with Clayton. As the moon distracts the other guys, explore Atlantis."

"Whatever you say." It's sunny out. All seems right with the world, but I feel responsible and apprehensive.

"You've always been the driver; but to remind you, I'll point out some rules and you apply them."

"What's the first one?" I scan the road ahead of me.

"The grease marks show where the resistance is weakest."

Focusing on the pavement, I see marks down our lane.

"Keep an eye out for the trucks. Watch the slogans and logos, forwards and backwards. Find the information."

"What about the bad guys?" John asks.

"Don't worry." Elsie pats his leg.

"That's good." John sounds relieved.

"They're around, of course." Elsie chuckles. "But we'll triangulate them."

Entering Clayton I realize I barely noticed Tiger.

"That's fine, Jay." Elsie responds to my thoughts. "You watch the road. I'll watch the rest. Just find the right place to park. It's an exercise. Find the place that's been opened for you."

Scanning the street, Sara seems pleased and excited. Turning back to Elsie, she says: "This looks different."

"Every thing is different, every moment." Elsie grins. "Ordinary mind fights that, but it's true."

I watch the main street traffic, shuffling for places, in and out of parking stalls, waiting at stop lights, spreading out before me like a chess set, seeing it from the level of the pieces rather than the players sitting above the table and yet I sense the higher level from which the directions come.

While we hover at our light, Elsie strikes a match. Holding it before her cigarette, she says: "I want the folks to see you, as if you belong. If you belong, there's a place for you. You have to know that. Practicing the 'as if' — suddenly it is. Being present, a place is prepared for you."

Accelerating slowly, I realize that the car pulling out of a parking stall, a block ahead, is leaving a space for us.

"That's right." Elsie stubs her cigarette out. "The next question is whether you're to get your hair cut or are we just checking in at the barber's pole? The razor blades are for more than shaving, you know." Pulling in, we face red and white stripes circulating up and down a candy-cane.

"Sara and Kathy understand blood mysteries. But there are a lot of things we don't talk about in town. Remember, dear," she pats Sara's back, "the cane is a transmitter."

Sara opens her door and gets out. Going to the window, she glances in like she's looking for someone, then turns and shrugs. A couple boys walk out. The old men on the bench to her right look her up and down.

Walking to the corner, her hair falls gently to the center of her back, riding above the line of her jeans. She glances both ways before turning back to us, her light blue cotton blouse tucked in at her waist.

I remember the service attendant's warning that I should caution her against the rednecks. My breath shortens. I'm alarmed, uneasy with waiting, aware that each of us in the car seems paralyzed to move, astonished that without warning she has gotten out, like a probe, to explore new territory.

"The chairs are full, with people waiting." Sara leans forward to address us through my window. "Maybe we should do some window shopping."

"Good," Elsie approves. "It's important that you see and be seen. Note everything carefully, but follow Sara's lead."

Getting out and standing in front of the barber shop, I'm hit by flashes of Larry's abduction, references to adepts misleading us, Kathy's dream, Larry's insistence that we have to be pushed ... Fumbling with her purse, Elsie bumps me. Shuddering involuntarily, I start to breathe again.

"Have a good time, kids." She raises her voice. "I'll meet you at the cafe at noon." Turning toward the men, she nods politely then shuffles down the sidewalk. Pausing, she checks her list before going into a store.

"We'll take this side if you'll take the other," Sara suggests, not loud enough to be overheard.

"Meet you for lunch," Kathy responds, louder, surprising me with her willingness to play along. Taking John's arm, she crosses the street. I am aware of Sara's eyes sparkling, pleased, like she's having fun, the sun shining in her chestnut hair, her arm looped casually through mine.

"What, Babe?" She purrs playfully. "Tell me."

"You may be comfortable," we move out of hearing distance of the men, "but I'm not."

"I'm just happy to be out and around." She points through the glass of a shop window. An old lady sits next to a card table near the back of the store, a Raggedy Andy in her lap, a corn dolly pinned to the wall behind her. Handmade quilts and baskets cover the tables. Pottery fills the shelves. Sara says: "A lot of Elsie's knowledge comes from the crafts-women in the mountains."

"How do you know that?" I start to relax as she guides me forward.

"I remember things later, just not when she said them." Glancing across the street at Kathy and John, she laughs easily. "Let's move. We're supposed to notice things." They do look like casual visitors enjoying the town.

"When I'm alone with Elsie," Sara starts again, "there's tremendous love and," she takes my arm, "she's been talking to me in my dreams. It's like ..." She pauses. "I just remembered I'm supposed to have a scarf."

On the corner of the next block, the building is marked "FIRST BANK AND TRUST" in gold letters on heavy plate glass at the top of massive, rounded concrete steps. A uniformed guard with big jowls, a round, friendly face, pushes the door open and looks down at us. "New to town?"

"Visiting our aunt," Sara responds cheerfully.

"Can we help you?" He smiles.

"I'm looking for scarves."

"There's a store in the next block." He points.

"Thanks." Sara waves as we move down the street.

"Could have visited, you know?" Elsie startles me, immediately behind us now. "You think banks would suffocate you." Digging in her shopping bag, she pulls out a blue scarf. "You didn't come here to avoid your family." She hands the scarf to Sara.

"It's beautiful." Sara is pleased. "Thank you, Elsie."

Taking the scarf, she puts it around Sara's neck, fiddling like an auntie would then hurries us toward the Atlantis sign hanging from the awning in the middle of the block, saying: "I'm starved. Let's beat Poseidon's crew."

"'Atlantis' and 'Poseidon' — that's pretty archetypal isn't it?" I say, and scan back over the shops we've passed.

"What isn't?" Elsie responds. "The sisters set this up. Keep your eyes open, or you'll miss what's in it for you."

Meeting Kathy and John at the door, Elsie points us in. All of the tables are taken except the one in the corner near the window, furthermost from the door — a pentagon set for five people. One of the waitress waves at Elsie then approaches, carrying a tray.

"Nice day, Miss Elsie." She sets water glasses before us. "Been busy?"

"Usual stuff, Madalen." Leaning toward us, Elsie says: "I always think chicken is good, even if you don't know the place. But here, it's excellent."

"Specials, then?" Madalen glances around the table.

"Yes." Elsie pauses. "These are my nieces and nephews."

"Family to us, then." She smiles before moving away, checking on the people at the surrounding tables before returning to the counter along the back wall.

"Do we know her?" I ask.

"Not here," Elsie cautions. "Wash your hands?"

Excusing myself, mildly disoriented, I get up and weave between tables. The cafe has become very busy. Looking up I see our waitress pushing through swinging doors into a large kitchen in the back. A group of workmen crowd in front of an old fashioned raised cash register booth. A line of women, from the opposite direction, are waiting to pay for their lunches.

Moving toward the back I enter an empty hallway with heavy dark mahogany panelling. Through a partially opened door on the left, I see several cooks working at big vats.

A little further along, an ornate foyer opens on the right. Fine upholstered chairs and baskets full of flowers frame an elevator. An attendant, dressed like the doorman at the bank, pushes the button. Inside, the elevator is burgundy with gold trim.

"Want a ride?" he asks, big faced, friendly.

"No thanks," I manage to say, wondering where it goes, amazed, but concluding the cafe must adjoin a hotel, although I didn't notice one on the way in. "Is there a men's room?"

"Opposite the ladies'." He tips his hat.

About twenty yards further, seeing the ladies' room sign on the left, I turn right. The door is unmarked, but swings open easily on big brass hinges. Inside I'm greeted by a large black gentleman, white haired, in a dress suit, sitting in a raised shoe shine chair reading the Wall Street Journal, the New York Times lying beside him, his patent-leather shoes resting on two foot stands.

Slowly lighting a long cigar and watching me, he says: "You read cartoons?" His voice is deep, with a warm, Caribbean accent.

"Sure." I move to the marble sinks, each with gold plated faucets, silver ash trays attached to the wall, and a separate towel rack with clean white linen. Drying my hands, I turn to him.

"Notice that one?" A big puff of sweet, white smoke circles above him. Laughing quietly, tilting his head back, he points to the wall beside his stand. "I'll take your towel." He reaches a big hand toward me, his fingers full of rings, gold cuff links extending beyond his jacket sleeve.

Approaching him, I see a wood-framed plaque of a Peanut's cartoon from a newspaper. Charlie Brown and Lucy are standing on a street corner facing a red light. In the next frame the light is green. In the third, Charlie is still standing on the corner and Lucy is yelling back from the other side: "You have to move your feet, Charlie Brown."

Laughing, the attendant says: "That's the hardest part."

Disoriented, I thank him and make my way back through the hall, emerging near the back counter, realizing I hadn't passed the elevator. The cafe is still busy, but the lines at the front are gone. Our waitress smiles, carrying a tray over her shoulder with five steaming dishes. "Over here." She cocks her head, indicating I should follow.

"Interesting, isn't it?" Elsie hands me a linen napkin.

"I thought he was a cook for a while." The waitress smiles. "He was wandering around in the kitchen." She moves plates from the serving rack to our table.

"They're all cooks," Elsie says. "I'm quite pleased, actually."

Sara takes a roll. "Did you get lost?"

"Wrong turn." I try to retrace the route backwards, knowing I came out a different way.

"Thanks, Madalen." Elsie nods. When we're alone, she adds: "One, two, three — Elsie do and Elsie be — thankful for hospitality."

After taking a bite of potatoes, she ceremoniously dabs her lips with her napkin, like a proper Southern lady, spreading it across her lap again before commenting: "Quite good, isn't it?"

"Elsie ... " I start to ask about the men's room.

"Just watch and listen," she interrupts me, then takes another bite. "It's not just what you eat but how."

Sara, John, and Kathy are concentrating on their food.

Glancing beyond the plants lining the front windows, I notice a black pick-up pulling into a stall in front of the cafe, and quickly decide to concentrate on my food.

"So," Elsie folds her napkin, "let's leave while the sun's out." She points. Following her finger, I see that the space, where the pick-up had pulled in, is empty.

"Should I pay?" I ask.

"It's taken care of." She pushes her chair back. The place looks like when we first came in, except most of the tables are empty now.

"Thank you, Miss Elsie." Madalen smiles at each of us as we head toward the door. "Have a good day."

Outside, Elsie says: "I left my hat in there. Why don't you split up, but take it easy, full stomachs, you know." She pats her front, then smooths her dress. "I'll catch up."

Sara and John head off down the side walk. Crossing the street with Kathy, I keep an eye on the Atlantis Cafe. On the side where I had found the hall to the men's room, a winged staff entwined by two serpents hangs in the front window of the Apothecary. The two floors above are boarded up, but arched, ornate windows look out over the street from the fourth floor. A plaque across the parapet on the roof reads: "Scottish Rite Temple."

Looking back while we move down the street, I see the faint outlines of a mural of Cretan bull priestesses on the cafe wall facing a walkway to the alley. Waiting for the light to change, I point it out to Kathy who, shading her eyes for a better look, says: "I have the feeling Elsie is manipulating all this." Glancing at me, she adds: "I had an experience last night with her."

Remembering Larry's comment, I start to ask what had happened but am interrupted as Elsie, standing immediately behind us, says: "We've done this all over the world. Keep watching." In her white hat now, she ushers us across the street. "Shall we?" She points. "For our picnic?"

The scent of fresh bread from a bakery, in spite of the fact that we've just eaten, is so good it stops us in our tracks. "Smells like the streets of France." Elsie winks. "Here's a dollar. Pick something for us."

While Kathy enters the bakery, Elsie sits on the bench, lighting a cigarette then stubbing it out, replacing it in a gold case. Across the street, Sara and John are walking by a Firestone store. Two men exit the door and get into a panel-truck with a Rural Electric logo on the side, beneath which Poseidon stands on a porpoise, holding a trident.

Carrying a white sack imprinted with the image of a stone oven in a wheat field under a radiant sun, Kathy rejoins us. Smiling, opening the sack, she says: "Can you believe this?" Warmth rises from three round loaves inside.

The light green ahead of us, John and Sara paralleling us on the other side, Elsie hums happily, then chants:

"Thrift shops and bakeries,
old rummage sales and spelling bees,
pennies for dollars, 'a' through 'z' —
you give us one, we make it three.
Dot your 'i' and cross your 't.'
You buy? We sell it cheap.
The world is full of sheep."

Stopping, she scans the intersection. The light turns yellow then red. "But what about the wolves, Elsie?" I ask.

As vehicles from the side start forward, she pushes us into the cross-walk. Cars and trucks halt suddenly, as if the light has shifted back to red for them. "Timing is everything." She grins. "A little match girl in the dark. An old sisterhood carrying torches. Stay the course and don't get lost. Insist on the light."

Pausing midway down the next block, Kathy reads a poster hanging in a window: "Living Water Symposium, Raven Gap."

"See the pattern?" Elsie points to gem stones displayed in a nine-pointed circle on an indigo velvet pad. Putting her hand on Kathy's shoulder, she adds: "You and Sara have an affinity with certain stones ..." then interrupts herself. "Calls coming in ... Humm," she exhales. "Yes ... Right." Nodding, she turns her attention back to Kathy.

"They say you will make stone jewelry. And Sara," she glances up as if hearing something else, "resonates with them. A team. Were and will be. For the present," she points back to the display, "we're coaching the instructor. Lots of resistance, but the information's getting through."

Kathy and I gaze into the window, Elsie behind us, our reflections in the glass. "See the announcement?" Elsie points to the white note card propped behind the display. "Folk art and healing. August 15, 1969."

Leaning closer, she whispers: "That's the anniversary of Aurobindo's seventy-fith birthday and India's Independence. Gandhiji, you know, understood sacrifice — respect for the sacred. The nine-pointed enneagram, identified by Gurdjieff, is the emblem of the Masters of Wisdom."

Kathy and I study the window display. Turning to ask for more details, I realize Elsie is gone.

Across the street, in front of the barber's pole — red on white, looking like blood circulating up and down a spine — two old men in hats are sitting on the bench. John and Sara, standing by our car, signal us to hurry.

Walking rapidly to the corner, the light turning green as we arrive, Kathy and I cross Main Street and hurry back to the car. John and Sara are already in. The old men are standing now. Other men, coming out of the barber shop, talk to them and point back toward the Atlantis Cafe. Clouds are rolling in from the south, hovering, dark-bellied like a cat over a mouse caught in a narrow corridor. A black sedan, with its lights on, waits at the stop light.

Sara stretches out the window on the passenger's side, projecting her voice: "Time to go."

Carrying the bread, Kathy slides into the back seat. Getting in, I notice the light changing at the next corner. The black sedan starts to roll toward the space now opened next to our car. The clouds look like they might spill any second. "Where's Elsie?" I ask, fumbling with the keys.

A match lights behind me, a puff of smoke. "Everything's fine. You're the driver. Just pull out. Follow the oil dots on the road."

No one has spoken since we left town. Following my instincts, I've driven north into the mountains. We've seen no other traffic. Leaning forward in the seat Elsie says: "Each of you saw something different in Clayton; but you worked very well together, really. Did you learn anything?"

Sensing that no one else is going to respond, I play with the word:

"Clayton: ton of clay, clay ... town."

"Clay Town, human base — which you can mold and hold — but mountain clay and living water, as well." Elsie approves. "Clay was," she emphasizes each word,

"First used to make Adam, then
the Breastplate of Aaron's heaven,
high priest after flood severed
Noah from the trees — delivered
the Ark of the Covenant for
God's men; but explore the roar
of Mother's fountain in the mountain —
clay mixed by the daughter
with her own living water."

She lights a cigarette. "What is living water?"

"Tears," I answer, quietly.

"Right." She pats my shoulder. "Now study the features in the landscape — the tiers of the waterfalls.

"The Oasis, Mahdah's, Certain Ritual Centers (understand now) CRCs are jewels at the base of the spine set up years ago, initially by the Cherokees who hold the secrets and guard the temples left by the explorers from Atlantis."

She stubs her cigarette out. "I'll give an overview. Keep your eyes on the road, Jay. Run at 55 miles per hour unless a guardian, by clear signs, slows or pulls you." Nodding my head, I try to concentrate.

"Good," she encourages. "Just listen and understand. The worlds hover, one in the other, seeming to overlap and contradict. But we've discovered a pattern based on equilateral triangles, dragon or ley lines between Oxford, Cambridge and ... You tell me the third point, Jay." She challenges me.

"Stonehenge?"

"You didn't even notice." Leaning near my ear, she whispers: "Eyes on the road. The rest comes of itself."

Attention back to driving, in the silence I'm also aware of Sara, Kathy, Elsie, and John, the landscape rolling past, then vividly remember hitching a ride, three years ago, across the Salisbury Plain, thinking about Sara, before we were married, being told Stonehenge was off to the left, that I could get out and explore, but chose to go on.

"You'll do it later." Elsie slides back. "But look at the map. Find the resonances between stone formations and the Grail Quest. Use a compass and straight-edge. Next time you go, find the city.

"But today," she pauses, "little stones in your pockets, big stones on the trail, we will discover and honor Seven Sisters: high priestesses, princesses of the Indian nations, holding the shrines, tears flowing, water falls, a mountain pass, preserving the temples, chambers and caves, each jewelled in the other — at the far corner of Atlantis — those who held the wall against the invader."

Elsie stops abruptly. "Got the picture? Keep the picture. Don't talk," she adds, emphatically. "Lay it across the roadways we travel. The stair steps are right and left, weaving up the mountain. This current, inhabiting our bodies, penetrates time, changes space, rises through chakras, temples, sacred maidens, tear drops, living water, and ... There's a trading post up ahead," she settles back, "where we'll pull over to tune up a bit. Anybody tired?"

"Actually," John volunteers, "I'm energized."

"Me too," Kathy agrees.

"Excellent," Elsie pats their knees. "We'll save the bread for the fourth chakra. May need it by then."

"Is this it?" Sara points to a rock shop.

"First stop after Clayton," Elsie announces. "Toot! Toot!" In the rear view mirror, she's moving her arm up and down, tugging the whistle on a train. Pulling in at the "Rock and Antiquities" store, I realize we're on an Indian reservation.

"Check around." Elsie hands five dollars to Sara. "I'll stay here. Have some work to do," she yawns, "because we're breaking up the afternoon."

"Hello." A middle aged Indian lady, a silver-chain belt around her waist, glances out at our car, then places three cartons of Salems on the counter. "Cigarettes are $2.50 each." Turning to the cabinet behind her, she pulls out a tray of smooth river stones and slides it toward us. "She'll want each of you to have one of these." Hands on her hips, she smiles. "Today, that will be $5.00 total."

Taking the money from Sara, she adds: "Give her my greetings," then moves toward some customers at the other end of the store while we run our hands over the tray, selecting our stones, then return to the car.

Eyes closed, Elsie mutters: "Keep moving."

We climb into higher land. Horses and cattle graze pastures on both sides, bordered by forest. In the far distance, blue mountains collide with clouds.

"The landscape is definitely changing." Kathy keeps her voice low to avoid disturbing Elsie. I wonder what she is thinking and sense that we are not wholly clear of the black sedan in Clayton. Sara studies the terrain.

The highway veers to the left. I slow to let a pick-up with a trailer marked "Sky High Ranch" pull out in front of us. Sara points to the oil marks it left behind.

"Correct," Elsie pronounces from the back seat. "Just checking in. Be careful now." I turn right.

Within a mile, the road narrows, snaking upward around severe turns. Forest and huge boulders impinging on both sides, we pass through a rain shower. Bright sun sheets and water fall together, cooling the air. The rain stops.

"You're watching those guys, aren't you, Jay?" Elsie sits forward. "Do you have the bread ready?" Kathy holds the sack up as, from a side road, which we had just passed, a black sedan pulls out and follows us. "Just an easy eye in the mirror," Elsie instructs. "First picnic area, pull over."

"Are they after us?" My fists tighten around the steering wheel. "They're getting close."

"They have no power unless we give it to them." She puts her hand on my shoulder. "Mind control is the first rule. You control it or they will."

"I feel responsible for your safety."

"And I for yours." She squeezes. "Remember the techniques. Practice the Presence. Start with 'as if.'"

"As if they weren't following us?" Everyone else is stone silent. My heart is racing.

"As if you were able to control your own mind."

"Can I?"

"It can only be occupied with one thing at a time." She pulls a piece from one of the loaves and hands it to me. "Smell this bread. Isn't it wonderful! Just taste this."

Biting in, feeling the texture mix with my saliva, sensing the transformation as the substance of wheat joins my flesh, I realize the sedan has fallen back.

Pointing to the right, Elsie says: "There's the spot."

Slowing, I prepare to turn in toward a wood shelter next to a stone oven. The sedan slows slightly then goes around us. Five large oaks form a circle around the picnic area. A white-water stream rushes along just beyond the trees. Fresh with pine scent, the air shines.

"Do you hear the waterfall?" Elsie radiates, pleased.

"Which one is it?" John asks as we disembark.

"All of them are 'Tears of the Princess.'" Absorbing sun and air, Elsie leans backward. "This is the fourth, like our earth. Touch the heart here."

"What if those guys had turned in?" I keep an eye on the road, wondering what they will do next.

"Serve them bread." Elsie laughs heartily. "Honestly, that's the best we can do." She steps closer. "Lighten up: picnic not panic."

Splitting the sack open like a table cloth, the girls place the loaves in the center of the table. Elsie chants:

"One, two, three:
His victory that we eat.
Her glory, have your seat.
Wish I may, wish I might,
Kiss the star in sudden flight
But if I miss the beggar's mite
Tell the sisters of our plight.
They will sing the sun king home
Or the bad guys all alone.
So tell me now my children dear:
Is there was, but have no fear.
If they follow soon or late,
We'll be gone to higher fate."

Each taking a bite, without speaking, we leave the remaining loaves and follow Elsie to the car.

As I turn back onto the road, the sedan pulls out behind us and rapidly accelerates. Panicking, my stomach tightens. I see Larry in the tunnel and start to bend forward, wanting to hold my middle and stamp my foot. At that instant, Elsie whistles shrilly, distracting me, then pulls down on an imaginary rope, chanting:

"Ka-Hoot, Ka-whammy.
There goes Uncle Sammy ...
Toot ... Toot ...
It's the old story
about fishes and loaves."

Glancing forward again, I see the sedan disappearing around the bend ahead of us. How did it pass us?

"The loaves are the female, the fishes the male, energy." Elsie claps. "Fused in the bodies of the disciples, miracles were possible. Some recorded in the Bible, some unrecorded."

She lights a cigarette and blows out the right back window across Kathy, then out the other side across John. Putting her cigarette out, she pats my shoulder. "Up to you, old boy. Steady now."

As the road straightens, I look for the sedan, not certain how I can protect us, but it isn't there. Studying the side mirror, I expect it to pull out and follow us. But we're alone. No one comments. Elsie seems to be asleep.

Ten miles further, curving steeply through a gorge, then sharp to the right, we see another beautiful waterfall streaming over a rock face in the distance.

"Any traffic?" Elsie scoots forward, Kathy and John leaning with her.

"We've been weaving back and forth. Haven't seen anybody for a long time," I answer.

"What's the pattern?"

"We've crossed the river several times," John answers.

"What else?" Elsie probes, like we are back to the testing which began outside of Clayton.

"Living water," I suggest. "Going both ways."

"Like the caduceus at the Apothecary," Kathy adds.

"And what is that?" Elsie closes her eyes.

"The winged staff of the surgeons," Kathy responds.

Turning back to face Elsie, Sara says: "The spiraling barber's pole. The blood mysteries you talked about."

Elsie nods. "And who laid down the pattern?"

"Hermes," Kathy answers.

"Uh huh," Elsie yawns, "precisely. Now watch for the temple."
She rolls her head against John, falling asleep. I want to ask Kathy
and Sara whether they believe we are safe now — but Sara touches
her finger to her lips.

We enter another gorge, both sides covered with trees but sparser
than before, mostly large pines. Mist rises into the sky. Rainbow
glistenings sliced by sun tunnels strike black marbled granite high
on the walls above us.

Climbing the rise at the far end of the canyon, the road straightens north across a plateau. Minutes later, the sun warm and crisp
now, we approach and stop at a white wooden sign: "Highlands —
Population 1869."

Getting out, I stretch and look around. We haven't seen any vehicles since the sedan passed us. In the distance I hear another waterfall. Breathing deeply, my ears pop. The air is full of the energy
like after an electrical storm.

The others follow me as Elsie slides to the side window, her eyes
bright. "Reminds me of Emerson and Thoreau." She grins. "The
whole lot of them, the Boston Brahmans." She touches her temple
like she's listening. "A Hindu group incarnated as Yankees writing
treatises on multidimensional chess. Visit the town, then tell me the
rest."

Climbing out of the car, changing levels, she draws us to attention. "What is the experiment which drives this condition?" She
stamps. "Attending the moon, the guys in black believe we picnic
while, in fact, we strike through our bones. Think less and understand." She pauses.

"Mercury flies between fire god and ice, earth garden and heaven.
A good day to dance, right? Toss the dice?" She shakes her hand,
like gambling. Moving forward, she chants:

> "Merge heart to head to ground.
> Snake flows all around
> Kundalini rolls up and down
> Pythagoras's division ...
> Stop and listen ...

For time warps along the edge of space — permeable, not permanent — in this place. If you're careful, you'll see what you've been
prepared to see and find the treat." Curling her fist down, she rolls

the dice. "Snake eyes!" she hisses. "Top Hatters know that when and where are all together:

> So why, why? ... Why do we wait?
> For goodness sake ... let's go!"

She laughs, and touches an invisible brim, bowing slightly, although her final chant had been plaintive and urgent. Slapping her hands, she directs us back into the car. "But do remember, the tears flow through seven falls along this body, down this mountain," she pats herself, "to red-footed Clayton and Raven — where we wash our souls in the pool at the base of the world."

Pointing ahead, Elsie indicates I should drive. As I turn toward Highlands, she leans forward. "While I sleep, you walk the streets, note the stores, shop and explore — in joy, find yourselves ... and," she digs in her purse and hands each of us $5.00, "find something which matches who you are."

Driving north, I slow for the first cobblestone cross-road. In the east, perched against the further rise of the mountains overlooking Highlands, the sun illuminates a grand old white board hotel. Deciding to ignore the hotel, I drive on north into the two blocks which appear to be the whole of downtown, having no idea what to expect.

Elsie's positive mood has provided some relief, but has not wholly dissolved my sense of potential catastrophe. I am honored that she trusts me to drive, but eluding the Black Hats by some type of split vigilance has taken its toll.

Looking ahead along the main street, a flutter of tension escapes my body, replaced by certainty that we are protected.

We pass a large auction house on the corner at the end of the first block. Two men are unloading crates from a haywagon in front of the main door. The sign reads: "Christy's International Trading Consortium."

Proceeding north, a beautiful limestone building, called the "Elysium," occupies the opposite corner — then a park, behind which a white steepled church rises over the green skirt of luxurious pines against the backdrop of mountains.

Further down the block, a series of shops fronted by a wood canopied boardwalk fade in and out of focus. Turning right at the next corner, I park in front of a livery stable, beneath the figure of Vulcan as blacksmith. Stepping into the splendid air, each of us grinning, we try not to disturb Elsie, eyes closed now. Behind the tall sliding door, the rhythm of bellows being worked accompanies the steady clang of iron.

At the east end of the livery, toward the mountains, two horses are tied to hitching posts, others lazing within the corral. Kathy points across a train-track to a ridge in the distance where riders weave in and out of the trees.

Leaving Elsie in the car, we round the corner and, turning back south, step up onto the boardwalk. Our reflections follow us along the window front. Pausing to peer in, I see a soda fountain at the back of the store. Two men in seersucker suits and straw hats, with a lady in a full length dress, corseted in the middle, wearing a large hat, stand with their backs to us. The sign in the window says: "Sundries and Dry Goods — Olsen's Since 1866."

"Should we go in?" Sara pushes her nose against the glass. Backing up, seeing our jeans and T-shirts, I realize we look like misplaced figures in an impressionist painting — that everyone else belongs in the 19th Century — and remember Elsie talking about a time warp.

"I'd rather check Christy's," Kathy answers for herself.

"I thought Christy's was just in New York and London." John looks puzzled. "What kind of town is this?"

"Could be Jerusalem, for all I know." Kathy responds, half-seriously. "You want to come?" While they move away I think of Sri Aurobindo's statement: "An eternal instant is the cause of the years," and have a sense of what he meant. But I am still ungrounded, not certain what is going on.

Smiling, Sara studies the windows, then moves forward. "Come on. We're supposed to enjoy ourselves. Don't be grumpy." She grins.

Shaking my head, I try to flip back to the present.

Glancing in at the next door we're greeted by a heavy-set lady in a white ruffled blouse, her gray hair in a bun. The sign, says: "The Cambridge Shoppe."

"Yes, young man?" She peers over granny glasses. "Anything in particular?"

Scanning hardbacks lining shelves to the ceiling, noticing volumes by Meister Eckhart, Jacob Boehme and Hildegard von Bingen, I conclude that all the books are expensive. "Maybe something contemporary." Knowing I can't afford anything rare, I grasp my five dollars.

"Interested in reincarnation?" She considers something. "We just received a book by H. D. Thoreau, one of Emerson's cohorts. You know him?"

"Not personally," I try to joke.

"*Walden*?" She glares at me, like the librarian in high school when she thought I was being flippant.

"Yes," I respond, properly serious.

"The material's embedded in a nature sequence based on the most ancient teachings of India. Did you know that?"

"No," I admit.

She considers me. "Let's see ... Yes," she pulls a copy of Thoreau off the shelf, then moves to a wooden crate on the floor and holds up *The Gospel of the Essenes*. "Know it?"

"It's a beautiful cover."

Pleased, she also hands me a small journal. "If you study the other two, you'll eventually understand this." Flipping the pages, I see sections in script, foreign languages, and cypher. "It was my grandfather's," she whispers. "Five dollars, please."

Amazed and exhilarated, I watch as she wraps all three in brown paper. Thanking her, I join Sara on the boardwalk.

"What was that all about?" Sara smiles.

"Can't wait to find out." I pat the package, still puzzled. "I want to put these in the car."

Nodding assent, Sara says: "I'm going ahead."

As Sara moves toward the park, the Elysium and Christy's Auction House, I turn back around the corner to the livery. Assuming that Elsie has gotten out, I open the door and slide my package onto the floor behind the driver's seat.

Lying across the backseat, Elsie opens one eye and nods.

Backing up quietly, I return to the boardwalk. A short dwarf-like man is pushing a small cart through a door over the top of which a sign reads: "Mountain Crafts."

"It's like we're in a movie," John chuckles, coming up beside me. "Maybe that's Snow White's shop."

"Watch out for the old witch selling apples," I joke.

"Right," John laughs, obviously in a good mood.

Crossing the street, we gaze through the window at a display of carved figures. The back wall of the store is one large bas-relief of a tree at the base of which a gnome, smoking a pipe, sits at the entrance to a cave-hollow hidden in the roots. No one seems to be in the shop.

Watching through the window, his pony-tail striking me as fairly typical of the era we seem to be in, John asks: "Did you find anything?"

"Yes," I report, pleased. "How about you?"

"Christy's was overwhelming, but I'm looking. You wouldn't believe that place." John shakes his head. We move along in front of a telegraph office then cross the street and gaze out over a terraced landscape with rock pathways and a manicured hedge labyrinth.

Enchanted, John's eyes float up to the church beyond. Moving past the gate which leads down into the park, we hear the steamhorn of the locomotive climbing to the east of town and stop at a bench in front of the limestone store front. Pointing at the sign, John asks: "What's an Elysium?"

"In old Europe," I think back to my mythology classes, "the Elysium was the sanctuary of the revered dead."

The train whistle echoes back to us again, chugging off into the distance. A small waterfall, or spring, whispers from someplace in the park. Blue sky cradles clouds forming and unforming, dragon patterns, in the west.

Looking at John, I appreciate his willingness to simply accept our experiences together. After a moment, he asks: "Do you understand what Elsie was saying about the waterfalls — between here and Raven?"

I shake my head, thinking about how much we've taken in. "She says they're in the landscape and in the human body."

"And that the base chakra is at Raven, near her house, and the top one is here?"

"Apparently."

Looking into my eyes, John says: "It seems like that, doesn't it, but," he lowers his voice, "I'm not sure where 'here' is or whether we're really 'here' — you know? I'm doing everything I can just to stay focused."

"Me, too," I confide. "You're doing great."

"It's like this place doesn't exist, but somehow it does, and we're protected." He smiles, like he is amused or fascinated, then, nodding to me, steps into the door to the Elysium and is startled by Sara and Kathy on their way out.

"Hi, guys." Sara beams. "We're going back to Christy's."

"Amazing place." Kathy comments to herself as they pass.

Oriental rugs are piled along the wall near the entry. Some people at the back are speaking in hushed voices, inspecting and admiring the goods, artifacts, and antiques which separate us from them.

"I've never seen a store like this." John lifts his eye brows in amazement. "Hope this is one of those places Elsie talked about." He clutches his five dollar bill and grins.

"Not a thrift shop," I whisper, then move between shelves lined with South American feathered masks, carved effigies, fetishes, pueblo vases, woven baskets, red stone pipes and drums, beaded buckskin shields. On the next aisle we see figures of the ancient Venus cave mothers, old beaten-copper bowls, helmets, trays of gem stones, and Celtic torques.

Emerging from the far end, John behind me, we are met by a dark skinned South Asian lady in slacks and an oriental jacket, wearing lapis, her black hair coiled back and held by a white ivory clasp. The room fills with low chanting, like from a monastery, mingling with sound of wind chimes and the soft rush of a fountain.

"Can we help you?" She bows slightly.

"Just looking," I reply respectfully. Nodding agreement, she returns to the back counter where sandal-wood incense is burning. I notice an opening behind and to the right of her, covered by strands of wooden beads.

Turning to the next aisle, we pass lithographs of cave paintings, maps, a Bali dragon mask, a scroll painting of Lao Tzu on a donkey, and, turning down the third aisle: a high Catholic reliquary, a tapestry of the Archangel Michael fighting a dragon, prints of megalithic sites, illuminated manuscripts, a carved statute of Krishna dancing with the Blue Maidens, an agate containing the blood of Kronos.

Dizzy, I sit on a tripod stool covered with sheep skin, leather side up, inscribed with a zodiac and archaic symbols, and watch John, unabashed and eager, inspecting the artifacts, searching through stone carved and brass cast figures. I sense that there are beings at the back of the room, perhaps not human, trading goods, and that we're in some cosmic free-zone in which anything can be material-ized.

"Look at this." John bends over a table.

"I can't bring myself to touch anything." I put my hand on my chest. "There's a strange, exquisite pressure here."

John nods his understanding.

Getting up, I move toward the last aisle where I discover stacks of tall woolen hats, and then a platform with a display of dwarfs, clowns, fools, tarot decks, violins, and a golden harp. Returning to the counter, my heart clipping, I hear John say we're visiting our aunt in North Georgia.

"Have you seen our garden?" She points at the beaded opening. A bell rings from the front door, as if someone has just entered. Stuff-ing a small sack into his pocket, John ducks through the beads, sig-nalling me to follow.

Our eyes adjusting, we see that we're on a platform at the top of three granite-slab steps descending to a grotto, bathed in sunlight and shadows cast from triangular windows and an arched gate which opens out above terraced gardens.

To our right, against the inner wall, a long eared, jewell-eyed fig-ure is emerging from the water streaming down the wall above its head, rolling across face, torso, hands, and fingers, down one leg extending into the pool filled with golden carp — as if growing from the pool, out of the rock, toward the sky, through sunlight dancing in mist.

"Reverence the sacred places." I hear Elsie whispering within the whirl of water. "This is the life-giving spring through which the tears of the Princess arise and descend."

While John moves down the steps, I kneel at the edge of the pool facing the stone figure, knowing I'm in a birth chamber where earth moves toward human form. The beaded drape across the top of the staircase is ages away, a faint memory or promise of future human-ity, of priests and priestesses, of commerce, of the sound of chanting mixed in the swirl of the fountain washing me with tears.

Eventually breathing again, partially blinded by sun, I follow John into the park meandering in slow coils toward the wrought-iron stairway to the street, rising through multiple dimensions, reorienting toward a community which, somehow, Elsie has set for us to observe.

On the sidewalk now, without speaking, we move north past the Elysium. Looking ahead, I note that the caduceus of Aesclapius, or Moses, two snakes twisting around a spine, stacks of gold bars on either side, decorates the sign hanging across the boardwalk in front of Christy's.

"Should we be getting back to Elsie?" John asks.

At that moment Sara and Kathy emerge from a store across the street. Sara waves. Pointing at her purchase, Kathy shouts: "Let's go."

"Apollo hit the moon as you hit Highlands. What do you think of that?" Elsie, wearing her white hat and blue dress, carrying a shopping bag, looks like a proper Southern lady standing by the car waiting for us. But something in the scene immediately unnerves me. It's like she has just re-surfaced and this whole community is a stage created in my mind, or hers, and she has stepped back in to take over.

Holding the bag up, she whispers urgently: "You can get us back, can't you? You know the way, don't you?"

Anxious and awkward, my mind floats back to the long-eared creature. "The Buddha?" Elsie gets right in my face. "The long ears for hearing? Siddhartha helping the Nazarene toward Christhood?" She hisses: "The Hathors of Ancient Egypt, Pre-Pharonic Venusians, long eared and caring?

"All those, yes. But hear this, too, about the dark." Sniffing at my collar, she puckers her mouth, nibbling. "The Mouse God was born in the cave of the Princess." She looks skyward. I get flashes of the grotto. Something is accelerating in my body, but I can't respond.

"Tic-Toc ..." She knocks on my head. "Who runs up the clock? Who stole the python at Delphi ... the Oracle of the Seeress? Son or not," putting her fist on her hip, she stamps, "he who denies his Mother, loses his tail. Well?" She trills her voice upward, clowning, but deadly serious. "He's cold now for awhile, but we're warm in these bodies."

She refocuses on me. "Understand? We're pissed at Apollo." She lowers her voice: "The chamber's in the bag. You were in it. We keep it here." She flattens the bag against her stomach then holds one arm out. "We made all this."

Composing herself, she moves to the car, chanting:

"All packages go in the trunk.
I've got a surprise for all those skunks.
Tweedle-dee-dee and Tweedle-dee-dum
Put Humpty together from just such a sum."

"What?" I ask, holding the door for her.

Eyes sparkling, she smiles affectionately at me. "Nothing's in the bag. It's all bubbles, spherical surfaces. Remember? Pythagoras? Hermetic Science." She clucks her tongue, shaking her head indulgently. I put my books in the trunk then slide into my seat.

"Don't worry. I'm a bigger spook then all the astral-knots. You drive and I'll ride shot-gun." She points for me to back out. "Common sense comes after supper. You talk to David? You know, Mr. Lawrence? If you don't get it, yet — just drive as if ... you do."

Pulling away, the livery with the sign of Vulcan seems to fade. Turning back onto the main street, the buildings look like stage-fronts with nothing behind them. Proceeding cautiously, I realize Elsie is manipulating my emotions, shaking me back and forth for some reason, then remember the Black Hats and Larry saying Elsie scrambles code with gibberish to throw them off and to teach us. But I still don't know how to get back.

As if hearing my thoughts, Elsie scoots forward and speaks rapidly in my ear: "Eyes on the road, take the opposite turns from the way we came up. Keep in mind that we're making a triangle. Return to a point, in Raven, from which we ascended." Taking a deep breath, she continues:

"Space and time, attention — a tension —
this whole sequence is a lesson
about weird packages, passages and shadows
in my room. Try to remember my kitchen
as you see the pieces of the mission
on the moon."

She laughs, but I feel vulnerable, unable to move. "Turn right, leave Highlands behind," she coaxes, "and remember," she sings, soft now:

> "The toad and the weasel
> Chase the mouse up the steeple
> While Alice careens through the woods.
> A Mad Hatter — yes,
> but with a few crazy steps
> She returns the temple to the world.

"By the way," she taps gently on the back of my head, "I'm quite sure this isn't Kansas anymore."

Yawning, she settles back. "They're watching, of course. But don't worry. It's okay now." She yawns again. "While I protect the Oz in us, you hold the wheel of our descent — just a slow, steady ride down the mountain of yourself. Night, night, dears."

Grasping the wheel, looking both ways, I turn right.

Multidimensional Chess

Sliding down the mountain, humming to myself, I hold the image of interlocking triangles, patterns suspended above the geography of our progression. There is no other traffic. As if they're in a trance, Sara, Kathy, and John say nothing. Within moments, they seem to be asleep.

"Where are we?" Sara looks around, dazed.

"We're home." I keep my voice low. Kathy stirs in the back. Glancing at my watch, I'm surprised it's only 5:30. I don't remember having pulled in. For a moment I think maybe we never left.

Leaning forward, Elsie says: "Change the flags. John, open the parasol. Larry should be here soon, so why don't you girls make a salad. Coffee would be nice. It's cold-cuts tonight, but worth it, right? Quickly, now," she chuckles and points for Sara to open the door so she can get out.

Going immediately to our tasks, I see each of us moving in a certain pattern, tracing geometries like webs of force Elsie is spinning — fitting whole weeks and months into single days, moving with a precision which seems wholly natural but is extraordinary.

"How do I look?" Elsie greets us as Sara and Kathy, carrying vegetables from the garden, follow John and me in. She's wearing an Indian sari now.

"You look beautiful," Sara responds warmly.

Extending her arms above her head, Elsie brings them down slowly as if caressing a subtle body some inches from her physical frame, then displays a silver bracelet on her left wrist. A small crystal ball containing a mustard seed accentuates the design. "For the guest, you know." She pauses and smiles.

"Faith," she points to the crystal, "even as small as this tiny grain, is the foundation of reality. Say to the mountain, 'move from here to there,'" she bows then looks up, eyes sparkling, "and it will. This is an open secret.

"As Blake said: 'See the world in a grain of sand, and heaven in a wildflower, hold infinity in the palm of your hand," she winks at Sara, "and eternity in an hour.' If you have faith, nothing is impossible to you."

"What's going on?" Larry opens the screen door then swings his shoulder bag down next to the wall. John is setting the cold-cuts on the table, Kathy tossing the salad.

"Have we got a story for you." Sara smiles.

Larry nods. "Let's eat first."

"How was your day?" Kathy asks while we gather around the table.

Instead of answering, Larry says: "One, two, three — blessings on you," his eyes touch each of us, "and me," then immediately makes his sandwich, cutting off conversation.

Just as we finish the meal, no one having spoken, Elsie re-enters. Rising on her toes, arms up, she looks thinner and taller than usual. Nodding at Larry, she backs away, reciting in a strange sing-song:

"Enjoy the little death. Make new dreams.
Be here at ten. Begin again. All Mercury is
What Mercury seems. Moon grow, moon know.
We come then go. Go come again."

About a mile beyond Elsie's, heading back toward Tiger and Clayton, John leans forward. "'Enjoy the little death'? We've been through a lot today, but ... what does that mean?"

"Sleep," Larry answers.

"And we're to make new dreams," I interject.

"I'm never sure what Elsie's saying." John pauses then chuckles. "Actually, I am sometimes," he corrects himself.

"How was your day, Larry?" I ask tentatively, remembering how he cut Kathy off when she asked earlier.

"We tried to calculate the effect of the Apollo Mission." He leans forward to pat my shoulder. "I'm interested in hearing about your adventures."

As he settles back, the road rolling in silence beneath us, I wonder how much of what Elsie said, about a new channel being opened, could be true. I hope Karin will be home so we can get some feedback from her.

"I had the T.V. hooked up," Karin folds her notebook shut and stands to greet us, "so we can watch the special on the moon shot later. Meanwhile, tell me about your day."

"You wouldn't believe where we've been." John gives her a kiss. "We did some type of time travel."

"Through a set of exercises, Elsie gave us," I add.

"We did have quite an experience." Kathy pauses. "I'm not sure what to make of it. But it was a treat."

"Let's talk about what we bought," Sara suggests, excited. "That's a good place to start."

"Good idea," Karin nods. "With all the attention on the moon, we can afford to be a little more relaxed tonight."

"My package is in the trunk." I fumble for a firm picture of what happened. "I almost forgot about it."

"I'll pour coffee if you'll get mine, too?" Kathy moves toward the kitchen.

"Something from your time travels?" Larry grins.

"I have to check first."

"Well, I have mine." Sara pats her jeans pocket.

"Me, too." John puts a small package on the table.

On the way to the car I remember hearing about a British film maker trying to document a fakir doing the famous rope trick in India. He saw a boy crawl up the rope into the sky and the fakir follow him, then heard screams and saw the boy fall, hacked into pieces, to the ground, after which the fakir descended the rope and put the boy back together.

When he reviewed the footage later, it showed the fakir talking and making arm movements, the crowd looking up, gasping in wonder and horror, then applauding, obviously relieved — but nothing else. Shivering slightly, I wonder how much, of what we experienced, actually happened? I know there is no way — in normal reality — that we could have gone back in time. Yet we did, or seemed to. But how? And who, in their right mind, would believe it?

Returning to the dining room with the packages, I hear Sara saying: "Highlands was wonderful. Elsie gave each of us $5.00 and said to find something which matched ourselves."

Unwrapping my books, it dawns on me that, probably by arrangement with Elsie, Karin intends to extend the exercise. She points at me to go first.

"I asked for something contemporary, because it looked like a rare book shop and I didn't think I could afford the prices. The lady pulled out this one." I read from the title page: "Thoreau's *Walden*, published 1854."

Examining the book, Kathy says: "There's no list of subsequent printings. This was from her contemporary selections?" She smiles as I raise my shoulders, recalling how puzzled I had been in the book shop, then unwrap *The Gospel of the Ancient Essenes* and hand it to her.

Turning to the introduction, she reads: "The Aramaic manuscript, from which this translation is made, was acquired by the Vatican Library from a Nestorian priest fleeing Central Asia during the time of Genghis Khan."

"When was it printed?" Larry asks.

Checking the front, Kathy says: "No date given."

John gets up for a closer look. "Who were the Essenes?"

"One of the branches of the Great White Lodge," Karin answers. "Many of their prophecies talk about the Millennium. Scholars know about them primarily from the Dead Sea Scrolls that were discovered in 1947."

Kathy glances through the introduction. "There's no mention of the Dead Sea Scrolls here."

"There wouldn't be unless it was printed after 1947," Larry observes. "This is obviously based on another source. Why don't you sort it? Just a couple lines at random." Flipping it open, Kathy reads:

> "'When the Earthly Mother's angels enter into your bodies, in such wise that the lords of the temple repossess it again, then shall evil depart ... and these things you shall see with your eyes and smell with your nose and touch with your hands.'"

She looks at me. "Was Elsie with you in the store?"

"Not physically. This lady ... "

"One of the Sisters, I'm sure," Karin comments.

"She said that the Essene Gospel would be an interesting companion to Thoreau and that this was mine." I unwrap a small, worn, black leather book with a snap cover and hand it to Larry.

Carefully turning to the front, he reads: "'New York, 1873,' by 'THE AUTHOR' — but there's no name. The first entry says: 'The Ancient Essenes ... Origin of the Order ... an ancient text of rituals and ceremonies.'"

"I haven't really looked at it," I nod, pleased, "except to notice that most of it is in cypher."

"That's definitely a match for you, Jay," Karin approves. "Kathy, do you want to go next?"

Glancing around the table, her grin barely masked, Kathy says: "Everything happened on several levels. What did Elsie call it? Multidimensional chess?"

"No one is better." Karin chuckles. "Do you agree?"

"There's no doubt about her skill." Kathy nods. "It all started in Clayton, a long, long time ago," she clowns, reminding me of Elsie's questions when we started up the mountain, then gets serious: "Sort of as a tune-up, where we were supposed to observe everything in detail and at the same time be invisible — like we fit in."

"Black Hats?" Larry turns to me.

"A whole other story," I respond tentatively.

Karin shakes her head and says: "Go on, Kathy."

"At first I was looking for something related to Elsie's thing about Atlantis and me protecting a relic," she pauses, "which I have to admit I am taking more seriously. Anyway, truth is, my experience ended up more whimsical than that. And I'm glad." She smiles, then pats her package.

"Everything was so different in Highlands that I really felt like Alice in Wonderland. Elsie had been ranting about the Cheshire Cat and the Mad Hatter — the spooky stuff — the other night then off and on today. Anyway, after going through Christy's," she turns to Larry, "honest to god, just like in the catalogues, only out of the 19th Century and in North Carolina — it all just seemed too strange ..."

"Weird?" Larry asks.

"Gorgeous, really, and incredible, or ... Yes, weird, but in a good way." She breaks into a smile, then releases it. "Anyway, I was definitely getting too serious. Like: What am I doing here? How am I going to find 'IT'? Just then, I see Elsie acting like the Cheshire cat, you know, grinning and switching levels."

"I thought she stayed in the car," I question.

"I didn't actually see her physically." Kathy pauses, thinking. "Just remembered, I guess. Anyway, at that moment I also started hearing Arlo Guthrie's song, 'Alice's Restaurant,' combined with Elsie's theme about the Cooks."

"You lightened up," Karin nods, "by switching channels."

"Yes." Kathy considers a moment. "Something I already knew came back and I exercised my right to switch channels."

Karin smiles. "Go on."

"Next thing I know, I'm crossing the street toward this thrift store humming Guthrie's song and knowing that I'm looking for something related to cooks and, when I enter and look around, the whole place is stacked with antique cookware." Eyes big, she conveys wonder. "I walked right up to the first table and put my hands on these."

She unwraps four white porcelain plates — "Alice's" inscribed in black letters across the center — and four matching cups. "Knowing Elsie as we do," Kathy pauses, a wide grin on her face, "these probably belonged to Lewis Carroll."

"Wonderful." Karin applauds. "Who's next?"

Pushing his package into the center of the table, John says: "Me, but first let me tell you about the store where I got this. I've never seen anything like it."

"In what way?" Karin asks.

"It was filled with museum quality antiques." John pauses, collecting his thoughts. "I found this shelf of miniature animals, all kinds, out of stone, brass, wood, clay. And I'm really nudged to stop there. Jay was just sitting on this stool fanning his heart." John chuckles.

"I was almost overwhelmed by the place," I interject.

"Same here," Kathy comments. "It was too much."

"Well, I knew there was something there for me." John pauses. "So I closed my eyes and ran my hand over it, like Elsie showed us, and got this fiery stab in my palm. Opening my eyes, I was shocked that I was over the only spot where there was a gap.

"So I tried again, only using my left hand. When I opened my eyes, my hand was above this." He pulls out a small brass turtle and holds it in his open palm.

"Using your left hand because it's receptive." Karin seems pleased.

"It's for you." John holds the figure out to Sara.

Her face spread in astonishment, Sara reaches into her pocket and, extending her arm into the center of the table, unfolds her fingers, revealing a small jade turtle, saying: "And this is for you," her eyes tearing up.

"Wow," John beams. "I can't believe we were focused on the same shelf. Out of that whole store to choose from. I had it in my mind that I wanted something jade, but when my hand was above the brass turtle and I picked it up, I knew it was for you. And I felt really good about that."

"Well, thank you from my heart." Sara takes a deep breath, wiping her eyes.

"Giving is getting." Karin affirms.

"This is strange." Sara pauses, considering what to say. "The store was overwhelmingly full. There was so much in there that I wanted to check everything out and not hurry. Going slow and steady isn't exactly my strength, but I'm working on it. The tortoise and the hare, you know? Anyway, that's the state I was in."

"Doodle do do a lot," Larry kids her.

"Being a typical hare, I had myself in a dither." She laughs at herself before settling back into her story. "I was drawn to the same table because of the turtles. The animal figures seemed alive, and I was immediately drawn to this one," she holds the brass one up, "but I told myself not to buy the first thing — my rational mind saying that would be too easy.

"Then I saw the jade turtle right next to the jade rabbit and thought that must be the one I should buy. Tortoise and hare image, again. Now I was really in a fix because I had to decide between the two turtles. I really wanted the brass turtle. But, second guessing rather than going with my initial intuition, I bought the jade one. Elsie talked to me about that. I even went back later to exchange it for the brass one. But it was gone."

"Because I bought it." John laughs, pleased. "You must have come back while we were in the shrine." He looks at me.

"Shrine?" Larry asks.

"That's another story." I try to smile, but am too uncertain what I experienced to even try to explain.

"So," Karin summarizes, "Sara and John mirrored and matched off of each other." Looking at Sara, she adds: "Elsie's right about your intuition. In this case you removed the one John was to have and you gave up the one you wanted so John could buy it for you. That's another level of knowing. Good work — all of you."

Leading us downstairs without allowing for additional comments, she remarks: "Let's keep an eye on the Apollo Mission."

The main room in the basement is filled with boxes, wood, paint, carpet remnants, and left over construction supplies. Opening a door, Karin leads us into her study. A board, serving as her desk, covers most of one wall.

Sitting on an old secretary chair, she swivels around to face a T.V. on a wooden crate opposite five folding chairs. Turning it on, John fiddles with the rabbit ears, teasing an image from the flickering snow.

Pictures of the moon, then of the earth floating in space — unlike anything I have seen or quite imagined before — come into focus. In the background, the anchor man announces that the race, which the Russians started with Sputnik, has now gone to the American team.

"But more importantly," the voice continues, "listen to Neil Armstrong as he takes his first steps on the moon." The transmission comes through live, full of strange, eery static:

"The eagle has landed ... One small step for man ... One giant leap for mankind."

"Today," the announcer breaks back in, "thanks to the heroic efforts of thousands of dedicated scientists, we enter a new era. As envisioned by William Butler Yeats, we will:

... pluck till time and times are done
The silver apples of the moon,
The golden apples of the sun.'"

Karin turns the sound off, allowing the image of the earth to hover silently on the set. Sliding her chair around so we face her in a semi-circle, she asks what we think?

"Fantastic. But what's really going on?" Larry's tone surprises me. "For instance, Steiner maintains that the moon, planets, all the stars which appear to be out there, are actually inside of us."

"Like a projection at the edge of our consciousness," I suggest, remembering Steiner's statement. Looking around, seeing Karin nodding instructively, I get the feeling she has just switched the stage setting and we're now in school.

"Elsie keeps talking about some type of space station," John offers, as if he's caught the new rhythm.

"On the back side of the moon." Karin nods again.

"She told me that there is a double helix, like the DNA molecules in the blood, at the very center of the sun." I pause, trying to remember when she said that. "And that relates, somehow, to what's happening on the moon."

"It's interesting they quoted Yeats," Larry comments. "He certainly knew astrology, at the occult level."

"It's like ... " I pause, uncertain.

"Go on," Karin coaxes.

"By referring to the sun as well as the moon, the announcer was suggesting that the Mission is metaphorical."

"Or occult," she adds.

"How so?" Kathy asks.

"Space-time curves back on itself," Karin scans each of us, waiting for a response.

"According to Elsie," I jump in, "we're on the surface of a donut-shaped multidimensional structure, the inside and outside of which are identical. Something like that. I remember the image, but can't describe it."

"Certain traditions talk about adepts going to the moon, through the etheric and astral worlds," Karin observes, thoughtfully. "Now, historically, we've put a man, in a physical body, on the moon. What does that mean?"

"I think it's a stage in a cycle." Larry sips his coffee. "We're expanding space, exteriorizing what has been an interior, or at least non-physical, phenomenon."

"In his book on spaceships," I pause, sensing that we're being observed, but it's not obtrusive or threatening, "Jung says that the archetypes are breaking through. By using the images of 'plucking the silver apples of the moon ...'"

"'The golden apples of the sun,'" Sara supplies the second line.

"Maybe we are," I think out loud, "as a species moving into some higher or further initiation."

"It's metaphysical as well as physical," Larry agrees.

"But plucking apples would also be a reference to the fall from the Garden," I observe.

"The Fall by which we rise," Karin paraphrases.

"According to the Kabbalah, the 'merciful fall,'" Larry adds. "Yeats's initiate name, in the Hermetic Order of the Golden Dawn, translates as: God is the Devil Reversed."

"The whole purpose of metaphysical exploration," Karin pauses, "is to come to grips with the relationship between good and evil. Would you agree?"

"That has to be the foundation." Larry nods.

"Using Elsie's simple cypher," I lean forward, "you know, substitute any vowel, rearrange the consonants, 'evil' backwards is 'live' but could be 'love.'"

"Remember the rap we had about Steiner's view that the earth represents the fourth chakra, the heart?" Larry asks.

"Yeah." I see us talking in my study late at night. "Move the 'h' back to the front in 'earth' and you get 'heart.' My mind floats to Elsie talking about heat, heart, the earth, and stopping at the fourth center in the mountains, giving us bread, nourishment. I see a pattern.

Focusing back to the T.V., viewing our planet floating in space, a blue living globe, I feel it as the pulsing, fragile and magnificent heart of the solar system.

The camera switches to a shot of Neil Armstrong encased in a silver helmet and thick space suit, looking like the hieroglyphs of alleged extraterrestrials who visited earth long ago. Standing next to an American flag, he bounces up and down, defying gravity, raising dust from a desolate, gray, and apparently dead moonscape.

"This is a critical moment in history," Karin observes. "The question is whether — as we put humans on the moon, thus moving our species physically out into space — we will also move deeper into ourselves. That's worth some prayers."

She smiles then leads us up the staircase. "I don't need to tell you," she turns back to us, spread like followers along the steps, "that if you talk too much you kill it. With Elsie the key is to act as if nothing too strange has happened but consider everything. It's a type of game where you have to find a rhythm, hold on, then reflect later."

Moving through the kitchen, I'm stimulated and want to talk about Apollo the Mouse God, the creature I saw beneath the Elysium, in the very depths of my own insides; and about how Elsie made everything happen in Clayton, then Highlands, or in her own kitchen without us ever leaving, because there is no such thing as fixed time and space, and everything which is there is also here, and every when is also now; and about how the Black Hats are trying to stop the scientists at Mahdah Hart's ...

The night withdraws softly, giving way to dawn. Sara, peaceful, like a cat next to me, stirs lightly. Going to the window I see Karin pulling out of the drive, lights on, moving down the street then turning left into Clayton.

Slipping into the kitchen, everyone else still asleep, the house easy, floating in the soft breeze and refreshed air of the coming day, I gaze out into the backyard, go to the patio and stretch, sense the eyes of protective Beings on us.

Flipping on the light, I find Karin's note: "One more tour to Atlanta, apparently. If you get a chance, haul the trash out of the basement. See you tonight. Love, Karin"

Crawling back into bed, pulling close to Sara, I wonder, vaguely, at what point we will know how long we are to stay, what will happen once Larry finishes his class, then release, falling back gently into dreamless sleep.

Love and Fear

Pencil in hand, an unlit cigarette propped behind his ear, Larry looks up from his work. "The sun enters Leo today."

"Leaving Jay's house, entering Kathy's." Sara sips her coffee and glances at me, smiling: "Where you been?"

"Asleep."

"I know that." She grins, holding her arms wide for a hug. "You didn't even roll over when I got up."

"Innocence means everything." I scratch my head and wonder what time it is.

"Better get moving, buddy." John thumps me on the back. "Half-hour to take-off."

"Where's Kathy?" I scan the room.

"She's organizing some stuff to clean out the basement," Sara explains. "Karin's gone to Atlanta."

Dropping Larry at CRC, sun shining, air fresh, we return to Elsie's by 10:00.

"Watch it." Elsie points as I duck through her door. "Either it's dropping or you're growing."

"I'm still fine." John studies the door-frame.

"It's close." Elsie seems younger, her attitude up. Barefoot, she wears a long checkered skirt with a white apron. The coffee smells great. Helping ourselves, we take places around the table. Doing a quick twirl, she announces: "Today ... we pluck apples, silver and gold, make pies, string beans and beads, learn to sew, clean, cook for a day, so you can pay, okay?" Clapping softly, eyes on us, she chants:

> "Though the stable is full
> the horses disappear
> when the spectators are fooled
> by visions of fear

but time is a space
in some other year
where we bear the sheer
burden of joy."

Pausing, she taps her foot. "Poetry isn't a play thing, not a blind exploration. What is it?" Her eyes pierce me, catching at my heart. "What does every creature feel?"

"The threat to his or her existence."

"And what does the creature do?"

"Protect itself."

"How?"

Shrugging, I say: "Write poetry to justify aggression."

"What distinguishes poetry?"

"It expresses essential substance."

"Crystalized emotion?" she asks.

"Essence secreted." I struggle, unable to be articulate.

"Like the piss a toad leaves on the brick when a human reaches for him?" She rolls her eyes up. "Really?"

"Like a slug's trail in the dirt," I respond, seriously.

"Sliding away from a rake?" Tapping my chest, she recites:

"There's a blue flag on the road.
The red bike leans against the shed.
Four crows on a line sing:
The white dove is dead.
But do we worry?"

"I feel it," I respond. "It expresses our condition."

"First you learn how things grow. Growing they die. Eating life, we die. It grows." She pauses. "None of our shells renders us impermeable to the pain."

"We distract ourselves. We forget for a moment." I feel sad.

"No, Jay." She puts her hands on me. "True poetry opens us, so we know better, so we feel more deeply. Learn to laugh so the crystal can wiggle." Grinning, she shakes her hips. Stepping back, she claps:

"To class, to class
The happy workers go
Today, though it's desert

We'll say it is snow
The clown's on the ceiling
Apollo's on the moon
Cheese he is dealing
For old lady Bloom."

Backing up further but leaning forward, her arms swinging slowly, wearing her mustard seed crystal bracelet, she's weaving plant life into the earth, her voice husky:

"It's a balloon, you know, my children.
It's an oven raising bread from hot slabs.
We're fish in the ocean with Jonah
Running from the whale with the crabs.
But the ship of the creature who fights her,
The shell he secretes from dead trees,
Will sink like a rock if he ignores her,
Will fall to the bottom of dead seas.
So sing now of boulders which bubble.
So sing now of lava which spews.
For the vision of Mama is monstrous
But without her the secreter must lose."

"Lose what?" Kathy gets up to refill her coffee cup.

"The hot moisture between the lines, the blood which makes our bones grow. Did you know," Elsie gazes out the window, "the moon grows by feeding on us? None of our joking stops that."

"Is that bad?" John asks.

Turning, Elsie faces him, but takes my arm, pulling me up to stand with her. "The Jews are a remnant of an earlier light-wave, left behind as the others advanced, thus ahead of us, thus despised. Is that bad?"

He stares at her as if nothing registered, but I hear myself whispering: "Who is Melchizedek?"

"John and Kathy," she ignores me, "would you do some weeding for dear old Elsie — starting at the far end and working back toward us? And close the canopy?" As they start for the door, she lowers herself to a chair at the small table, suddenly looking very tired. Sara joins us.

Blue eyes sad, Elsie lights a cigarette, and watches white smoke curl in the light, then, stubbing it out, says: "There are Orders of the Right and of the Left. I want to write poetry. Sara wants to nurture us. You want to do good. But we don't always know whether what we are doing is right or left. The opposite of right is not wrong. The opposite of wrong is not always right.

"Melchizedek took tithes from Abraham. Melchizedea from Sarah. King and Queen of Salem, they offered their children. Jesus and Mary loved each other. Her hair on his feet. His fingers along her neck. Their breath in each other. Their children could rule the world in kindness and grace if it were not for ... If we could just ..."

"What, Elsie?" Sara asks, concerned.

Her eyes on Sara, almost pleading, Elsie says: "We've carried it longer than I can remember. It's almost time for you to take over."

"How?" Sara asks.

Leaning forward, her arms around Sara's middle, she says: "Even while you raise your children, you will be doing it. But we do something else, too. We understand. It's the work, in here." She pats Sara's solar plexus. "And here." She leans back and points to Sara's heart. "What we give of ourselves. There are no words for it." She points to Sara's head.

"And for you, Jay, it's hard." She looks over at me. "Elsie here, Elsie there. You remember, don't you, how I used to sing to you when you were a little boy? In German?" She stands, her voice deep, caressing, the stanzas flowing one into another, the words forming patterns which I do remember, rhythms which carry, reassure, and concern me, though I don't understand the language.

Finishing the song, Elsie smiles, her blue eyes moist at the corners. "You want to learn German, don't you?"

"So I can read Steiner in the original."

"And Goethe." She nods. "Steiner carries it on, but it's in Goethe first. Go back to the source. Are you ready for the English. Do you know why you're so scared?"

"No," I admit.

"Then listen." Elsie sings:

> "Daily went the Sultan's beauteous
> Daughter walking for her pleasure
> In the evening at the fountain
> Where the splashing waters whiten.

Daily stood the youthful bondsman
In the evening at the fountain
Where the splashing waters whiten.
Daily he grew paler and paler.

Then one evening stepped the princess
Up to him with sudden question.
'You must tell me what your name is,
What your country, who your kinsmen.'

And the bondsman answered:
'Mahomet is my name; I come from Yemen.
The Asra are my kinfolk —
They who die when love befalls them.'"

Humming a moment longer, hauntingly repeating the refrain, Elsie turns her attention to Sara.

"Sing to your children. Work with Jay on the stories. Rewrite the fairy tales. Give them better endings. Not just light. Beauty and truth, but also purpose, shadow and direction. Don't repeat the old patterns."

Filled with emotion, I say: "My mom sang to me."

"She held you to the light." Elsie whispers: "I'm here to break the window." Then, looking at both of us, she says: "There is a mystery in your fear, and in your love, that has brought you to this life. Don't deny it. Don't smother it. Don't let go."

She glances toward the ceiling. "But while holding on, let go of the old stories. As you die you are reborn but, this life, do it over and over without leaving your bodies. Do it as a sacrament to love. Neither lose yourselves in each other nor draw back and break the bond. What you will give is unique and beautiful and needed."

She looks at Sara. "You are of an ancient school. You have waited at the well. You have provided the living water drawn from deep within the earth to the thirsty traveller. You have raised his light, and nurtured, and taught him.

"He whom you have accepted wants you so much he's afraid. Nothing easy about accepting the light I carry, which is yours also, which we have prepared for each other down through the millennia, working in a world which is filled with ignorance and cruelty but also," she kisses her forehead, "great joy and blessing."

Relighting her cigarette, scanning Sara then turning to me, Elsie continues: "The Order of Melchizedek draws you and repulses you. Portions of that school have been captured by other forces. The bridge between Wales and Salem is fraught with danger and tragedy. The Johannine Mysteries rise. Michael descends.

"Sara is of the school of Mary — the Mother and the Magdalen, the virgin whore, they say because they're frightened by our love. Yet, were we to give what we can, the world would be saved. Hold her or she leaves you. Hold her too tight and you both die. For now," she takes a puff and blows it into the center of the room, "change the flag, open the antenna, work while we can and when you are ready, remember the parts I have told you which are true."

Doing a little tap dance, pumping her arms up and down, Elsie whistles like a steam engine, then circles: "Because, 'choo, choo ... I think I can, I think I can' becomes: 'I am ... I am ... I am ...' in the school I teach." Nearing the door, increasing speed, she grabs her straw hat and scoots out along the cabin and disappears into the trees.

Alarmed, Sara and I try to follow her. John and Kathy, startled, look up from their work in the garden. "Open the sun shade," I call to John as Kathy stands and points to the path Elsie took. A shadowy man is looking at us. The clothesline is bare. Turning back to the cabin for a replacement flag, I hear a vehicle hovering at the end of the drive. Two men in dark hats stare at us.

The door is stuck. Pulling frantically, I pop it open. "Hurry," Sara pushes me from behind. "Should I call them in?"

"No," I respond with absolute certainty, "we should be in the garden," and race into the workroom, retrieve a towel checkered like Elsie's dress, and dash to hang it on the line while John finishes opening the canopy. Signalling him to follow, I notice the pick-up backing away. No one stands in the opening into the woods.

Dropping onto hands and knees in the onion row, Sara and Kathy opposite us, John whispers: "What's going on?"

"Bits and pieces, words and phrases, here and there," I mutter under my breath, not understanding, pushing my fingers into the roots, trying to focus, to find a rhythm. Finally slowing my breath, the sun warm on my back, I look up. Images of time and space, past, present, and future, light memories of what Elsie had said, just moments before.

"Good work." Her hat square on her head, the big pockets of her apron bulging with mushrooms, she stands at the edge of the garden smiling at us. "As soon as you're done here, come in and I'll show you some more about the beads."

"Line up now." Elsie lights a cigarette, inspecting us from behind. We're facing the shelf along the back wall in the workroom. "Each has a box. Each has a talent. Each has a string. You have plenty of time before we fix lunch. He's been working hard, you know. Have to feed him right."

Kathy turns to Elsie. "You remember what you said about us being Indians?"

"About your having another purpose for being here? Yes."

"Well," Kathy takes a breath, "I need to explore now."

"I'd like to go with her," John volunteers.

Stepping up to each of them, running her hands over their heads and down their bodies, Elsie says: "Be back by noon. Keep your words in your hearts. I'll follow you in a moment. Sara and Jay can tell the beads for us."

Kathy pulls a red bandana up over her hair and starts toward the door. "Here." Elsie stops John, putting an old brown felt hat on him. "Now hurry." She pushes him gently, then goes to her room in the back, leaving us alone.

"Telling the beads?" Sara glances at me then holds her hand out over the box, sensing the individual pieces.

"Like a rosary, I guess." I follow her lead.

Fully concentrated while selecting then stringing beads together, neither of us speaks during the next half-hour.

"Let's see them?" Elsie reappears from the back room — wearing the same skirt and apron, but with the addition of her bracelet and jade jewelry — and reaches for Sara's delicate and precise, perfectly symmetrical bead necklace.

"Like Indian sacred work." She moves the strand between her fingers. "I like your work." Then, accepting mine, her head jerks back. Feeling a different intensity surge through the room, I step back.

"Other lives, other connections." She lowers her eyes to me. "Said this before — did you get it — Bremyer? Drop the 'Br' and you have 'Emery' left. Search for meaning? It's everywhere." She grins. "I used toads to chase mice at Emory U. in Atlanta. I cooked for the boys during initiations — those who could stand it. Took them on digs even. Stirred up the past — flew with the falcon. Understand?"

"No." But deep down I feel a quickening.

"Merlin Emrys, boy!" She huffs then, striking a match, seems to refocus. "With the body marks, with the name, with the asymmetric design in your bead work — certain schools you've attended are attested. From Atlantis to Wales and back, Emery is a clue to the mystery of Salem-Melchizedek."

She holds my necklace up for Sara to inspect. "Sort of drives you crazy, doesn't it?"

Sara laughs. "Totally the opposite of mine."

"But it's very good," she comments, apparently normal again. "Against your order, what he does is very good. Yes, but he definitely needs your order, your balance. Don't forget his song — nor the song of Nimue. Anyway ... " she slides our necklaces over our heads, "let's get ready for Mr. Lawrence. Set the table and call the scouts home."

John, still wearing his hat, walks through the door behind Larry. Looking tired, Larry settles by the window. "Where's Kathy?" he asks.

Elsie blows a puff up into the air, watching it curl before responding: "Where is she, John?"

Hanging his hat on the peg beside the workroom door, John turns back to us. "We crossed a stream. Then she told me to go back because she needed to go on alone."

Larry stands up. "Should I go for her?"

"No." Elsie pushes him to sit down. "Sara, go to the clothesline and holler that lunch is ready. Act casual and come right back." Looking distressed, John stands at the window until Sara returns.

"Kathy's got her things, you've got yours." Elsie examines Larry's fingers and palms. "Are they sore?"

"What can I do?" His voice is raspy.

"Besides letting go?" Glancing at me, she moves around to work his shoulders. "Have you talked about Honigberger?"

"The scientist at the Hart Retreat?" I ask. She nods but keeps her eyes on Larry, concentrating, working her fingers into his back. "Not much."

"There are a lot of people whom you haven't met yet," Elsie comments, casually. "When you're done with class," she slaps his back, "you can be a helper here, for a big feed, with the others. Sound good?"

"Sure." He looks up, appreciative.

"Mahdah, Sadie, Galen, and several others. It will give them a chance to look you over. If all goes well, you can get a healing. Now," she squeezes his shoulders, "to the table."

Lighting a cigarette and blowing smoke into the air, Kathy's place empty but set, Elsie chants:

"One, two, three, a blessing in the trees.
Bring her back between the cracks.
One, two, three."

Clapping three times, she backs into the workroom as Kathy pulls the screen door open, walks to the sink without a word, washes her hands, then takes her seat.

"What happened to you?" Sara asks. They're at the sink. Seeming reflective and troubled, Kathy has barely spoken since she came in, not even when Larry hurried back to class.

"I don't know whether I can talk about it." She hands a dish to Sara to dry. John and I are standing right beside them, not sure what to do.

"We all have separate tasks." Elsie emerges from the workroom. "Close the shade, would you, John? And wear your hat." She hands it to him. "And duck when you go out. I'm starting to worry."

"About what?" Perplexed, John looks at the door frame.

"Maybe," Elsie inspects him, speaking softly, "you are John of New York now — but before that," her voice rises, "was it Patmos? Are you that courageous?"

John holds his hands out like he's confused.

"St. John of the Apocalypse?" I ask.

Turning to me, suddenly fierce, Elsie bites off each word, backing me up:

"Of the sacred college of Wales, Languedoc,
the Adriatic then Aegean Sea, and further east
still — waiting — the ancient keeper and
singer of songs which will come of our past,

future and present longing for what we've done,
will do, are doing, must do —
the falcon of the argonauts, all alone
on an island in the sea, all alone,
waiting for you and me and ...
Merlin's bell, Mephistopheles in Hell,
Old Faust, faithful mouse ... Out!.Out!"

She turns abruptly back to John. Stunned, he pulls on his hat and hurries to close the sun shade. Settling into the chair by the front window, Elsie keeps an eye on him. When he returns, she lights a cigarette and paces in front of us.

"We're covering a lot of things here. We're putting things together in different combinations and," she pauses to put her cigarette out, "always, at the same time, we're doing something else," she pulls on an imaginary train whistle, "and learning to see ourselves doing it, but," she puts her fists on her hips and cocks her head, then stamps her foot like an exasperated, spoiled girl, "nevertheless," she sing-songs, swinging her head back and forth:

"You see red, I see blue.
All the little children
Go two by two
But beneath the sky
In the morning so true
I still see red
and you still see blue."

She points at Kathy. "Do you know why ..." she squints upward, looking through the ceiling, tapping her foot, not allowing a response, "someone closed the windows? Where did the sky go?"

Eyes back to Kathy, she continues: "Sometimes, in the forest, the illusion of the world slips away. Why didn't you let John follow you?" She holds her arms open, radiating warmth and care. "I love you, you know, but you scared me."

"I scared myself, Elsie," Kathy responds, still serious and semi-withdrawn.

Tapping her head, Elsie winks and says: "Got to get a new tuner. Anyway, dears, get coffee and sit. There's something I want to say. Something they want to hear."

When we've shifted the chairs to face her, Elsie nods. "Now, tell me first and I'll relay it."

"What?" Kathy responds, a bit distant, although I had noticed her smiling when Elsie tried to tune her head.

"In every piece of art there must be a defect." Elsie takes a deep breath. "On this plane, perfect good, or evil, would disappear. Why didn't you let John follow you?"

"The hat bothered me," Kathy speaks slowly. "I felt like it was a marker and I needed to be totally alone."

Elsie whispers: "For a moment I couldn't find you."

"I'm sorry, Elsie." Kathy lowers her eyes.

"What did you see?"

"Is it safe?" Kathy walks to the door and looks out then, as if she has made a decision, turns back to Elsie. "I had a dream ... the night before we went to Highlands."

"This is safer," Elsie leans forward and thumps the floor, "than in your dream, know why?"

"No." Kathy returns to her seat.

"Because there are witnesses here. You're not alone."

"But in the dream ..."

"I was there." Elsie marches in place. "I told you not all the 'me's in 'I am more than I am,' are easy to take, but — for goodness sake — Hell!" She stamps. "You've read the billboards, haven't you?" She slams her fist down, "BOOM!" sounding like thunder. "'Lucky Strikes make fine tobacco!' So," she spreads her arms to the ceiling like entreating the sky, "sometimes a girl's got to push or be pushed."

Kathy laughs uneasily.

"We're," Elsie lets her voice run up, "listening."

"This is like the dream." Kathy hesitates. "I was bothered because you were trying to make me do something."

"Haven't you heard?" Elsie leans forward. "People in dreams are projections of the dreamer."

"No." Kathy is adamant. "This was you."

"Not so nasty as I was to Jay, a minute ago, was I?" Elsie raises her eyebrows.

"Why did you jump him?" John asks. "It was my fault."

"About Patmos in Wales — the search for the Golden Fleece?" Elsie chuckles. "Oh for the water of the Adriatic. Oh how I love to kick ass in Athens. Told you about that, didn't I?"

She looks up at the ceiling. "They're not getting much," she comments to someone. "Yes," she looks back at John, "you didn't follow instructions but Jay gets the best stuff when I'm a little crazy and he's a little scared.

"So," Elsie paces again, "we're pulling teeth are we?" She gets up in Kathy's face as if to inspect her mouth.

Reluctantly breaking toward a grin, Kathy leans her head back, slacking her mouth open while Elsie draws tools out of an imaginary carpenter's belt, miming a big chisel and hammer, wholly exaggerated in her concentration.

"And you have such beautiful words, Kathy," Elsie says. "It's a shame you won't speak." She backs up and takes her seat again, tapping her head. "Or that I can't hear you. Was it something about tobacco? This is Turtle Island, you know. Big deal tobacco. Carrier of prayers? Messenger between worlds? Something to do with the Indians, was it?"

"Okay." Kathy finally grins. "But it wasn't funny, and I don't know what to do now." She walks to the screen door again as if checking something. "I guess," she pauses then pushes the solid door shut, "I have the feeling that if I don't say it, it will go away."

"Just the opposite," Elsie advises, serious now.

"After we crossed the stream, and I asked John to leave," Kathy paces between us, "I realized that I was lost, or at least couldn't recognize anything, not even the landscape. It was much lusher, almost tropical, and I was hearing drumming in the distance, like an enemy was advancing toward us, but there was nobody with me.

"Starting to panic, I wanted to yell for John to come back or to run to where he was, but the drumming was coming from the direction which I thought he had gone and I knew that if they caught me the secret would be lost."

"What secret?" Elsie asks, gently.

Stopping and looking at Elsie, Kathy says: "The relationship between tobacco and lightning." Beginning to pace again, Kathy goes on: "That's your Lucky Strike image, probably. All I know is that I smoke Luckys, at least before we came here, and that even though you're always talking about Salems, in my dream you were telling me that was wrong, that I have to find something, that Wales and witchcraft come later but there's something below that which you told me I have to do on my own. Do you remember that?"

"That's what we're all doing, Kathy." Elsie nods. "This is the re-membered present. The point in space-time where we can express all that is. And these are your witnesses."

Glancing at us, Kathy goes on: "In the dream you said Larry is to take over the Harwood Foundation, and grow tobacco again, and I am to handle the weaving. I know I'm a weaver, so I was inter-ested." She stops and thinks a moment before starting again. "But I also knew, somehow, that we would have to take the plantation, or what ever it is, by force ..."

Elsie reaches out and stops her. "They took it from us by force, Kathy. Nobody said this would be easy."

"But I have no right," Kathy protests.

"Did they?" Elsie asks, dropping her voice.

"It's an actual place. I know that, Elsie. I saw the literature in Clayton. In the crafts shop. I didn't want to tell you, or anyone," Kathy sits down. "It was so weird."

"Tell us now," Elsie whispers.

"John and I were on our side of the street, going to the restau-rant." She glances at him. "I went into the back to see the weaving, while you went next door. Well," a quick spasm goes through Kathy's shoulders, "Mrs. Harwood literally accosted me and read me the riot act about you, Elsie."

"Not my best friend." Elsie grins. "Go on."

"She said you were invading her dreams to force her to will her property to Larry, she said Lawrence; that you were practicing the left hand path, and we were being duped, and that if we couldn't protect ourselves, that was our problem; but she had her own forces and we better stay the hell away. I didn't say one word before, dur-ing, or after her tirade."

"I know," Elsie shakes her head. "Dear Mrs. Harwood is quite a card, isn't she?"

"I'd hardly call her a card."

"Who was the red queen?" Elsie smiles, then gets up to re-fill her coffee cup. "Do you remember her?"

"More like the High Priestess in the tarot deck," Kathy retorts. "It wasn't a casual exchange. I didn't want to say anything to any of you until I figured it out."

"Figured what out?" Elsie sips her coffee. "We both know she's powerful. I didn't mislead you. Alice was scared, wasn't she? If not, she should have been."

"Then, why did you let me go out there alone?"

"You decided that." Lighting a match, she gazes through the flame toward Kathy. "Tell me what happened and they'll tell you what went wrong. Honest Indian, really."

Pacing again, Kathy says: "I knew I needed to keep going and find what you were talking about."

"Is it a relic or a secret?" Elsie coaxes her.

"I thought it was a relic, an artifact of some sort, and spent most of my time in Highlands looking for it."

"But the Order of the Cooks brought you to the warehouse and sent you home ready to feed the tribes, uh huh." Elsie looks up and acts like she's twisting a knob in her ear. "Coming in better now, thank you. So," she winks at Kathy, "what you found in Highlands was just right, but what you almost lost out there ..." She points through the wall. "Well?"

Kathy sits down. "It's hard to describe."

"You're safe now."

"I had this pouch, containing the last seeds of our sacred tobacco, what the sky god had given to my people, what the mother had borne for us. I was the keeper and they were searching for me."

"This is a memory, Kathy. Just let us know how we can help."

"They didn't know what I had." She turns pleading eyes to Elsie. "Who were they?"

"Atlantean technicians. So much went wrong. It shouldn't have been that way."

"Who was I?"

"Caretaker of the Peoples."

"Cherokees?"

"Their ancestors." Elsie relights her cigarette. "The Black Hats were determined to destroy your culture, enslave your people. Where did you hide it?"

"I ran through the woods, the drums getting closer and closer, then buried it in a circle of trees."

Holding up a brochure for the Harwood Foundation, Elsie points at a picture on the back page showing a tree circle.

"That's it." Kathy stares. "How ...?"

Laying the brochure down, Elsie puts her hand on Kathy's shoulder. "You're taking on too much alone."

"Who is she?" Fear shows on her face. "Why is she against us?"

"She was the leader of the invading troops." Elsie backs away. "One of our purposes is to regain Her Wood. Because it is your life, I pushed you. Why else would you have come?"

Kathy fingers a strand of her long dark hair, but says nothing.

"You didn't remember that. Most don't. If they did, they might give up. Fear could stop them." Elsie smiles. "Alice tumbled down the hole, not quite by choice. Did I push her?" She cocks her head sideways. "Because I understand the importance of a Lucky Strike? That's why we call it that, you know?"

Kathy looks up. "The sacred tobacco?"

"The birth of tobacco seeds from lightning." Going to the cupboard, Elsie pulls out a carton of Luckys and hands them to Kathy. "Been saving them until you asked. Can't respond, not directly, until there's a request.

"Yes?" She checks the ceiling. "Alright," she seems peeved, "I'll admit it. Sometimes I push and sometimes I answer — hoping the questions will come later." Fist on her hip, she stamps. "But it's because I love you. Toot. Toot."

Holding her hand out, Elsie asks for a Lucky. Returning to her chair and lighting it, holding the flame up for herself and Kathy, she says: "But you planted the seeds and you're alright now. Understand?"

"I heard Sara calling me."

"Elsie's Restaurant almost always works." Elsie winks.

"Was I really in danger?" Kathy, seeming more relaxed now, smiles, almost shyly, at the rest of us.

"There are so many forces here," Elsie looks at each of us, "and so many reasons for being cautious." She pats John on the shoulder. "Sometimes it's important to follow what I say." She nudges him to stand up, blows smoke into the air, then moves it around his body.

"He was to take the heat for your journey." She returns to her chair. "Showing himself to the others, your path was open. He was safe, thoughts covered." She makes the image of a hat on her head. "Sending him home, you were vulnerable.

"The owl screeching," she jerks toward the window as if something has caught her attention, "is both ally and death. Your attention was distracted. Death is one thing — if you're ready. But capture ... "

"Capture?" Kathy tightens.

"We can reconstruct the physical if we catch the etheric in time. But, to be perfectly frank with you, we have to know you're going to jump in order to get it right. There's always danger." Elsie pauses, holding her jade necklace.

"I told Sara that I'm tired. But it's hard for any of you to imagine how tired. There comes a time when we all want to jump, but it will be my turn long before yours."

Elsie leans forward, speaking softly: "In our various combinations, those of us who are native here are holding the limits, protecting our families, our ancestors and descendants." She slaps her side gently. "In our bodies by right. In this place by right. You understand?"

"I think so," Kathy whispers.

"Your children are what you create, Kathy — what you tend. You are the Keeper. We are your witnesses."

Elsie leans back. "The great God Pan fathers many kids. But it's Her Wood and he's just the guest."

"Harwood?" Kathy asks.

"The Old Bag stole the name. Just keep it straight, in your heart, because that's where the battle will be won."

"We have to make our own decisions, though, don't we?" Kathy seems to be searching. "Decide what to accept?"

"Sure." Elsie backs toward the workroom. "Whether to clean up or leave the dishes. Whether to wear the hat or go bare-headed." She winks at John. "Whether you're a poet or just a drunkard." Her eyes scan me.

"Whether we are Indians or just live once." She glances at Sara. "In fact, it's a burden off my back just to know that you know that none of this is real for — I do assure you — only love and fear truly exist. One expands and the other contracts you, like breathing, like laughter."

Disappearing into the workroom, her voice floats back to us: "Strike when you hope you're lucky — that's what I say."

My heart aches. I feel that Kathy was in real danger and that Elsie is giving us something, and protecting us, and that it costs her immense energy and care. As in a daze, Kathy says: "We need to clean out the basement at Karin's," then moves toward the door and pulls it open.

Approaching our car, the sun bright and hot, I see a note stuck under the windshield wiper: "Put the shade up. Wear your hat. See you at 5:00. L.C." Slipping back into the cottage, John returns quickly, hat on now, and cranks the canopy open.

"Was she in there?" Sara asks.

"Are you serious?" He grimaces. "There's no way I'd look in her back room."

Dancing in the Dark

Returning to the Oasis for supper, I glance in the rear view mirror and notice John fidgeting with his hat, pulling it down tighter. The line is full of fresh clothes. Leaning back against the cabin wall, Larry waves. "Better hurry."

A warm and spicy aroma permeates the room. A mess of fresh beets boils on the stove. Coming in last, John hangs his hat on the peg while Sara and Kathy dish the food into bowls and put them on the table.

Wearing a maroon dress, a thick black belt with a large silver clasp, black shoes, a black pill-box hat with a lace veil piled on top, and carrying some type of case, Elsie stands in the corner watching us. Once we are seated, she announces: "Check yourselves on the way out."

"You never eat with us!" Sara protests mildly.

"I'm running behind." She starts for the door. Sara gets up. Turning tired eyes to her, Elsie nods.

"Sleep well and sleep enough
Or the clean edges get rough.
It's positive prerogative
To balance the negative.

So, if you don't remember anything else, do remember: if you don't get enough sleep, you get negative."

"Should we wait for you?" Sara asks.

"No." She puts the case down and stares out the screen. "But if David could hold the harp, that might bring Jack home. Karin is looking for him. Someone plucks the strings for the Teachers in Bukhara." She cups her hand behind her ear. "Did you hear?"

"Gurdjieff's group?" Larry stands.

"The Masters of Wisdom," she squints into the distance, "study the dance while the giants advance. The point is to ..." she focuses on him:

"see the dancing figure in the fire,
know the one still point spinning in the center,
hold the image while the strings form a chord,
cross the chord to the cave of memory.

By the harp the Davids hold the treasure," she hands the case to Larry, "the instrument of their healing. Through the veil approach the sound. It's for Jack if David holds it." She taps gently against her forehead and looks up. "Any messages before I go? No? No mo' messages for me?"

Holding the case, Larry asks: "Are you okay, Elsie?"

"Just keep grinning." Pulling the veil down over her eyes, she backs out through the door, letting it flap shut behind her, then knocking, calls back in: "Sara?"

"Yes?" Sara answers.

"You might bring the wash in before you leave and, Jay, black and white tonight, for balance." She pauses. "And John, attend the shade, will you, dear?"

"Wherever she's going," Larry holds his arms out, indicating we should all join hands around the table, "she wants us to stay calm."

Outside we hear the canopy over the picnic table being opened, then a vehicle pulling into the drive. We don't move. A cloud passes over the sun, casting a shadow, darkening the room as a door slams and the vehicle pulls away.

Eating then cleaning up quickly, we head for the car. Remembering the flags, I turn back and go to the shelves in the workroom. Glancing along the walls I wonder where Elsie is, what is happening with her and Jack and Larry and ...

"Don't think about it too much." Elsie's voice startles me.

"I'm taking it very seriously." My heart is pounding.

"Then you're not playing enough." She laughs. "The Star Children die when love befalls them but must," she holds her arms above her head like a ballerina, "dance the enemy which sustains the universe, the one poem, while they die."

Staggered as she disappears, seeming to swim through shadows, I tell myself I must have imagined her.

Weaving back toward Clayton, in silence, the sun stretches red night across the road.

"Thanks for cleaning up." Blue eyes moving toward Larry, Karin adds: "Did you bring anything?"

Opening the case, Larry runs fingers over the strings, raising a strange cacophony. "Elsie emphasized to me that certain sacrifices are being made, or demanded." He looks directly at Karin. "Can we talk?"

"We have to." Karin sets the coffee pot down.

"Okay." Larry glances at Kathy. "Elsie says that in a sense there's no right and wrong, just the fullness of light and darkness, the dance between life and death, but ..."

"There are certain things which are very wrong," Karin completes the statement then looks at Kathy. "What do you think of Elsie?"

"She's an alchemist, and ..." Soft harmonics rise beneath and mix with the weird, almost wailing cry of the autoharp. Karin interrupts:

"She's one of the great sisters who has given everything in order to channel messages, angels and demons, for her students. One of the most powerful and most vulnerable of all of the great Mistresses of the Ancient Schools." She pauses, "Each of you have to understand how we got here and what is at stake." Karin rises and pulls the sliding door shut.

"There had been an attack on the rehabilitation center where Jay and Sara met Jack. When he went back to the complex after taking them to Elsie, he was abducted, although he probably didn't know it because they're using one of the oldest tricks known to the left hand path."

"How did it happen?" I ask, dismayed, remembering how positive and yet, in a way, disoriented Jack had seemed.

"Elsie was sending him to one of the sacred lodges in Atlanta, which would have protected him. But Jack was misled, because the men who took him use the name of Melchizedek and all the slogans about serving the masters."

"Black Hats without the black hats." Larry nods. "Where is he now?"

"Elsie says he doesn't know what he's doing, but apparently he's recruiting boy prostitutes for them through the Y.M.C.A. in Atlanta." Karin shakes her head. "She's had me looking for him there. Needless to say, it got a lot more serious when I realized what was going on. I don't know how much more involved I dare ... "

"You shouldn't mess with it at all." John is emphatic. "For God's sake, Mom, we live in New York. You don't have to go to Atlanta to get mixed up in that sort of thing." He paces. "What does your teacher say?"

"That something went wrong." Karin looks into his eyes.

"What does Elsie say?" Larry asks.

Karin glances out the window before answering: "Elsie told me it's imperative that we find him. She has fixed him, spiritually, so his memory body is suspended in a cave. But she can't hold him there much longer. You know she gave you his autoharp for a reason, don't you?"

"He's attached, somehow." Larry pauses. "And I'm to help hold him."

"This is crazy." Kathy stands, obviously agitated. "Larry, you can't be taking this literally."

"Figuratively or literally," Karin puts her hand on Larry's shoulder, "I can use your help and will do what I can to help you. Now," she takes Kathy's arm and leads us into the living room, "let's change the energy." After pulling the drapes, she forms a circle with the five of us holding our arms out so the tips of our fingers barely touch.

"Love is the greatest protection." Karin turns inside the circle. "Conscious love brought us here, provided this house, sends you to Elsie's and CRC," she nods at Larry, "each day, brings us home safely each night. What I ask now," she touches her own heart then each of ours, "is that you extend your protection to Jack."

She pauses, reflectively, her eyes closed. "My teacher says: It's through memory that we can know all things. The changing times come through the work of the cosmic Christ." Letting silence encircle our breaths, she waits a moment then smiles and waves her hand over us. "Thank you," she whispers then moves toward her room.

"How are you feeling about all this?" Sara pats John's shoulder from behind as Larry scoots up to the table.

"Got my hat, you know." He cranes his neck to see her. "I'm worried about Mom, and a lot of things."

"This is serious stuff." Sara considers him for a moment. "But your mom knows what she's doing. Right?"

"She usually does." John gets up. "I'm learning more than I ever thought possible, but I don't know what I'm supposed to do or how I fit in." He pauses. "Where do you think Elsie went tonight?"

"Where do you think?" I ask, reminded of my encounter with Elsie, or someone, after we thought she had gone.

Taking a breath, John says: "To make some sort of deal."

"What kind?" Sara asks.

"It had to do with me leaving Kathy this morning." He looks down. "And it cost her something."

"I'm sure she can handle whatever it is." Larry attempts to reassure him. Nodding, John walks to the hall then turns back before disappearing toward his room. "I hope so."

"Have any of you noticed anything strange about the granite monument on top of the rise, on the way to Elsie's?" Larry lays the autoharp aside. "Ever since the night I got caught in the storm, I've felt certain things." He turns to me. "One of which is that Elsie put me there on purpose, or let it happen, then ..."

"What are you talking about?" Kathy seems distressed.

"Bad Guys." Larry puts his hand over hers. "Elsie has been hinting to that effect but when I tried to ask her she cut me off. I don't know how many levels she's playing, but, especially after listening to Karin tonight, I think that much of what she's doing is designed to get Jack back. And, needless to say ..."

"She's putting us at risk, too," Kathy interrupts. "You know about my dream; then Clayton and Highlands — L.C., Alice, all that." She pulls her hand away. "This morning she sent me, or allowed me, however you want to put it, to get out in the woods and I had this experience with ..."

Vividly remembering Kathy's recounting of her experience, I say: "Atlantean Technicians and Mrs. Harwood ..."

"Yes," Kathy confirms, staring at Larry. "I told you the dream, and that she was in Clayton. Here's the worst, Elsie had a brochure on the Harwood Estates and admitted that she intends to use you to take back the sacred wood there, by force. There's a real battle going on, Larry, and you don't seem to know it. You think this is some game."

"I do know it," Larry responds seriously. "And we're in the middle of it. The question is what are we going to do. I have absolute faith in Elsie's intentions ..."

"But how much can she control?" Kathy interjects. "And I'm not sure about her intentions. She may be a Mistress of the Old Schools, whatever Karin said, but she's human ..."

"Or working through a human," Larry suggests. "You can't fault her for not warning us. About half of what she says is laced with warnings and coded hints."

"And gibberish," Kathy retorts softly. "I mean maybe if you could unravel it, it would make sense. A lot of what she says does make sense poetically and mythologically, but ..." She shakes her head. "What makes the most sense is the heart stuff, I admit that. She pulls at you, and you're convinced at the moment. But when she tells you herself that you can't trust her — how can you, or any of us ..."

"Jump into the breach." He glances up at Sara. "There are certain things we signed up for just by coming here."

"You still have choice," Kathy asserts.

"Not once you've accepted the gifts," Larry replies earnestly. "And what I've accepted I have to complete."

"What about the monument?" Kathy gets up.

"I think it has something to do with Jack," Larry answers. "I didn't want to say anything until I had checked it out." He pours coffee for himself. "But I've watched for it every time we've gone by. Sometimes it changes shape and even locations. Anyway, Kathy," he pauses, "whatever I've got to do, it relates to the monument and I need to know everything you remember about Harwood."

"So you think there's no getting out of it now?" She slides reluctantly back into her seat.

"What about us?" Sara asks.

"I guess our training was for more than fun and games, Agent Uh Oh." He tries to joke.

"It's not funny anymore, is it?" Sara comments.

Closing the door and pulling the drapes shut in our room, Sara turns to me. "I am totally serious, Jay. Whatever Larry and you think about all this, I'm scared and so is Kathy."

"We're all scared." I drop to the mattress. "But what can we do at this point?"

"We can pack up and go home." She starts to open her suitcase. "We can do what sensible people would do."

"And leave Larry?"

"I'm sure Kathy is talking to him right now."

"And I'm sure she knows he won't leave."

"Then maybe Kathy and I will go." Sara shuts the suit case, frustrated, and looks at me pleadingly. "You thought this was all great when you thought it was about poetry."

"Listen, Sara ..." I'm frustrated, uncertain what to say or even what I feel.

"Well?"

"You're as close to Elsie as I am."

"I'm not sure of anything." Sara turns away.

The Stand

In the morning, as if we've all determined to act like nothing is wrong, we drive toward Tiger.

"Stop," Larry signals at the foot of the rise. Leaning forward, I let him out and watch as he climbs a trail between tall trees. Back to us in five minutes, he looks puzzled.

"There's a clearing up there but nothing else."

"Today ... " Elsie, sitting at the table by the window, lights a cigarette as Sara and I walk through the door, the sun bright behind us, "you should visit Paladin, start working on your long term commitments."

John hangs his hat up and goes to pour the coffee, Kathy helping him, while Sara and I stand before Elsie.

"We met him at CRC," I say, feeling awkward, "but I don't know that we can just drop by."

"He'll be glad to see you," Elsie states flatly. "Don't you think it's time, Sara?"

"He seemed to like Jay," Sara answers noncommittally.

"I really was drawn to him, but ... "

"But," Elsie abruptly stands up, "wash the hog, Jay." She looks worn through the face, seems impatient today. "You're supposed to be my student and here you are," she rams her finger against my chest, "stammering like a kid-goat. You want bacon? Got to slaughter the pig. Who's bringing it home in your home? Sara maybe? Want her to do all the work? It may be wrong," she backs up, "but the real fact is that the perfect world is dead. They leave that out of the movies but the fairytales don't. The tail twisting is total — not just pretty. Grimy, gutsy, violence may scrape your fine, delicate, face ... Understand?" She curtsies sarcastically.

"I don't, Elsie," I stammer.

"Well?" She taps my head, leaning close. "It's not like Jack being sent off to fight the horrible giant, you know, for dear ol' Britain."

"Should I just crash in and say I'm a writer?"

"Crash?" Elsie opens her eyes wide like she's shocked, then pokes me in the chest again. "That's just the edge of graphic. You don't know anything about crash. I'm the white witch, right? You've been fantasizing that, like Jack did, saying Elsie do, Elsie be — but what about you doing something?

"Let's think a moment, okay?" She backs up again, glancing at the ceiling. "Yes, I see now. You think it all just happens. Well ... Hell, Jay ... it's not perfect. That's true. Let me see ... " She taps her foot, finger at her temple. "Yes. Dorothy?" She cranes her neck, peering at me, then asks: "Do you know why your shoes are ruby-red?"

"Me?" I ask, backing up.

"Yes," she snaps. "Isn't this Oz? Aren't you looking for Toto? Let me tell you something young man." She screams: "It's because the bloody house fell on my bloody sister. We're all family. All of us. And you're the sweetheart from Kansas who got her slippers, blood and all. But you can't get home without seeing the wizard and dirtying your fingers. Is he the wizard? Am I?"

"What do I say to him, Elsie?" I ask, backing toward the door, feeling like I'm being beaten away.

"That you have to save Toto because the Flying Monkeys got him ... And that, although she's a good witch, she's really pissed because your house fell on her sister and smashed all her blood into her shoes and ... " Breaking into laughter, Elsie chokes off the rest, no doubt because my mouth is hanging open.

"Honestly, Jay," she doubles up, holding her stomach, "you're so serious." Putting her hands on my shoulders, she adds: "I've put sandwiches, cheese and fruit in the basket. Sara's not Little Red Riding Hood," she crouches and turns swiftly, making her voice deep, "though she is ... " then winks, straightening again, and looking back to me, continues: "We are all characters in archetypal stories we're re-writing together." She smiles reassuringly. "Today's assignment is to go see Paladin. He's a knight in the old tradition. Then have a picnic. It's time the two of you talk. It's just that simple."

"Me and Paladin?" I ask.

She takes a deep breath. "You and Sara."

"What about Paladin?" I'm still confused.

She taps my forehead and looks up. "Can't find all the buttons this morning. Yes, okay." She looks back at me. "If he is for you, you'll know it. All of this makes sense, if it ever does, by looking back on it. But for now ... the way I figure, you can't look back if you don't first do it.

"Image the Sorcerer. 'I-Mage' is to 'Source-Her" ... er ... I mean." She glances up. "Yes, we'll talk about it later. But, for now," she focuses back to me, "there are certain 'mini-mal' demands on your time and mine. But just know," she chuckles, "I keep you busy so you won't waste time reflecting before the image I'm painting is done. So," she looks at Sara, "you better grab the basket."

Moving toward the door, I glance at John and Kathy. They seem totally confounded.

"And be back by three," Elsie appears on the porch stoop, spreading her arms like pleading with heaven as I open the trunk to put our basket in, "to help with the supper."

Driving toward Paladin's I'm uncertain what is happening to me. I don't know what Sara and the others are experiencing. Elsie was pushing me away and pulling me in at the same time. She has definitely put this into the frame of her multidimensional chess projects, partly related to my learning to write and making a connection with another writer. I don't know why I resisted. Dan said we should visit him.

But there is much more at stake here. Sara is concerned about Elsie, or my relationship to Elsie. She turned away last night when I tried to talk about it. This morning Elsie immediately started talking about long term commitments. But I don't know in what sense. I recognize that there is something wrong with just wanting to stay with Elsie. It's like I can't think for myself.

Parking our car on the sand shoulder opposite the lake, I dismiss my questions. Wanting to make the best of this meeting, we climb the stone steps through the trees toward the porch. Dark haired, shirt sleeves rolled up, a broad, benevolent smile on his face, Dan greets us: "Where have you been all week?"

"In town with a lady we met at the Jarvis workshop."

"And with a woman named Elsie," Sara adds as we step into the coolness of the big house, several children running past. I remember them playing in the yard and fishing across the road while we were at CRC, a lifetime ago.

"So," he points for us to sit, "how did you hook up with this Elsie?"

"It's quite a story." I hesitate.

"Did you know I'm working on a new novel?" He changes the subject.

"What's it about?" Sara asks.

"The struggle between extraterrestrial beings and the contemporary representatives of an ancient cult, called the Olympians, who were known as gods in the old myths but are in fact natives of this planet." He pauses, letting it sink in.

"The Olympians insist that Earth must develop from within herself, free of outside influences. The alien teachings are disguised as technological progress so normal humans, like us, you know," he raises his eyebrows, "accept them. Yet we are nervous because we see the beginnings of the catastrophes which result from exceeding the limits set by the Old Gods.

"We know that all this had been predicted in the ancient occult sciences and when we listen to the Olympians we feel the truth of their warnings. But we're skeptical because so many groups have believed the prophecies in the past. Yet nothing, too bad, ever happened."

"Who wins?" Sara asks.

"That's the conflict, of course." He nods. "Will we wake up in time to avert the disaster?" He glances at me.

"The risk is heightened because, like the disciples following the Crucifixion, even the Olympians assume that the Apocalypse is beyond their control. They know this is not simply a mining colony for other planets. We do have a unique responsibility here. Earth is in the balance. But in their despair, they almost wait too long before reacting."

"What do they do?" Sara pursues it.

"They prepare for the worst, or the best, depending on your viewpoint. And," he laughs introspectively, "try to keep one foot on the ground, so to speak. Fortunately, they do eventually engage the enemy in an all out showdown."

"One of Elsie's metaphors is about keeping one toe on the ground," I say, but I'm actually thinking about her urgent insistence that we be ready and willing to fight.

Looking puzzled, Dan says: "Which Elsie?"

"What do you mean?" I ask, surprised.

"Will says there are several mediums in the area who are called Elsie."

"Our Elsie lives at the Oasis," Sara interjects.

"The Oasis? Isn't that where Dr. Honigberger lives?"

"The scientist?" I'm uncertain how much to reveal. "Is he pretty well known around here?"

"I've heard he was a protegee of Dr. Hart, who was Mahdah Hart's husband, and of a group of other scientists who had centers here and in Florida. His wife, Sadie, is Cherokee."

Sara focuses us: "Do you know the Elsie we're talking about?"

"Not really." He pauses. "Ned and I have tried to distance CRC from the other groups in the area. So I've never paid much attention, but Will told me there's a cook at the Hart Retreat called Elsie." He chuckles.

"What do you know about Mahdah Hart?" I ask, a little uncomfortable.

"Just that she claims to work with her deceased husband. Actually that was the point of Will's story." He grins. "One evening an entity, speaking through the cook, claimed that he represented Dr. Hart and that Mahdah had to sell her place. According to Will, Mahdah really raised hell with him." His eyes twinkle with amusement. "That's an image, isn't it?"

Somewhat taken back, I say: "How do you feel about all that?"

"Like old Yeats," he grins, "I gather scraps for my story bag." He leans forward and pats my shoulder. "Want to see where I write?"

We follow Dan through large glass doors into a beautiful paneled library. Gazing out the window onto the lake, he asks what I've been working on.

"Poetry, mostly."

"There's no money in writing unless you get the pattern right." He turns back to us. "So, what do you think we can do together?"

"I really have no expectations. What are your plans?"

"After *The Olympians*, I don't know, but once you're bit, you can't stop." Putting his hand on my shoulder, he guides us back into the hallway.

"Are you going to stay with CRC?" I ask, feeling awkward again as we approach the front door.

"No. I'm more likely to be productive in the city. At least for now."
I feel a sadness in him and yet a will strong as steel. Eyes intense, he
adds: "Let's stay in touch."

"That went well." Sara seems relaxed and comfortable as we drive
away.

"Now we can picnic, Little Red Riding Hood," I say, half sarcastically. The experience with Paladin is forgotten as Elsie's ranting about
witches, Oz, and danger, combined with the sting of Sara turning
away last night, flood back to me, making me angry. Wanting to be
insistent, emphatic, or turn away myself, I add: "What about the
wolf?"

"Elsie was really tough on you this morning," hurt in her eyes, I
know she is trying to reach me, "but beyond all that I think she
simply meant for us to stop by Dan's and make contact, then just be
together. We need to talk. I'm sure that's why she set up this picnic."

Immediately sorry for my tone, I struggle to breathe regularly.
My anger starting to defuse, we pass the Sea Captain's lodge, then
turn right, following a side road weaving between pine trees and
stop in a meadow.

Pulling over, I want to hike up into the woods among the wild
flowers with Sara, knowing that our love is the only thing that will
never change. But I'm also determined to face the questions we
aborted last night even though, if I'm not careful, I could forever
jeopardize our relationship. I can't find an even keel.

Coming around the car, Sara takes my hands, and looks up into
my eyes. "You don't want to go home, but we have to."

Somebody is squeezing my heart. "That's not the way I understand it." I try to stay calm. "We could stay here, if we're strong
enough to hold the vision."

"Are you forgetting about last night?" She drops my hands. "Elsie
told us we're supposed to decide what's true. That includes deciding what is right for us."

"I'm just afraid you're not willing to consider our alternatives —
that, like the stragglers who come too late and find the door locked,
you've lost your nerve." I'm sincere, but felt an insane meanness in
myself as I said it, something that is self-destructive, destructive of us.

"You don't get it, do you?" Sara is angry now. "Because it's sunny and we're together, you think this is all that exists. But it isn't." She tightens. "If you're so committed to staying," I feel a bite in her voice, "make sense. Do we drop out of school? How do we make money? What's real?" Tears form in her eyes.

"I love Elsie, too." She searches me. "And I know our lives have been immensely enriched by her love. But we can't stay here. Not now. Not until we've figured things out. It's like you're blinded to the obvious." She walks away.

Following her, knowing she is scared and hurt, I search for words, but feel myself slipping between different personalities which I can't control. I can't hold the picture of what is happening to me. I know she understands something which I'm missing. But I won't acknowledge it. I have to win. Stopping and turning back to me, she says:

"Elsie is full of wonderful, but also weird stuff, and I just think ..." She takes my hands.

"I know," I soften, "but I don't want to screw anything up. I just know you can't go back to ordinary life once you've had these experiences."

"Yes," she leans back, looking at me, "but we'll always be on the path. We're changed by these experiences. But this isn't our home." Releasing me, she spreads the blanket and then our food. Settling down, I try another tack.

"According to Elsie, magicians seed certain points in the space-time continuum. I think that's what she's been doing, to make us grow."

Thinking a moment, Sara speaks carefully: "A lot of Elsie's instructions have been about holding images in order to precipitate material forms. But she said it's critical that we not 'image' anything that we don't want — because it's our responsibility once we create it."

She hesitates. "She means it when she says not to accept everything, and that she doesn't want you just following her around. She's not like that." In the silence I hear snatches of Elsie screaming at me, tearing apart ideas I thought I had understood, but I say:

"You're simply not willing to accept the complexities of dealing with her."

"Not on your terms," Sara fires back.

"But I'm talking about meaning and value ... what drives our lives."

"So am I." She is exasperated. "What's your point?"

"That what's true at one level," I search for a connection, "is not always true at another."

"I don't disagree," Sara pauses, "but we have to make choices. We have to check things out for ourselves."

"That's right," I concede, "but she's teaching us that our ideas are too limited, that we have to read more complex patterns and see how they relate from various levels."

"And?"

"Pieces in this game are also pieces in other games which are going on simultaneously. From the perspective of other levels a 'wrong' move here could be the best possible move in terms of our further progress. Elsie intends to stretch us, to show us new possibilities."

Sara stands. "All I know is that it's not the right time to make a permanent decision. Elsie is saying to me — go home, let it settle, decide what's right for us. She's telling Kathy the same thing about Larry."

Re-packing the basket, Sara moves to the car. Following her, I feel she is slipping away. Turning to me as I get in the driver's side, she says: "Will you listen?"

"Sure." I feel a fist in my stomach.

"We have to go back to Elsie's now and act like everything is okay." She takes a deep breath. "I love you and believe that we'll get back on the same track; but there is something terribly wrong with how you're reacting. You're not thinking for yourself and you're not yourself. Elsie has told me that, and that I have to figure out how to get you back."

Turning away, she is unwilling to meet my eyes. Driving past CRC, I hear Ned O'Riley, as if he's talking to me: "Elsie is a sorcerer — a black witch. All she wants is to control your soul. She'll say all the right things to keep you in her power. All her shenanigans are props to convince you she's innocent, to set you up to make the decision to serve her and to abandon Sara."

"No," I speak out loud, startling Sara.

"What?" She glances at me.

"You're not saying Elsie is bad, or evil. You're saying she's trying to help me."

"Yes." She turns away again.

"She's the Teacher I've waited for," I whisper inwardly. "She's breaking my boundaries. She has given me so much. If I stay with her I'll grow faster. She loves me. Sara doesn't understand."

"She loves having you love her," O'Riley's voice interrupts me again. "It's all a counterfeit to make you lose yourself. She's giving you just enough truth so that you'll serve her. She wants it to be your own choice, against her advice, so you can't blame her. She's brilliant and evil."

"She's trying to help me," I insist, realizing that's what Sara said, but from a different angle.

"Part of her, perhaps," O'Riley's voice relents slightly. We're passing the turn-off to the rehab center. I reach across to touch Sara's arm, to break her silence. "What about Jack?" I ask, wanting her help. "He was devoted to Elsie?"

"What about Jack?" Sara looks at me like she can't believe what I just said.

Questions and Answers

Kathy is sitting on the tree stump near Elsie's door. Larry and John are talking intensely at the far edge of the garden, Larry explaining something with arm movements. Elsie doesn't seem to be around.

Looking up, Kathy says: "How did it go?"

Sara shrugs. "How about you?"

"Elsie was full of it this morning, wasn't she?" Kathy holds her hands up like not knowing what else to say. "After lunch, she sent John and me to the Hart Retreat. A lady was doing past life portraits. Wish I had volunteered. I could use some insight."

Seeing a match light behind the screen, I walk to the door. "There are a few things they want to say to you. Was I right about Paladin?"

"Yes," I answer slightly apprehensive, and enter the house.

She smells of carnations. Gold and silver bracelets dangle from her arm. "You can go sideways too long. Hear what Sara is saying, too." She points for me to sit opposite her at the little table.

"See the levels, the four directions, plus up and down, in and out. The center point spins but never moves. That's nine levels, connect them. Remember, I'm working with twelve."

She raises a glass to the window. Returning it to the table, it's full of sun dancing with ice, sparkling. "Fire and water, Sara and you are ... Ram and Crab by sun signs. Look at everything invisible."

As bird songs float toward us, she whispers: "I'm the nightingale separated from the rose. Song pours from me like a waterfall. The individual songs, the notes, dance, cascade, swirl, and are gone."

She swirls the ice again. "You and Sara are potent seeds, chymical fire and water. Astrologers warn against it, but you must fuse the elements, meld the metals, transform each stage from first matter into purest gold."

"How?" I ask, feeling stupid.

"Start with your birth sign, Jay. Kepler had it: soul light fixed, a crystal moment which moves through time." She rolls the ice again. "Cancer, from the sea crab, the home, yin/yang, female/male 69 ... See the code? Plato's separated twin soul, water seeking fire. This is 1969. See it reversed. What of 1996, back to back, facing out, one life, death, and resurrection from now, four years from the big bang? From the Millennium! What then?"

She makes big eyes. "Mr. Hardshell, you've got to use the brains in your heart ... Quick! Do something while there's still time!"

"What?"

"Follow up with Paladin, for instance. He's witty. Doesn't take himself too seriously." She slows down, seems to settle. Looking at me caringly, as if just back from somewhere and noticing me for the first time, she continues: "He's open to a tremendous stream which will work through him, in fact, already is." She taps the table then sits down. "We can set it up, if you really want to write, but you have to find the balance and choose. You have many possibilities."

"I want to make the right choices."

Standing, her eyes blazing dark now, her tone masculine and accusatory: "You believe you should never take anything."

"I don't want to violate anyone's boundaries." Memories of Jack and Larry, and something having gone wrong, flood into me. I stand. "And I don't want anyone to violate mine."

"You think you can reject what Elsie gives you — bits and pieces of her self! Then you don't understand. Gifts that you have already accepted," the last six words are emphatic, "must be paid for by actions. Work by indirection!"

Elsie staggers slightly. "I need some air." She pushes me to move so she can sit by the window. Taking a deep breath, she leans forward pointing at the floor, muttering: "Don't mention the harp. I've already told the others." She raises her voice: "Put the incense out, would you?"

Shocked, I weave toward the sandalwood scent which is pungently intense. When I return with another chair, she pats my knee. "That guy is good, but abrupt. Sometimes it's like I'm burning inside. And he doesn't like dresses. He likes pants and wants to have a big sword at his side." She chuckles then focuses on me. "He wants you to know that we can't lay it out unless you're willing to steal it."

"I thought we had to pay," I respond, confused.

"It's almost like stealing ... at these prices."She looks around, then relights her cigarette. "Anyway, what was your concern, dear. I'm sorry. I'm not quite centered, yet."

"Well ..." Vaguely aware that I've been scolded for even thinking about Jack, I stifle the thought this time and try to think of something else. "Paladin told us that Mahdah Hart really got after some entity who was talking through Elsie, the cook. I wondered about that."

"None of your business," comes through, loud and gruff. Elsie stands up and hurries outside. Through the screen, I see her stamping her feet in the dirt. Pushing back in, she says: "I know what's coming through, but can't censor. That's why the authority must be here." She points at me, reseats herself and leaning forward, indicates I should scoot closer.

"Some things I want to say, I can't say. Be patient. Try to be open, without losing yourself. Just wait. There's a lot in store and," she glances outside, "we can not afford to be indiscriminate as we approach the change over."

"Change over?" I ask.

"The great pancake flip." She gestures in the air like a cosmic cook. "In the twinkling of an eye, while we sleep on the roof tops, a thief steals through the night and the whole world is changed." She pauses. "Some of us are already living in the new world ... and ... somebody has to pay. We do that for each other. But, I'm tired. And if you are not willing to steal it, I can't keep putting it out."

Clapping her hands, Elsie changes the mood as the others file in. "Tomorrow is big, for our guest," she points at Larry, "is done with class and is free to help here and to be helped by our other guests." She grins infectiously. "And old Mr. Lawrence, of course, is tired and beat-up with studies. So maybe he will be asked to a healing. Just payment for what he's already done for us, to turn his hands new born and fingers smooth as hounds' teeth."

Calling us close, leaning forward, she whispers: "Larry has to take it seriously. They listen through him." She winks. "So ... check with Jay about what I said."

Raising her voice, she backs up with a flourish. "Now for the cooking: Kathy, potatoes, please. Slap and slice them with carrots and nuts. Sara, my dear," she curtsies and Sara responds, "will you do the salad with vinegar and oil? And my good lad," she turns to me, "practice the Taoist blade trick with pork. You remember, don't you? Not a molecule disturbed. Warm it first, of course, and you, too, John, with the bread, while Mr. Lawrence practices a superior super-vision. Lead and be led, I say, then," she claps, "be fed."

Pointing at the fridge, she skips into the workroom and then sweeps back through the door with a big straw-broom, as if she's with a dance partner, a feather duster, like a sword, thrust through her apron belt. "Tomorrow's the big meeting, you know. So we clean-up and practice today!"

Catching the broom as it starts to tilt sideways, she whips out the feather-duster and in a series of deft strokes fans the shelves, cupboard doors, counter, tables, all of us standing back and watching, trying to stay out of her way, singing and whistling as she goes.

"Fie on the Englishman, you know?" She straightens her back. "He needs such exquisite care." She squeezes the words out the side of her mouth, raising the tone. Tossing the feather duster to Kathy, raising one leg, then the other, she stomps out of the room like a giantess.

"The Englishman?" John glances at Larry.

"Jack? And the Bean Stock." Larry pauses, puzzling a second, then quietly recites: "'Be he alive or be he dead, I'll grind his bones to make my bread.'"

"Now you're cooking, Larry." Elsie bolts back into the room. "'Got to be nimble. Got to be quick.'" She points at the table. "One, two, three ... The man climbed up the tree. Finding a world both green and curled, the atom's light, the glorious night, singing a song he whirled."

A smile on her face, Elsie bows low, her jade necklace dangling forward. Then, instead of leaving the room, she pulls her chair over. "Go on. Eat. And while you do, this is my chance to talk to you. Sree Thakur," she points at the food, "whom we'll discuss later, knew, even as a child, that no two things are ever identical. So one and one are two ones. And, yet, the giantess and Jack contain each other."

While we pass the food around, Elsie says: "There's a yearning in your heart — all of your hearts. We've seen certain things, had certain adventures. Your brains are filled-up but your hearts know we've just skirted the edge of something really important. This is our chance to talk straight. So let's do some questions and answers."

When no one responds, as if to reassure us, she says: "This is the old me with a few simple lessons. Just accept that. Tomorrow we feed Mahdah's crew, then you can visit the Retreat for a full tour and get a treatment for Larry."

"Great." Larry nods appreciatively.

"Then, before you go, Saturday or Sunday, if you go," she glances at me, "you must go to the waterfall where I bathe, because all of my sisters will assist you there. What you image there, with our help, literally will be what you'll get. So be cheerful but be careful and think clearly because the consequences of wrong imaging, in a set up like what we will do then, can be horrendous. So I have to know, tonight, whether you're ready. Your choice.

"At the waterfall we will join you, give you a boost. So," she tilts her head and smiles coyly as she settles back onto her chair, "just to have a practice run," she scans the table, "what do you want to do, with your life, Kathy?"

Laying her fork down, Kathy says: "Art."

"Your vision is clear, your heart strong." Elsie focuses on her approvingly. "You'll need to watch the landscape, how things grow, take your time. People will love the beauty which you produce. You might work with stones, as well, and silk-screens, meticulous layer over layer, building up the composition. You'll need to spend time in the wilderness, and among the pueblos, because you're connected there."

"What about me?" Larry asks, apparently pleased to be included in one of Elsie's group exchanges.

"You may not relish this, but all of us face things that are not easy. You have the power to control great fortunes. Even now there are funds set aside for you in trust in New York, Philadelphia, and Boston."

"I don't want money." Larry pushes his plate away.

Smiling, Elsie says: "Like I said, you don't relish this, because money can be so easily abused. You know about that and about yourself and consequently you hold back. Jay, on the other hand, can handle funds."

She turns to me. "You're frightened, too. But for different reasons. You're trained to it, but resist. The point is to find your proper relationships, here in matter. When you arrived, I already knew what you brought to us, what was likely to develop. We've done this together before. Once in Egypt." She points at Sara. "Don't you remember me?"

"Yes." Sara hesitates. "But I don't know how."

"It's only by following certain rules that we can make sense of it. I'm Elsie. You're Sara. I remember more consciously, so I'm connected to other events which proceed according to another set of rules. Those rules can apply here as well," she smiles, "so long as we don't blow it up.

"What I'm doing," she pauses, "is poking you, each of you in different ways, then, when I've got your attention, I pull the veil back a little. I couldn't be here without you. You are me, in all the permutations of your relationships. By our combinations we define and express each other."

"What will all this mean once we're home?" Sara asks.

"I am with you so long as you remember."

John says: "I can hardly remember yesterday."

"What you'll remember, at first, will be putting the shade up and down." Turning to me, she adds: "And you'll remember the importance of the flags."

"What is your highest teaching?" Larry asks.

"I already told the others." She smiles affectionately. "I'm a Quaker girl. Sara and I are goose girls, match girls, lighting fires, herding the little ones toward safety, holding the dark back, accepting the dark. All I know is the Perpetual Practice of the Presence of the God-Goddess in us."

"What about the bad guys?" John asks.

Elsie walks into the workroom and returns with the picture of her husband lighting the cigarette with his finger. "He fights them. He guards the gaps by which they enter."

"Do they attack you?" Larry asks.

"I can't be this open without taking the chance they'll enter." She props his picture against the wall. "So," she turns around, "I give you certain talismans which ground you to the work we do. It's what we've always done but you may be just now starting to remember. Or you may not remember for years. But take something of me, if you want to." She disappears into the workroom.

By the time she returns we have finished our food, cleaned up, and are waiting at the table.

"You have Thoreau, don't you," she looks to me, "from Highlands." I nod. "Read that," she adds, "with Emerson's 'On Compensation' — the best treatise in English on karma."

Scanning the others, she says: "*Ockham's Razor* and *Ocean in a Tea Cup* — here's a new combination for you." She lays both books on the table. "What are they about? Good question." She straightens up, ready to address us.

"Ockham is the master of parsimony — that is, founder of good practice in science — an English pastoral theologian of the 14th Century. And this is," she pats the book, "about minimal surfaces and bubbles, worlds interpenetrating, the periodic universe, and indeterminacy.

"The title," she holds up *Ocean in a Teacup*, "says it all about Sree Sree Thakur Anukul Chandra, a great Bengali doctor and mystic, a Kirtan dancer, and everything else." She grins. "I ghost wrote it for a lovely couple. One and one, alchemical correspondences, remember?" She nods. "Also, I suggest that you read Isaac Asimov. We use him. Everything he writes is informative."

"He's no spiritualist," Larry comments.

"Doesn't need to be. Never," she stamps her foot down hard, "never accept anything you can't verify for yourself."

After a moment, Larry asks: "You work with the White Brotherhood, don't you?"

"The White Lodge," Elsie corrects him. "They contact me. They work through me. They use this." She touches her body. "Again, how do you know whether what I am saying is true?"

"When it works, and not otherwise," Larry answers.

"Ultimately," Elsie walks over and puts her hands on Larry's shoulders and moving her eyes across Kathy, John, Sara and me, says: "you learn to identify yourself, what you really are, which will take the form of a living crystal. You are a light who can see through that crystal. You hold it up against the impulse which approaches. If it matches you can accept it. If it doesn't, then that which approaches is not true, or is too dangerous, and you should reject it."

"Can you tell the difference?" Larry asks.

"Not for you." She walks back to the window. "I've given up something. I'm old, tired, and doing all I can."

"You're not old," Sara says, almost pleading.

Elsie smiles in appreciation, then goes on: "In this body, now, I'm like a receptor set. If I step back, information from other galaxies can come through. But if I hold it, and judge it, it stops. The Sisterhood protects me, and Vern protects me. But this week, with the five of you, someone else is here who is greater than myself."

Elsie turns to the window before looking back to us. "Your love protects me and through me protects the guest." She smiles. "I'm burned but not consumed by what comes through. The bad guys tear me, but I recover." She takes a white apron from the peg and wraps it around her middle. "I keep cooking. I keep feeding kids like you because the hope of the world rests with you."

"But if the world isn't real?" I ask.

"Oh, it's real." She enunciates each word. "Don't ever doubt that."

"It's a stage and we make the rules," Larry summarizes.

"You can change your role," Elsie corrects him. "You can experience levels beyond those most people are prepared to recognize. But the rules are set. They apply to the role. You can change the role, not the rule. Most people live just within a narrow spectrum, one weighted with stones. What we're doing is pushing the stones up. Lighting matches in the cave. Dancing with the shadows. Finding the light in the dark. You challenged Isaac Asimov?" She sits.

"I-seek As-I-Move. See the code? We use him because he doesn't bullshit. Like using comic books, or operator's manuals. Remember why?" She looks at me.

"Because the channels aren't cluttered."

"Not exactly." Elsie rolls up her sleeves. "All channels are cluttered. All lines carry layers of information, cluttered by noise. We use the ugly ducklings because no one else looks there: advertisements, truck panels, cookbooks, science fiction, fairytales and fantasy. We don't have to worry about the pretenders who read, even write, treatises on magic — screwing everything up. That's their nasty business, of course." She doubles her fist. "Anyway," she sighs, "we use the ugly ducklings. Do you know why? Because while other's think they're ducks, we know they're swans who carry the light. So we're keeping it light, tonight, right? But ..." She starts marching.

Startled by thunder, I glance out the screen door. Sheets of rain fall through dark air while Elsie circles, swinging her arms up and down now as if crashing cymbals together, creating the thunder, grinning at us.

"Whoa, partner ..." she slides a horse to a stop by pulling back on the reins, then turns to Larry who is laughing, delighted with her display, "are you ever glad to be out of class. Am I right?" She taps him affectionately as the rain stops and the sky streaks yellow and red over the forest. "Talk to Karin tonight. Be here by 9:00 tomorrow." Smiling at him, she turns to the rest of us: "Run along now. Shoo ... " She flips her fingers out like herding mice from her kitchen.

Remembering

Driving through Tiger to Clayton, each of us absorbed in our own thoughts, we seem to be the only life forms along the darkened and now quiet road.

Approaching Karin's, I think of all she has been through in order to facilitate this time for us and hope we'll be able to talk tonight. I need to get a handle on what has happened.

"How was your day?" Dressed in jeans and a frilly shirt, still wearing earrings, looking tired but pleased, she greets us at the front door. "I know it's too complex to say all at once." She runs her hand back through her hair and, pointing to the tea pot and cups on the low table in the living room, adds: "But at least we can try. Okay?"

"Absolutely." Larry takes a cup and, his mustache wet from his first sip, settles back against the big overstuffed chair. Kathy, long dark hair wound and held behind her head by a leather clasp, loose strands falling around her ears, kicking her sandals off, joins him. Glancing at Sara, I imagine all four of us back in Manhattan, working on *Outlet*.

While John, Sara, and I get tea and arrange ourselves on the floor, Karin says: "From the moment I first met Elsie, I knew this was an experiment. It's been tough in some ways; but we're doing pretty well, overall. Don't you think?"

"My finger's in the wall socket." John shakes his head. "I like it, but I'm not sure how long I can last. Honestly," he blows out while pushing his wire-rims up on his nose, "I feel like a ball hooked to a paddle by a long rubber band."

"And Elsie's the paddle?" I salute, knowing the answer.

Puffing his cheeks, big eyed, holding his own ponytail from behind, he nods then grins. Karin laughs and pats his shoulder before shifting down in front of the couch. Turning to Larry, she says: "So what happened today?"

"After explaining our assignments for tomorrow, she sent us home to talk to you." He pulls the autoharp, still in it's case, from beside the chair and places it in the center of the room. "I finished my class today. New role. New opportunities, I hope. How about you?"

"I'm doing better."

"What about Atlanta?" John asks.

"My concentration there has been necessary in order to allow certain things to happen here." Leaning against the couch, she looks back to Larry. "And because of Jack."

"I know." Larry nods. "And I think I understand what happened. According to Will, who works at CRC," he glances at me, "there's an underground system dating back to Atlantis, which was discovered by Dr. Hart and the other scientists who built occult laboratories here."

"Actually, there's a whole web-work of etheric tunnels through these mountains," Karin refills her cup, "connected to the center in Atlanta."

"That makes sense." Larry pauses. "I've been trying to figure it out, but couldn't get the image until ..."

"What?" Karin asks.

"On the way home tonight," he thinks a moment, "I got a very precise impression that the monument, which we've all seen outside of town, marks the point where a tunnel or cave is accessible. And that, in effect, Jack had been captured there, or part of him."

"You mean literally?" John asks.

"Literally," Larry responds, "but not materially. On the physical level, he probably is working for the Order of Melchizedek; but like you said," he glances back at Karin, "it's not the true Order."

"By literally," Karin pauses, "you mean astrally?"

"As Elsie says, sometimes you laugh at the devil," he glances at Kathy, "sometimes you just stay calm. I've been trying to stay calm. But if I've got it right, his emotional self had been free floating and scared. I saw him jumping on your back, like a monkey, so you could carry him home, and that it had to do with getting out of the tunnels."

"Elsie sent me out to fetch back the parts." Karin nods thoughtfully. "When did you first sense him?"

"The second night, between CRC and Elsie's. I was caught in a horrendous storm and went into the woods. Somehow I found the monument and went into it. There was a lot of strange stuff going on." He glances at me. "Remember?"

"It was real spooky," I answer and look to Sara.

"It was," Larry says and looks back to Karin. "Basically, I think Elsie used us like lightning rods. Me to distract the bad guys and then Jay to pull me out. You were grounding Jack, spiritually, right? Or out to do that?"

"Attempting to." Karin pauses. "Go on."

"I think Elsie had already caught his memory, part of his mental body, and linked it to his harp." Larry glances at Kathy. "Those are the kinds of levels she's working on and it's pretty amazing." He turns back to Karin. "Anyway, eventually his astral body rode you home so Elsie could ..."

"Put him back together again." Karin completes his thought. "What do you think, Kathy?"

"Maybe that's not so crazy." Kathy sets her cup down. "During shamanic warfare the object is to take the other shaman's medicine pouch because it contains his initiatory talisman. Given the types of things Elsie has done ..."

"Jack, or part of his power, could be deposited in the autoharp." Karin nods and turns back to Larry. "Do you feel that the openings between the worlds are closing?"

"Shifting." Larry pauses. "When I find the monument, it might be absolutely ordinary, just like it would be for anyone travelling through here with no connection to Elsie."

"So you think Elsie is manipulating the gaps?" I ask.

"Partly," Larry turns to me. "And partly it's that this has been an extremely potent time for magical operations, the moon shot and all." He pours himself more tea.

"What about Jack, then?" I ask.

"Karin was the stabilizer and I'm the keeper for him." He pulls the autoharp closer. "I hope he's safe now."

"What if he isn't?" John asks, obviously concerned.

"Nothing important is easy. You might not realize that Jack was already injured, psychically, before Elsie started working with him." Karin stands like she's ready to go to her room. "We've all had to do our part, but we should recognize that Elsie is the one who has really taken the heat. I don't want this to sound wrong, but what the rest of us have been doing is minor compared to her efforts."

"I totally agree. One other thing, Karin." Larry holds up his hand. "Would you tell us about your book?"

"Sure, but just a quick summary." Karin smiles as the rest of us, eager to have an explanation, re-settle ourselves.

"When you get through all the data, it's really about memory and language." She thinks a moment before continuing:

"Language holds the key to a dimension of memory, a re-membering, a putting the pieces back together so that they not only make sense but are changed. The meaning is richer and improved. It's a text book for understanding the changes which are going on now, and the shift in consciousness which is now possible, and a warning against going wrong."

"How to re-make history?" I interject as she pauses.

"It's about history, and the role of the Western Mystery Tradition — about planetary initiation." Her glance flows around our circle. "We're at a cross-roads. The war in Vietnam is tragic in a way which is unprecedented."

"Aren't all wars insane?" Kathy comments.

"There's a difference." Karin pauses. "World War I was territo-rial, like the old wars. Then we had to fight Hitler. Some knew that the negative magicians were behind him, but most wanted to deny that — still do. Anyway, when Japan attacked us, we finally re-sponded. The Korean war spun out of that. But Vietnam," she takes a deep breath, "withdrawing from Vietnam — which will happen — won't heal the wounds of the people who had to fight and suffer without justification.

"The politicians move the pieces around on the table, but the unity of purpose which had held this country together has been spoiled. Until that is remembered, actually reassembled, new alliances struck and old wounds healed, the kids of your generation will be living in the world which is struggling to move forward while the older gen-erations, to the extent they hold to the former path, will be living in a world which is disappearing but can still wreak terrible damage."

She holds her breath a second. "Anyway, that's what I was writ-ing about, as background, even before the Teacher sent me here to learn more about the higher orders, particularly the Sacred Lodge. And that's where Elsie comes in."

"How so?" Kathy asks.

"I think that's a big part of her work." Karin studies us before going on. "She refers to esoteric orders, visible and invisible, High Masons, Templars, the Followers of Melchizedek and Melchizedea, and points out the obvious — that what they call themselves doesn't guarantee who they are.

"And, more fundamentally, that accepting anything on someone else's authority is a mistake. We have to think for ourselves." She holds her hands up. "So that's it."

"What about your painting?" Sara asks.

"I think I've had better success," Karin smiles at Sara, "expressing myself in simple images,"

"Profound images," Kathy corrects her. "Let me get it." Returning with the painting, Kathy turns it toward us as Karin, wholly serious but almost shyly, says:

"Those are the stages I believe we're going through. It's called 'The Stairway to Initiation.'" She leaves us facing the painting propped against a chair.

Amazed by the precision and vividness of the oils, I am drawn up the seven steps: ruby, amber, gold, tourmaline, turquoise, sapphire, and amethyst. From the floor to the pinnacle on which a silver winged, hawk-headed entity waits beneath the angels of the ceiling, crystal light flooding the chamber, I know with absolute certainty that the painting represents the technology of initiation, an image of what we have been experiencing.

And I also realize that I've seen it somewhere before, in a dream, perhaps, or in a vision when I first became aware of Karin and knew, somehow, that we would be working with her. And that all my struggles, with Elsie, with Sara, with the threat of the Black Hats, with whether to go home or stay here, have to do with the transformation of my self.

Feeding the Guests

Larry knocks on our door, his voice gravelly and excited: "You guys need to get moving. Elsie said to be there early."

"Go away, Larry," Sara mutters, rolling toward me and checking the clock. "It's just 7:00, what's his hurry?"

"First day without class." I kiss her on the forehead. "He's eager." Cuddling together, we fall back asleep.

Leaving Clayton, John asks about the monument. The sky is clear, the air fresh around us. "Next curve on the left," Larry says; but when I slow for the curve, two kids in a car honk from behind, wanting us to speed up. Craning out the side to the right, he concludes: "I can't see it."

"Is that good?" John asks.

"I think so." Larry shifts back in the seat. "If the tunnels are closed, we shouldn't have to worry about Jack."

The sun shining around her, wearing a light blue smock with her white apron, Elsie waves from the door. She's smiling.

A man in a hat, like the one John is wearing, and overalls, carrying a rake, disappears into the woods. Steam rises from the compost heap. Bright red tomatoes, green, orange, and yellow squash sparkle with dew. Black and blue berries glisten in bushes behind which several dwarf fruit trees form a semi-circle.

"It's so different this morning, Elsie." As I approach, her blue eyes welcome me.

"Every day is different. Watch your head now." She points to the door lintel. The scent of fruit pies, still hot, rises from the window sill. My mouth waters.

"Had to put the cats out." She nods. "You haven't seen them? Aren't they familiar?" Cat-like, she paws at me. "How many levels are you playing?" I back up. "Don't worry." She bobs her head from side to side and laughs.

From the corner of my eye I see Larry and Kathy moving toward the workroom, carrying cups, John following.

Taking a half-burned cigarette from the tray, Elsie sits, then giggles, eyes on me: "We really should talk more, with you and Sara." Sara slides into the chair next to her. "What do you want to do with your life, dear?"

Apparently having carefully considered it, Sara says: "I want to work with nature, be a good mother, teach."

"You'll do all that." Elsie extends her arm around Sara. "And much more, but you're not quite ready to admit it."

"I don't know, Elsie." Sara seems shy, innocent.

"There's a quality you have, like me. We're caught with a knowledge which can't be expressed in words." Sara's eyes are down, elbows on her knees, watching the floor. "We're holding on, but we're desperate, right? It's like we're being pulled apart, like we're falling behind, and we can't let go. But we must let go. It's a pain and a struggle because you don't accept who you are and what you can do."

"What can I do?" Sara searches Elsie with her eyes.

"Whatever you set out to do." Elsie brushes her hands over Sara's head, then, with her fingers at the back of her neck, thumbs under her chin, holds her face up. "You carry the Virgin who, even though a crone, is always young. You can heal by your touch. But let it go, Sara. Don't hold what you relieve in other people. It's a great gift; but you must give it. When you try to figure it out, you hold what they had. Give it. Let it go."

Lighting her cigarette, she blows smoke over Sara's head. "Breathe out, Sara. Don't hold it. What flows from them to you will flow out; but you must ground yourself in water, in fresh air, in movement, in working with plants, in walking on the earth — WITH BREATH-ING. The earth will absorb what you take in, if you breathe out. Let it go.

"And," she pauses, "you grasp when all you need to do is accept. Keep your arms open, your shoulders back, your head high, your palms facing the world."

Stepping back, Elsie spreads her palms. "See these fingers?" she asks. "Hold yours to mine." Sara touches palms with her, short little fingers mirroring each other. "See what we've lost. See what we've gained. Now, make a list, and follow it. Start nothing you won't complete. Avoid fear. Don't judge yourself. Avoid the rubble of always questioning, always second guessing what you know. Like me, you can be eaten up and still find yourself."

Sara looks up. "But what about Jay?"

"The two of you are like a lock, a pattern which can help others. You've done it before. But your struggles, and his, are separate. Don't accept his, or anyone else's. Just know that if you are open ... " She holds her hand up, spread. "Not closed." She forms a fist, then opens it. "Whatever Jay faces, he will always come back."

"Won't we stay together?"

"You can be together, here." She puts her palm over her chest. "Fear is the only thing which can stop you. Fear is an illusion, but it has such power. And he has fear. He fears you will let go. You fear he will go on. Just remember, you are the butterfly."

Looking to me, Elsie says: "And you know she is. And you're scared."

"I am, Elsie." I lean forward, watching the floor like Sara had been. Putting her hand on my shoulder, she leans close to my ear. "What are you going to do?"

"I just want to serve you." My heart aches.

"No one serves me," she whispers, voice harsh. "Wake up, Jay. You're dreaming again."

"What can I do?"

"You have to pay the world. If you don't want to be a flyer, then be a lawyer. You have to serve the world. Then die. Let love transform you. The world is changing — but it's still a stage. Read Whitehead's conversations with Lucien Price." She thumps me. "The formal stuff's good, but get to the man, understand how he got there."

Taking a breath, Elsie turns to Sara. "He's willing to work. His dad, and his mom, gave him that, but his discipline might drive you crazy, because he hides in it. He's on a tight rope." She smiles. "But he's a good heart."

"I want him to write," Sara states forcefully.

"Once he's paid back, sure." She strikes a match and blows on it while studying the ceiling. "Yes," she nods, looking back to Sara, "someone is saying he's to re-write Steiner. Each generation, you know," she turns to me, "has to have it in new language. You have a particular assignment."

She stands and takes the mop, swishing it back and forth across the floor. I see her as a God-mother, white witch with a broom, in a pointed blue hat, with a big brim. She laughs playfully, like she's caught my image.

"It's from here," she lays the mop aside, points at my throat with both hands, spreading one up and the other down, then collapsing them to the center again, "where the mind and heart meet in the struggle with words. Remember I said I would help and ..." She glances up. "Yes. You need another ring, one from the black forest where my sisters live.

"Close your eyes." She holds a box of stones in front of me while I pick a dark green moss agate. "Put silver with it. While it's here," she touches the ring finger on my right hand, "you speak for me."

Feeling her words deeply, conscious that I will never forget, I say:"I want to stay here, Elsie. I can learn from you and help you. I can pay back here."

"Now, Sara," she turns away, "pick a rubbing stone that connects you and Jay." Sara scans her hand over the stones and selects a larger, lapis-blue, streaked agate.

Elsie nods. "Life moves in it when you touch it. Watch it change. It grows as you and Jay grow. Share it between you." Then, standing, she calls to Larry, Kathy, and John. "You have your stones?" Coming through the door, all three hold up small agates. "And you have your personal one, Sara?"

Sara digs in her pocket and pulls out a light blue agate.

"So," hands on her hips, feet spread, she runs her eyes up and down each of us as in a military drill, "let's get to work and make sure that everything goes smoothly. But one secret, troops." She clicks her heels, back straight, head high. "In the Himalayas, we provide yak stew, spiced with herbs from China, just the right sauce, deep rich bread — vodka. Gourmet. But this is Georgia, right?"

Everyone nods.

"So we make stewed chicken, lots of mushrooms, onions, toma-toes, celery. Sara's in charge of the salad and bread with real butter." She points to the oven. "It's ready to come out now." I realize I've been smelling it all along, mixed with the pies which have been cooling in the window. "Jay, you set the tables. Larry and John, give the wood a quick scrubbing. We have an hour and a half, so don't tarry."

"Right," Larry responds.

I realize I've been hearing verbal directions but seeing an entire flow, how these events curve into Mahdah and her guests coming, how everything will get done, how we'll behave.

"Good." Elsie turns to me. "Because it is very important that we treat our guests properly. I work for them, you know. This is their place." She spreads her arms. "This is my privilege." She turns to Sara. "You'll make noodles, okay? A big bowl we can set the chicken in, and, all of you: feel free to visit with them. Answer any questions they ask. But if they don't see you, or don't seem to, just do your jobs. You can eat afterwards. And John," she nods at him, "help Jay with the tables. They're under the back porch. Clean them. Also the folding chairs. We're going to open this up." She gestures around the room. "You'll put flowers on each of the tables, won't you, Kathy?"

"Sure." Kathy smiles. "How many guests?"

"Depends on how many are embodied. Set for thirteen."

Cocking her thumb back toward the workroom, she adds: "Got it?" Then, in the silence, fresh bread, pies, the woodlands in sun, bird songs floating through the window, she backs past me, leaving us alone to slide into our assignments.

Standing in the door from the workroom, dressed in purple now, jade necklace, earrings, and perfumed, Elsie looks the perfect hostess. She inspects our work. "Ockham's Razor," she puts her cigarette out, "is science in the kitchen as well as the laboratory."

Taking her apron off, she walks to the stove for one last stir, smelling then tasting the chicken, adding a variety of herbs and spices to it. "Yes," she turns to us like we're the staff readying ourselves for a grand event, "it's alchemy — fundamental alchemy. The spirit in which you approach cooking is critical."

Signaling Sara and Kathy to bring the serving bowls, they put the chicken with mushroom and vegetable sauce over a plate of noodles, garnish the sides with parsley and black pepper, then fill bowls with a green spinach salad. Displaying each in turn along the counter, they present an elegant buffet.

Standing back to survey it, noting the table settings and salads, Elsie signals Larry to ice the wine bottles sitting on the counter and John to fill the glasses with water. "Leave a pitcher on the tables," she says. "Refill it when it's low, but let them handle their own glasses. This isn't the Hilton." She laughs, pleased.

"Color, arrangement, rhythm, smell, lighting," she claps while turning in a circle, sounding like a cinematographer, "all are equally important. Ockham's Razor requires that we use the least number of assumptions sufficient to explain a phenomenon. Likewise, in the laboratory, the least number of variables to accomplish the goal."

The room is transformed, the effect splendid. For over an hour we've worked in perfect synchrony. We're happy. We look fresh, excited, focused, clean.

Elsie lights a cigarette. "They want to talk about elementals."

"Nature spirits?" Larry asks.

"Salamanders, crickets, butterflies." She sends a smoke curl into the center of the room. "Mice, humans." She laughs. "We're all composed from the ground up. Your rhythmic self, instinctual, was built up in Lemuria. Emotional — now that's a bit more troublesome — Atlantis. The others," she points at Kathy, Sara, John and me, "had some Atlantean adventures, right? Black Hats crowding us, Clayton to Highland and back, while the cold ones rode rockets into space.

"Yes," she turns back to Larry, "you missed that, but you've had your own, right?" She stubs her cigarette out in the tray by the window and takes a deep breath. "I meant the elements, they meant elementals, you know, so they got combined. Good dining, good pleasure, that's the level we should be on; but, since you're on the other," she looks around:

"Just watch their toes and their hats
and if any have tails, well ... "

She grins, actually beams, at us, leaning back and breathing in with obvious pleasure.

"Just tell them ol' Elsie sent you.

"Now ... " She taps her foot and holds her right elbow in her left hand, right finger on her temple, looking around, making mental notes. "Elementals ..." She pauses. "Yes," she answers herself. "Devas ..." She focuses. "Right. They have helped a lot by providing the building blocks, the cleaning, the sweet scent of the flowers."

She points out the window. It seems much larger now, light streaming in, a glow rising in the room. "The fire, water, earth, and sky helpers. They want to help, you know. When you mow, for instance, and it's about to rain? Just ask them. They'll hold back until you're done. It's like the parking stalls in Clayton, remember?"

"If you ask, they answer," Sara says.

"Yes," Elsie agrees. "If you don't ask, they can't."

"And watching the tire marks on the highways," I suggest.

"Puddles and marks. Rain storms and signs." While she talks, Elsie walks around the room, touching her finger to furniture like doing a military white glove inspection, then props the screen door open. Inside and outside merge. She turns to us.

"For today, all is prepared
So our guests can arrive."

"Good day, Elsie B., so these are the young people you spoke of?" A tall woman, eyes dark and deep, dignified, tilts her head toward us then takes her hat off and slides it over one of the pegs next to the door. I hadn't heard any one drive up. We're all standing with our backs to the stove.

"Mahdah," Elsie turns to us then back to her, "we're so glad you could be here today. Wonderful day, isn't it?"

"Delightful, Elsie." She moves directly to the table. "We've had quite a schedule, haven't we?"

"Indeed," Elsie answers.

A man in a baggy but fine seersucker suit and white straw hat, puts his cigarette out in Elsie's tray on the window shelf, hangs his hat on the next peg, and follows Mahdah to the table. "Any wine, Elsie?"

Larry immediately takes a bottle, already opened, from the iced thermos on the counter, and fills a glass for him.

"This is Dr. Galen Honigberger." Elsie stands behind the gentleman. "This is David, Galen."

Dr. Honigberger sips his wine, nods acknowledgement, then turns to the door. "Over here, Sadie." A sweet looking lady, dressed smartly like Mahdah, but less formal, enters and joins him and Mahdah.

Larry says: "Can I get you any wine?"

Shaking her head, brushing a loose strand of hair out of her eyes, she smiles at him. "No, Dear," she says, then extends her hand to Elsie. "Chicken and pie, how lovely. Thank you, Elsie."

Another man, two older couples, then a woman who looks a lot like Karin, enter and take places at the other tables, leaving a space empty at the main table where Mahdah and the Honigbergers are visiting quietly. Sara re-fills the water pitcher and starts moving among them.

Another couple enters, in their forties, perhaps, then a man looking like Will from CRC, or perhaps the gardener who lives at the back of the Oasis or around here someplace.

Elsie acts as hostess while Larry moves from table to table offering to serve wine and Kathy, following him, suggests salad and bread. The warm buzz of friendly and familiar conversation hovers around us.

I watch from the stove, amazed at the speed by which we've progressed from visitors to a team, by how Elsie has orchestrated another event which fits with an outside view of what we're doing and yet, simultaneously, is a magical and mysterious ritual.

"Interesting people." Sara brings me back from a daydream. I remember moving among the tables. One was on the patio, but it was behind the house. Elsie was singing or a record was playing. Dr. Honigberger was saying something to Larry. Everyone was thoroughly enjoying the food. Somebody, maybe invisible, was sitting at the front table with Mahdah. I had the sense Elsie's husband was at the outside table, with the gardener, but can't remember what he looked like — maybe like the picture, but older.

Glancing outside, the sunshade is down. Larry and John are carrying tables and chairs out. The flags have been changed to blue. Kathy is washing dishes. Sara, drying them, is handing one to me. I am returning it to the shelf.

"Jay," Sara repeats herself. "Didn't you think so?"

"Amazing. How many people were here?" I try to focus.

"Thirteen, I think."

"Where's Elsie?"

Larry comes up behind me. "She just changed the towels. Don't you remember?"

"Was she singing?"

"She did at the last — humming, actually," he responds, "as they were leaving."

"It seemed like there were more people here than would be possible." I glance around the room. "Only one piece of pie is left?"

"You want it?" Sara asks.

"I'm full," I respond, but I can't remember eating.

"She said to be back by five." Larry pats my shoulder.

John comes in, whistling. Putting his hat on, cocking it to the side like an explorer, he says: "Better get going."

"Where are we going?" I ask.

"To the Hart Retreat. Jay to earth," Larry chuckles. "Are you back now?"

"I think so." I have vague glimpses of conversations on the patio, of Elsie applauding our discipline, of Mahdah inviting us to stop by, of a man lighting a cigar, of sitting at the table eating.

"Said we should drive," Larry comments. "Didn't you walk the first time?"

"Where?"

"Past Mahdah Hart's, by a path, from that place where you met Jack?"

"Where?" I have no idea what he's talking about.

"Past the Hart Retreat to here," he explains, pointing to the floor.

"Yes," Sara answers, drying her hands and passing the dish towel to Kathy. "But she said to drive."

"Right," John joins in. "Let's get going."

Pulling through the stone entry way, slowing and stopping at the side of a large meeting hall, which looks like a New Hampshire barn, precise and solid, I get out and feel better. Sun, brilliant, friendly, and warm, dances off trees and shrubbery, weaving down rock walkways through the clean precision of the landscape. Toward the center of the compound, the large purple flag flutters majestically from a tall white pole. Larry starts for the entrance to the lodge. Except for the breeze, everything seems to be completely still. "You'd think there would be somebody else here." I seem to be talking to myself.

"Apparently not." John holds his arms up, and shrugs. "Come on. Kathy and I were in here for the workshop but didn't get to look around."

The inside of the hall is lined with double levels of monastic cells. The ceiling, vaulted wood beams, like a church, arches above us. Holding Sara's hand, I sense we are moving between dimensions — that this retreat for spiritual contemplation is in fact a front for something much more mysterious and active.

Doffing his hat and opening the door, John says: "Let's tour the grounds."

In the blue sky-dome above us, white clouds form and unravel in patterns suggesting birds and huge sailing ships. Pebble walkways meander through manicured grass, sculpted hedges, flowing down the slope of the landscape, widening at various points to accommodate stone benches overlooking the slow ballet between earth and heaven.

Stopping with Sara, we watch Larry, Kathy, and John descend the stairs to examine flower beds. Chatting quietly, they walk to a row of raised vegetables and something that looks like a shrine, a concrete post with a pyramidal cap, in a clearing between several of the plantings.

Further down the slope, an older man, or being, swings gently within a geodesic sphere constructed of white tubes. The others walk past him, but he doesn't look at them. Beyond him, the landscape slides into a green belt of trees through which a stream runs, above which the sky pulls mountains up to clouds, merging at the horizon.

Holding the bannister, we descend toward the garden. The being has disappeared, but the swing is still moving. A book lies open in the grass. Looking up I see Larry, Kathy, and John moving up another path past a sign reading: "Temple of Silence."

Entering the temple at the edge of the trees, Sara settles in the center of the room while I walk the edges, glancing at pictures, like the pictures Jarvis had of Yogananda and his masters, but these figures are of a Western tradition, male and female, some maybe a century or more ago, some quite recent — then join her.

Disembodied presences surround us. The room hums with an inaudible, peaceful chanting. Though the walls are closed, we're covered with light. Though my eyes are shut, I see someone doing a ritual — then Jack, and someone else ... holding a harp.

Touching my arm, Sara moves up the steps. Remembering to breathe, I reassemble myself in bits and pieces then follow toward the buildings, past the stone wall and gate through which we gazed with Jack when he took us to meet Elsie and, beyond that, the path to the landing site.

Larry is standing with a woman on a patio in front of a concrete block bungalow. She is moving her hands over his body. We join Kathy and John near a white pick-up with shovels and a wheelbarrow in the back. Sara asks:

"Is Larry getting a treatment?"

"Yes." Kathy brushes hair from her forehead and squints into the sun. "I hope it's like what I saw in the temple."

"What do you mean?" Sara asks.

"In the middle," Kathy turns back to Sara, perplexed but serene, "a column of purple substance, but spirit, rose right before me. Whatever it was," she shakes her head, "I don't want to talk about it, but I know it could heal Larry."

John holds a match out, watching the flame, then, as if honoring Kathy's desire not to discuss it, says: "They've been up there quite a while."

Following his glance, Sara says: "Who is that?"

"Mahdah went in to get somebody." Her eyes are distant. "She said for us to wait here."

"How do you feel about this place?" Sara asks.

"This was the site of one of the last battles to preserve the treasures." Kathy looks away again.

Larry comes up behind us. "You ready?"

"Are you?" Sara grins at him.

"What ever she did, it helped." He holds his hands up to inspect them. "You know, her name was Elsie, too? A really sweet lady." Larry smiles, then leans over to Kathy and, his arm around her, whispers: "They've taken over. Both Jack and I are safe now."

The crease, at the corner of her eye, moist, Kathy turns and hugs him — then leads us back to our car.

"How was it, Munchkins?" Elsie grins then laughs gently. Beneath her smile, I see a sad-faced clown. Following the others into her house, I still feel dazed.

"This is a stage in your progression." She swings her hand around the room. "And everything is different now." She cocks her head sideways, listening. "School children," she shakes her finger at us, "how do you know the dancer from the dance? Is the soul in nature or nature herself? Are you the monkey? Am I the white witch? And ..." she studies us, "what choices do you want to make, now?" No one responds. "If you hold your hearts open this will come back, but it may be twenty-five years, and then it will be different." As if startled, she hurries outside. Coming back in, she's pale. "Some of you only hear part of this. That's your business. I don't listen to all they tell me, and I only relate part of that to you." Taking a deep breath, she composes herself then points at the chairs. "Sit." Her voice deeper, more instructive, she picks it up again:

"The moon's cycle affects each of us. It's growing now. Apollo feeds it. My sisters feed you, but we don't know what you like best. Lots of my voices have no bodies, but they're not necessarily ghosts just because they speak through me.

"You can keep the ghosts out, but remember," she puts her fist on her hip, "when you drive one out, unless you occupy the form totally, seven rush in. Create space with questions, yes — but follow with answers. What are you going to do?"

"That's what we have to decide, right?" I interpret, still tentative.

"Everything is a choice at this level." She pats her diaphragm. "You are dealing with will, now. Your parents, your friends, have brought you this far. I hold the window up, then break it so you can get out."

"Out of what, Elsie?" Sara asks.

"Staying here or going back are earlier stages." Elsie looks at the ceiling and nods. "Switch to a new level of who you are. Alone and side by side. This is an acceleration. Get out of prison. See and act upon multiple levels, where ever you are. Getting out means dropping your preconceptions and exercising your choices.

"Tomorrow," Elsie paces before us, "as we've discussed, go to the waterfall. All of us will be washing." She points at Larry. "You do need one more scrubbing. But once you're clean, all of you, while we're together, imagine what you want to do with your future. We will put flesh on your images. And take care because we live with the consequences on this level." She moves her hand in a circle over her stomach. "Some of what we create is hard to digest.

"In this world," she points around the room again, "I teach reading patterns, precipitating images, playing chess, practicing the presence — that's all. Because we love you we will be there. It's dangerous, though," cocking her head to the side, she puts her finger to her ear, "because what you image with us is what you get. It's our gift to you."

Suddenly quiet, looking at the floor, she whispers: "We all are vulnerable because," she brings her eyes up to us, voice stronger, "we are attempting great things."

Striking a match, gazing into the flame, turning it toward us, she adds: "And where there is great light there is great darkness. We've all come together again to face that."

The Waterfall

"Has Karin already gone?" I ask.

Larry, at the table, the sun shining through the sliding door behind him, the *I Ching* open, glances up from his notes. "She left a copy of a Russian folk song and said she'd write." My heart sinks. I can't believe we are not going to see her again.

Joining me at the screen door, watching a robin, wet with morning dew, hop around in the still glistening grass, he says: "It's hard to believe we're leaving."

"I still don't want to go." Pulling the screen open, I go out on the patio. Spreading my white terry-cloth towel over the back of a lawn chair, I think about the flags and wonder whether, once we're back in Kansas, Karin will continue to provide a bridge to Elsie.

Rejoining Larry at the table, I say: "I wonder to what extent, even when we're all in the same room with Elsie, we all experience or even see the same thing."

"Karin told me an interesting story about her." Larry waves as John crosses the hall to the bathroom.

"When was that?" I ask, surprised.

"This morning before you got up." Larry chuckles. "You know how Elsie talks about her husband being in the Pentagon? Well," he leans back, "the day after you and Sara left, after your first trip down here, Karin and her realtor friend took Elsie to the airport in Atlanta to fly to Washington. When they went through the terminal, there was a Marine escort by the ticket counter." He pauses. "Karin assumed some dignitary was arriving but ...

"Apparently," Larry continues after letting the image settle in, "Elsie walked right by the ticket counter, the Marines falling in behind her, then out the gate and up the ramp onto the plane. Karin actually saw lines of military people on both sides — holding flags. Great theater, right?"

"Absolutely." I shake my head, imagining the scene.

"But," Larry pauses again, "the point is, once they were back on the highway, Karin asked the realtor about it and he swore that he hadn't seen a single person in uniform."

Kathy and Sara walk past us to the kitchen, visiting quietly, and fix themselves breakfast.

"Did Karin say anything else?" I ask.

Larry hunches his shoulders. "Just that what you see with Elsie depends on how awake you are."

While sun shines through the windows of Karin's house, and we pack, clean-up, and load our car, I'm suddenly aware that John is remote and quiet. We're leaving, but he's staying. None of us seems to know what to say to him.

In the car, John leans forward, breaking the silence. "What about the space ships?"

"What do you mean?" I ask.

"Since I'm staying, at least for now ... I just ... You know, a lot of weird stuff has happened." John pauses. "Stuff I never even thought about."

"You're concerned about us leaving?" Larry asks.

"I don't know what future contact I'll have with you, or Elsie." John pauses. "Or what my mother will do. Or what I'll do. It's like I've stepped into some other world, and now you're going away; and I'm left with the space guys, the transistors, or whatever the sunshade is ..."

Slowing to turn into the Oasis, I ask: "What would you like to do?"

"I don't know." John sounds like he's withdrawing.

Elsie's front door is closed, a note pinned to it. Everything looks smaller than the day before. Five red towels hang from the line. The picnic table has been moved closer to the cabin. The canopy is closed.

"John," Sara turns around in her seat to face him, "you're very special."

John mutters: "So much depended on us being together."

"At some level we've always been together," Sara holds his eyes, "and always will be."

"All we know is that we have perceived and learned certain

things." Larry pauses. "And Sara is right. One of those things is that we are a group."

"But Elsie has made it clear that there are these other forces around us." John looks away.

"There are, in fact," Larry confirms. "But the only question is how are we going to conduct our own lives."

"What about Jack?" John asks.

"I gave his harp to your mom this morning." Larry smiles reassuringly. "I'm sure he'll be back to claim it."

John looks at me. "Do you think it was all staged?"

"Couldn't possibly have been." I grin and grab for his ponytail, both of us laughing softly.

"Hold us in your heart." Sara places her palm on his chest. Silence washes around us. "I better see what's on Elsie's door." She moves through the world we five had entered together then returns with the note. "Elsie's left instructions on how to get to the waterfall."

Another hundred yards further along a dirt and rock track beneath the canopy of trees, we reach a meadow spreading green through purple, yellow, bright orange, and red flower clusters — clover and butterflies. Thinking about the tears of the Indian Princess, I take Sara's hand. "Did Elsie tell you anything specifically about this waterfall?"

Concentrated and far away, she says: "They protect this place," then looks into my eyes. "It's a temple to them." The scent of wild flowers permeates the air. "You do remember, don't you?"

"What?" I'm surprised how far ahead the others have gone.

"This is the time and place where we are to decide, really deeply decide. And then they'll help us."

Silent again, we move through the meadow and along the path through the trees, the rush and spray of water drawing us closer. Leaving the veil of the forest, suddenly we're in bright sunlight facing cascades tumbling down shelves from a high cliff one hundred yards up and ahead of us, splashing off ledges, rising in breath catching rainbow mists, collecting in a pool swirling at the base, moving then into the stream alive with clean promise — what you could drink from with fish, frogs, turtles, the teaming union of life — then pushing on as a stream meandering into the trees, sun speckled, leaves swaying, vibrant, off through the back trails of the Georgia highlands.

Astonished, I realize this is the secret place, a living monument, a moment suspended, the Temple of the High Priestess where Elsie bathes in all her splendor.

Waving his arm for us to follow, moving ahead quickly, John right behind him, Larry shouts: "Let's get in!"

"What do you think, Kathy?" Sara asks.

"This is it." Kathy walks forward, her eyes on the cliffs above us. I sense Sara's excitement, her hand on my shoulder while she slips her sandals off to follow.

"I'm going to play." She smiles as I reach for her hand, wanting to hold her. Blue eyes reflecting sky and waterfall, her arms spread as she turns. The entire surround flows into and out of her. "Remember the first I Ching reading we got?"

She stops to address me. "This is the source of the lake and the heavens. The helpers have brought us here. Now each of us has to decide about the rest of our lives."

"This is holy." I nod. "Do you sense Elsie here?"

Moving toward Kathy, sitting on a great gray stone, watching cliffs above us, over which sheets of water tumble, a guardian, a warrior priestess from millennia past, Sara turns back to me and answers: "Elsie and all the Beings."

Barefoot, I wade into the rush of swirling water. Following Larry and John, I climb the hidden stairways up the rock face. Rainbow showers and hydrants crash, separate, and recombine in crystal tears, latent with a new order.

By earth blood channelled from the mountain shrine at the Elysium in Highlands, to the heart springs where we stopped to share bread, to the birthing stone, where we wait now, we have fallen and risen, cold and hot, in light splintered spirals. Together we look out upon Sara and Kathy sitting at the edge of the gathering pool, sun on them in separate funnels of light against the green felicity of the trees.

Males, lacking language, we settle on ledges. The cold spray exhilarates the heated air. Each from his own perch, we are lost in the roar, the sound below appearances, the collision and exaltation of chaos, labor pains, the long and short vision of excited emergency. A cosmos of confusion, I search for an image by which I may re-order my shattered self. Sara stands. Radiant water streams down her face. T-shirt flat against her breasts and stomach, in jean shorts, sun glistens along her legs. Eyes bright and shining, face alive with joy and peace, she smiles at me.

"I felt you. I felt what you were seeing." I whisper, love stretched through the roar which carries the bridge between us, then dig in, searching for the figure of myself, what I shall choose to be.

She climbs the stones, kisses me, hugs me, pulls me up. Larry and John have moved to the pool below us. Kathy is talking to them, pointing around the rim of the basin from which the new world rises.

Holding each other, we speak the truth of bird song, the scent of flowers, of deep green, of dark rich loam, of light through water, of stones washed from the beginning of time beneath a sky shining in splendor on new beginnings.

"So now you know." Elsie stands behind the screen door looking out at us. Wearing a forest green dress with her jade necklace and mustard seed, crystal bracelet, lighting a cigarette, the flame reflected on the point just above and between her eyes — brilliant blue — she studies us. The sun at our backs, I sense the quiet, the cool depth behind her.

Pushing the screen door open, she hands us five purple towels. "Dry off with these." She laughs. "You do look great. Loved how you were dancing around."

Taking the towels, we back up. "Then, John," she steps out, bare-foot, "hang these up and bring those in," she points to the clothes-line, "and put the sunshade up. David," she looks at Larry, "will you gather greens for the salad?" She winks at Sara and Kathy. "The girls will help, of course."

Elsie chuckles as they turn to their chores, then signals me to fol-low her. "Hungry?" She grins. "Might have sandwiches and cook-ies for you but," she turns and thumps my forehead forcing me back against the door, "what we have here is a loss of character. All beauty contains a thorn. I'm like a rose." She softens. "Hold me too tight and you die." Breathing hard, I sputter that I want to stay. "Hush."

6

Whispering, she backs me around the room. "Like a slave you'll be lost, unless you become the master of your life. We don't need spineless snakes lapping cow's milk."

"But if you'd talk to Sara ... We could help you."

She smiles, gentler now. "See these eyes?" She steps back. "See them in Sara. Go home, Jay. I've already given you, and her, the best of my love."

Slumping to the seat by the window, I watch the others file in. Elsie chants: "One, two, three. What's left of you and me? What's right?" She looks like the first time I saw her. "Come on now." She claps. "Don't be sad!"

John puts cold cuts on his plate, smears mayo on his bread, then mustard. Like the pump has been primed, we all dig in as Elsie pulls her chair into the center of the room and leans forward, speaking seriously:

"I'm leaving, too, part of me, you understand — because you're leaving. I go with you. You stay with me. Right? So here are the rules. Some things we don't talk about. Some things we do."

Looking up, Sara says: "Can we take pictures?"

"Photographs never work," she answers matter-of-factly.

Swallowing hard, I ask: "Can we call you?"

"I don't feel good about the wires." Leaning forward, whispering, she says: "You can write, but keep it general. In an emergency, call Mahdah. She can get me. Don't say too much, but the world will be different when you get home. The road is cleared, the guardians will cover you. Each event is discontinuous. Consciousness is the bridge. I'm there in who you have been, in who you will be." She touches her heart. "In who we are." Walking behind Sara, bending to kiss the top of her head, she adds: "Listen to each other."

"Can we come again?" Larry asks.

"Each time you come, I will be different."

"So will we," Larry acknowledges.

"And you will be welcome." Her eyes move to John.

"What about me?" he asks.

"You will decide that." She smiles warmly at him, then backs up to her chair, lights a match and studies each of us through its flame while saying:

"None of you will understand much of what has happened. The

world has already changed, but will never change. This is not a matter of government, of statecraft, although you will each do what you can. This is the perpetual practice of the presence of conscious-ness of self. We're just friends huddling together, finding the 'I Am' in the silence, the golden chemistry of our bodies alive with light.

"You, John, have a mother who carries you, like Jay's mother car-ried him. All the mothers here are sisters. All the fathers, brothers. Some don't know it. Some have suffered more than others, but for their own reasons. Each has participated in the creation of the bod-ies which you now inhabit. We're in a temple. The stained glass is beautiful. I break the glass. Let sky in. Let dark in. Let you grow your own wings."

In the silence, Elsie watches her garden while we clean the table, wash the dishes, move like a team through her home, quiet, no one with a voice, with words which find the air. As the others finally move outside, I hesitate, my heart crying.

"Elsie ..."

She stands and takes my arms. "You were born to practice the presence, not serve me, not ... the killing rose. Go home to what you were born to do."

Dizzy, following the others, I move through the door.

"But one more thing." She takes my hand.

"What?" The word sticks in my throat.

Leaving Larry, Kathy, Sara, and John to wait beneath the golden sun in the arch of the blue sky, gray clouds shifting into white swans, Elsie leads me to the back of the Oasis and points to the shed at the edge of the woods.

"There is an ancestor shrine from Tibet, which I have carried for you. It's yours. Remember me."

Gently pushing me forward, she slides the door open. Shafts of light, from cracks in the walls, illuminate crystal goblets, boxes of books, manuscripts, clothes, old rugs, blankets, and artifacts. The air shimmers with treasure. A small black and gold ornate shrine sits on a table in the middle of the shed. Lifting off the top, Elsie slides prayer panels up and says: "For the ancestors."

Carrying the shrine back to the car, and carefully packing it in the trunk, I am amazed to see Karin pull in beside us, get out, nod at

John and greet Elsie. Spreading her arms, she embraces Kathy, Larry, then Sara, while Elsie pulls my face down to her.

"Remember the ring and watch the patterns." Grinning, her eyes crystal-blue, she whispers: "I'm the goose girl, the match girl, with whom you live."

Holding her arms out to Sara, she laughs then says: "Watch out for Jay."

"Okay." Sara smiles, her eyes flooding as Elsie embraces her. Tears of the Princess. Laughter of the Queen. My breath catches then releases as my heart breaks then grows.

Hugging Larry, Kathy, John and Karin in turn, Elsie turns abruptly and walks to the clothesline, takes five blue towels and two white ones out of the basket, hangs them, pulls the purple ones down, then carries the basket into her cabin, never looking back.

The lump in my heart swells with the waterfall of sadness and pain, humor, hope, and absolute knowledge that we have been uniquely blessed.

"So," Karin holds her arms out. "God's speed. You will always be safe in my heart."

"And in mine," John adds, stepping back, his arm around his mother.

"And you both are in ours," Sara responds.

All in a circle, standing together, arms around each other, the center of the world at our feet, we breathe and hold one last moment.

Looking to each of us, Karin says: "Our time together never ends."

Breaking at last, reluctantly, we follow Larry and Kathy into our car, pulling the doors shut as silent lightning streaks across the sky, then the rumble of distant thunder. Cloud shadows cover the ground. Karin and John get into her car. As rain starts falling, Elsie reappears at the door to the Oasis, waves a big broom at us then tosses a kiss.

Turning the lights on, I start the engine and windshield wipers, then move toward the road. Karin and John follow.

Larry, leaning forward, places one hand on each of our shoulders. Kathy does the same, their arms crossing. I reach for Sara's hand. She receives me. We connect. A strength rises between us.

The storm crashes through the trees, sweeping across the road in dark fury. Watching the tire tracks in the flickering light, I ease out onto the asphalt, turning toward home.

Following trucks through the rain storm, reading messages in their slogans and road signs, watching the puddles, I am certain that we are protected, as Elsie promised, that the Beings she works with have provided this storm as a cover to disguise our exit, as they did our entrance.

Just beyond Memphis, Larry leans forward and asks: "What time is it?"

"It's 4:00 straight up," Sara answers.

"How is it possible?" He checks his map. "That's over three hundred miles from Elsie's, in a storm, in three hours."

"Not bad," we all agree.

Epilogue

Even now, more than twenty-five years later, I vividly remember our excited speculation about what the world would look like upon our return to Kansas. We tried to explain what had happened, but could only give examples. We struggled to understand Elsie's insistence we face the contradictions, which we perceived as monsters, in order to push forward.

Our excitement settled into a buzz just beneath the surface. Eventually Kathy moved to Santa Fe to concentrate on her art. While pregnant with Seth, Sara finished her teaching degree and I switched from philology to law school. When she got pregnant with Aaron, I joined my father's firm.

In 1976, on our way to a seminar in Florida, we stopped in Georgia so our boys could meet Elsie. We had exchanged Christmas cards with appended notes. Elsie's had been loving and full of good, grandmotherly advice.

Living in a small cottage on the edge of Tiger, Elsie took the boys into her workroom to choose stones. The magic was present but subdued. Karin had moved to the Hart Retreat. She was happy and full of references to esoteric projects.

Three years later, John drove a motor cycle up to our front door. He had left Georgia a year after we did, but had returned to be with his mother when she died. He reminded us that during the summer of 1969, something extraordinary and inexplicable and exciting had happened.

Early in 1985, we received a letter from a man saying that Elsie had died. Our names were on a list to be notified. He wondered whether we had a picture they could use as part of a memorial to her. No picture of Elsie was ever found.

In 1994 Larry, who continues to live in Manhattan, reminded us that Elsie had said it would take twenty-five years for us to understand what had happened. He suggested it was time to write about our experiences. Four years earlier, I had left the law firm to write full time, initially about children in need of care and community systems. Seth and Aaron were in college. It was time for the next stage.

Sara, Kathy, Larry and I differ in regard to certain details; but that had been the case even when we were there. We considered including multiple viewpoints, but decided to leave the experience in the first person, present tense. Elsie stated all she would do was set stages. She insisted each person must determine what is true or useful.

She said this is not a perfect world. We were then, and are now, living in challenging times. What appears as madness and chaos on one level can be genius and beauty on another. Elsie taught us to see other levels.

Sara, Kathy, Larry and I all agree that for reasons we do not understand, Elsie singled us out and devoted astonishing resources to expanding our boundaries. She fed us, then sent us home. We are grateful to have been given this gift. Our purpose is to pass it on.

About the Author

Jay Bremyer, author of *Walled-In*, *Soul in Nature*, and *The Dance of Created Lights*, practiced law from 1973 through 1990 when he returned to writing full time. He and his wife, Sara, live on the Kansas prairie. Together with a planetary network of friends, they celebrate creative diversity and the emergence of the ability to think with one's heart.